I Am Dangerous

JOHNS HOPKINS: *Poetry and Fiction*
John T. Irwin, General Editor

STORIES

BY

I Am Dangerous

GREG

JOHNSON

The Johns Hopkins University Press
Baltimore and London

This book has been brought to publication with the generous assistance of the G. Harry Pouder Fund.

Printed in the United States of America on acid-free paper
05 04 03 02 01 00 99 98 97 96 5 4 3 2 1

The Johns Hopkins University Press
2715 North Charles Street
Baltimore, Maryland 21218-4319
The Johns Hopkins Press Ltd., London

Acknowledgments: "A House of Trees," *Southern Humanities Review*; "Hemingway's Cats," *South Carolina Review*; "Uncle Vic," *Southwest Review*; "Evening at Home," *Prairie Schooner*; "Scene of the Crime," *The Southern Review*; "In the Deep Woods," *West Branch*; "Little Death" (under the title "His Name Was Lennie"), *Virginia Quarterly Review*; "Sanctity," *Cimarron Review*; "Leavetaking," *Antigonish Review*; "Last Night," *Boulevard*; "Primordia," *Chariton Review*; "Alliances of Youth," *Kansas Quarterly*.

Library of Congress Cataloging-in-Publication Data will be found at the end of this book.
A catalog record for this book is available from the British Library.

ISBN 0-8018-5375-3
ISBN 0-8018-5376-1 (pbk.)

—*for* John Barrett

Contents

A House of Trees, 1
Hemingway's Cats, 18
Uncle Vic, 39
Evening at Home, 60
Scene of the Crime, 76
In the Deep Woods, 88
Little Death, 104
Sanctity, 117
Leavetaking, 136
Last Night, 149
I Am Dangerous, 160
Primordia, 170
Alliances of Youth, 191

I Am Dangerous

A House of Trees

THE summer he turned thirteen, my brother went up to live inside the trees. Our back yard had several pines, a gnarled old elm tree, and close to the elm, their branches intermingling in a way that suggested a complex shaking of hands, a tall, many-branched mimosa. This was the tree that Cody chose as his principal residence, though the smooth bark made climbing treacherous, and the slender uppermost branches looked as if they'd snap beneath the weight of a small monkey, much less my ninety-pound brother. There were a couple of close calls, but on each occasion he was near the larger elm, and as his branch began trembling and bowing, Cody reached for an elm branch and kicked away from the mimosa just in time. Then he'd stay in the elm tree for a while, as if the maneuver had been a deliberate bit of daring. He'd sit with his legs and arms folded, his face blurred by shade and distance but his posture, his silence, his perfect stillness suggesting the complacent serenity of an Eastern idol.

At such moments I'd call up some ineffectual taunt. "What's the matter, Cody, can'tcha get down?" Or: "Guess the mimosa isn't so comfy after all, huh?"

I was two years younger, and these queries had a boyish desperation that even I could hear. All during the eight days my brother spent in the trees, I was torn between disdain for his showy foolishness (on several occasions, my father had remarked that I was his sensible son) and a heart-twisting, envious affection. This was another example, after all, of a puzzling change in my brother during the past several months. He'd become moody, sullen, preoccupied; when he noticed me at all, he spoke in a hurried, offhand way, as though I were a mere gnat-like annoyance. I'd always adored Cody—he seemed taller, stronger, and smarter than I could ever hope to be—but the close camaraderie of our childhood had all but vanished, our incessant chattering replaced by a sore and bewildered silence. Cody's voice had now changed to a commanding deep tone that was all but identical to Dad's. Yet there was now a strange tension between them, a tendency to argue over nothing, a subtle but fierce tug-of-war in which I played no part. In my prepubescent ignorance, I had no idea what the struggle was about, though I knew enough to hate the echoes of my own plaintive, high-pitched voice. In my father and brother's company I sounded like a pipsqueak, like someone who no longer counted.

If Cody had spoken the handful of words I longed to hear—"Hey, Scott, come on up!"—would I have been able to join him? Would I have cast a final glance toward the den window, where my father surely stood watching with a drink in his hand, and then turned defiantly and shimmied up the smooth pale-tan trunk, heart pounding, scalp tingling, as I tossed my reputation for level-headedness to the winds? *Could* I have joined Cody in his stubborn independence, his theatrical gesture of protest? To this day, I still don't know.

The invitation never came, in any case. It was clear that Cody felt nothing but distaste for my mother and me, both fence-sitters in his eyes, both timid and weak and hopelessly compromised. When my mother came scurrying out the back door every few hours, bringing sandwiches, slices of cake, pint-sized cartons of milk, Cody would wait in dignified silence as she arranged the food in a small wicker basket on the ground. The basket was attached to a heavy rope that Cody had looped around a medium-sized branch perhaps a dozen feet up the tree, and when Mother stepped back he'd slowly haul the basket upward, watching its progress with his blue-eyed, steely gaze, careful to avoid glancing directly at Mother or me. We stood there foolishly, necks craned, as though waiting for some word of acknowledgment or thanks. But Cody said nothing; it was clear that we were beneath his notice, in both senses of the phrase. When the basket reached him, Cody would take the food around to the back side of the tree, behind a screen of branches that shielded him from our unwanted scrutiny.

During those first couple of days, my mother would make feeble jokes. "Well, Scottie, looks like Cody's still up to his monkey business" or "How does it feel to have Tarzan for a brother?" Then she'd give her hollow laugh. In the mornings, she'd still be wearing her shapeless pink housecoat and matching flip-flops; later in the day, she donned one of her plain cotton blouses and a blue-jean skirt she'd worn around the house for years. She claimed it made her look thinner, a comment I didn't quite understand at age eleven, since I'd never had the idea that she was fat. Like the mothers of my neighborhood friends, she seemed a familiar and unchanging domestic fixture, like the refrigerator or the bathroom tub.

I'd understood at once that her efforts to reason with Cody were futile. After a few attempts she'd shrug, cast a quick blurred look toward me, as if I were somehow complicitous in my brother's prank, then shake her head and retreat back into the house.

She made other futile gestures, too. One evening she brought a white cotton blanket and placed it inside the basket. But this was June, the nights were warm, and Cody didn't bother to pull the blanket up. Yet each morning she'd come out the back door with determined good cheer, her plump face lifted toward the fragrant pale-green branches, and say something like, "Hey, Cody, how about if I take you and Scottie downtown this afternoon? That new Western is playing down at the Lovejoy. . . ." But Cody, who slept in the back part of the tree, out of sight in a cradle of the thickest branches, gave no response. Mother would stand there for a few minutes, hands on her hips, waiting. Once I said, in a voice shaded with contempt, "He's not going to answer you, Mom," and a flat look of despair fell across her eyes, making my heart writhe with guilt.

She made one last attempt that surprised me with its subtlety, and even made me think she might succeed. It was Cody's third afternoon in the tree; he sat perched just above us, eating the lunch my mother had placed in the basket. As he was finishing a square of apple strudel, Mother suddenly held up a pink-tinted envelope, wriggling it in her hand so that Cody, despite himself, looked directly at her.

My heart began to pound when Mother said, in a casual, by-the-way tone, "Oh, Cody, you got a letter from Sandra today. Would you like me to send it up?"

Sandra was Cody's girlfriend, a dazzling dark-haired beauty whom he'd lost twice to the junior-high football star, a grinning kid named Brad whom Cody detested. For the past few months, Cody and Sandra had been going steady, but now I wondered if she'd spurned him once again, in favor of Brad; perhaps it was just a broken heart, after all, that had sent him scurrying up into the trees? Standing next to Mother, my neck craned exactly like hers, I waited tensely for his answer. It had been clever of Mother to ask Cody a question, instead of just putting the letter in the basket with his lunch. If he wanted the letter, he'd have to speak to her. It seemed as though half an hour passed, but it was probably only two or three minutes. Cody stared down at Mother, his conflicted emotions evident only in his free hand, which he kept clenching and relaxing. But finally he turned away, tossing down the foil wrappings from his lunch and again scurrying out of sight, into the rear branches.

My mother sighed noisily, then bent to pick up the wrappings. "Well, I'll save it for you, then," she said. "You can read it when you come down." She kept her voice casual, but I could see the disappointment in her eyes. Her best effort had failed, and I knew she wouldn't try again. After that day, she had me deliver the meals to Cody's basket. She'd begun wearing her housecoat well into the afternoon, saying that she didn't want to go outside, that she looked and felt too awful.

My father stayed inside, too. He'd lost his job near the beginning of that summer, and though he spent most of the day alone in the den, never joining in my mother's efforts to talk Cody down from the trees, I always felt that he was watching us. Sometimes I caught glimpses of a whitish flickering at the den window—he still wore his white dress shirts each day, though they were dingy and wrinkled by now, and soiled at the armpits. (Once, at the dinner table, when Mother said something about sending the shirts to the cleaners, he snapped: "Forget about it, Ellie!" She hadn't mentioned the shirts again.) The thought of his cold angry gaze made my scalp tingle sometimes, as I stood uselessly out in the shade of that mimosa. Did he consider my behavior as treacherous as Cody's? Was he simply biding his time, or did he plan on doing nothing at all?

Even at age eleven, I had the cursed ability to view any situation from another person's point of view. I understood my father's angry entrapment, my mother's befuddled perplexity, Cody's flamboyant rebellion. It seemed necessary that I take a side, act out some dominant emotion of my own, and yet this was impossible. Inside the house, I took meals with my parents, watched some TV in the evenings, went to bed at the usual time. But in the morning I was back outside again, an unwanted attendant upon my brother's new life, lingering through most of the daylight hours. Sometimes a twig would fall, landing in my hair, but I didn't know if these wordless acknowledgments represented affection or ridicule. Once, in the late afternoon, it suddenly began to rain, though the sky had been cloudless that day. I took a couple of quick steps toward the house, shielding my wet head with both hands, but then the rain stopped abruptly. I heard Cody's distinctive laughter: a *huck-huck-huck* from the back of his throat, a kind of disdainful chortling. I looked up and saw that the sky was blue, the sun shining. Only then, sniffing my hands, did I understand. I looked up into the mimosa just as Cody, his knees straddling two branches, was zipping up his jeans, his strong-jawed face set in a smug look of triumph.

I walked calmly inside the house, took a shower, washed my hair, and allowed myself a few bitter tears. But I put on the same clothes again, so that Cody wouldn't know I'd gone to such trouble, and went back outside. This time I sat on the cement back steps, chin in my hands. I glared at Cody, who sat reading an adventure novel I'd slipped into his basket the day before. He was eating from a bag of Hershey's kisses that Mother had brought him. When dusk began to fall, he closed the book but continued sitting there, his jaws working slowly as he ate the chocolate pieces one by one. Gradually my long-limbed brother became a figure of shadows, as though he were dissolving along with the daylight. He kept his arms and legs perfectly still, and I could no longer distinguish them from the tree's limbs. But I could be stubborn, too, so I waited in my own silence, watching as every few seconds an empty foil wrapper fluttered down through the branches and onto the grass.

The argument had flared quickly, out of nowhere. It was so sudden, and so unprecedented, that no one could have foreseen or prevented it.

We had never indulged in violent emotions, and once or twice I'd overheard my mother, talking on the phone to her sister in Alabama, claim that we were a "close-knit" family. Even that young I sensed the incongruity of this description and felt a shimmer of denial, like gooseflesh, spreading down my back and along my arms. But I couldn't have translated this perplexity into words, for it was true that the Stuart family was outwardly harmonious—the father taciturn but courteous, the mother blandly cheerful, the sons well-behaved and industrious at school. People noted often that Cody was a virtual replica of Dad: the same high, broad forehead, the same wide-set dark eyes and strong jaw. Both were long-limbed and had a commanding poise; when either of them entered a room, all eyes tended to shift in that direction. My father had been promoted swiftly through sales and management positions (he worked for a life insurance firm), and during the school year preceding the summer of our family's crisis, Cody had been elected president of his seventh-grade class. He had the sort of charm and popularity that could inspire both desperate idolatry and stinging resentment in a younger brother. Even physically I didn't seem a worthy sibling. I was stocky, round-faced, freckled, while Cody had Dad's elegant slenderness and his smooth pale-olive complexion. Several times my father had joked that I looked just like the milkman, a remark I resented long before I understood what it meant.

My father seldom joked, but when he did, his sarcasm could be cutting. I remember that once, waiting for Mother to finish dressing for his firm's annual Christmas party, he sat with his third or fourth drink in the living room, watching television with Cody and me. When Mother finally appeared, wearing a billowy red dress that she'd bought just for the party, Dad laughed angrily. "For God's sake, Ellie, don't you have anything else? You look like a Russian battleship in that get-up." Mother had left the room quickly, her face crumpled, and had returned minutes later in the dress she'd worn to last year's party.

Dad had used similar methods over the years with Cody and me. In the evenings, especially, when he stalked around the kitchen as Mother prepared dinner, ice cubes rattling in his glass, he'd deliver some harsh assessment of the way Cody had trimmed the hedges out front ("Were you wearing a blindfold, Son?—they look like they've been attacked by piranhas"), or of my less than sparkling report card ("Well, Scottie, are you planning to *be* a milkman when you grow up?"), or of the way we sat at the kitchen table ("You kids look like a couple of chimpanzees—Ellie, can't you get them to sit up straight?"). I responded swiftly to that last remark—to this day, my posture is ramrod straight—but Cody made a joke of the criticism, scratching his sides like a chimp and slouching down in his chair until his eyes were just visible above the table top. Mother and I laughed, and Dad couldn't keep a straight face, either. He grinned, then shook his head and left the room.

After my father lost his job, his criticisms became fewer but meaner. Within a few weeks he'd made the den into his solitary retreat, emerging only at mealtimes; even Mother had grown quieter, more somber. She said only that Dad had experienced a "personality conflict" with his boss, who was undoubtedly jealous of Jake Stuart's abilities and perhaps feared that Jake would be promoted above him. There wasn't a hint that Dad's drinking and erratic temper were behind his dismissal, though I would learn the truth soon enough. As was often the case in our family, palatable lies were the bricks and mortar of our illusory togetherness. Perhaps it was a weariness of lies that drove Dad into his glowering, drunken silence; or perhaps he glimpsed in Cody an unbearable reminder of his own lost youth and good health. Whatever lay behind the rupture of our family, I must assume for my father's sake that the consequences of his behavior horrified no one more than himself.

On that evening, Cody had been playing baseball with some neighborhood kids and had been a few minutes late for dinner. Mother kept his plate warm in the oven, and she chatted and cooed over him, as usual, as she delivered his plate, a glass of milk, some hot rolls. She took her seat again, and she and Cody began idly discussing an old movie they'd watched on TV the night before. All this time Dad had kept eating in his mechanical, joyless way, not even glancing up when Cody entered the room. His first reaction came a few minutes later, when Cody turned to me.

"Hey Scott," he said, "guess what, the Cooper twins are building a cool treehouse in their back yard. I was thinking we could build one, up in the mimosa. We could sleep up there and everything."

"Oh honey, wouldn't that be dangerous?" my mother said.

I wasn't too enthusiastic, either. But I said, "Sure, why not. Is that okay, Dad?"

Everyone stiffened at this question, including me; it had slipped out by habit, I suppose, though in recent days Cody and I had seldom addressed him directly. Now we watched as he chewed a bite of food. An unpleasant grin had contorted his big unshaven jaw.

"Sure," he said slowly, "if this house isn't good enough for your brother. If he can't even bother to eat his meals on time."

Cody gave him the tilted, sideways look that meant he was trying to control his temper. He said, "We were at the end of a game, Dad—the last inning." He was smiling, uneasily. He'd been buttering a roll, but he put the knife down. It clinked loudly against his plate.

"Well, God forbid we should interrupt *that*," Dad said. "Do feel free to come and go, just as you please. Don't trouble yourself about anyone else."

Mother said, touching Dad's forearm, "Jake, it doesn't matter—" but he jerked his arm away.

Cody turned back to me. "Ron and Randy have some boards left over, they got them at a construction site or somewhere, so tomorrow we could—"

"Don't interrupt when I'm talking," Dad said coldly. "I won't have any sons of mine stealing lumber, I don't care what it's for. Besides, what's this garbage about a tree house? Have you turned into a goddamned ape? I guess I shouldn't be surprised, the way you've—"

"Maybe we don't care for *this* house!" Cody cried. He pounded his fist on the table, sloshing milk from his glass. "Why would we, when it stinks of liquor all day long!"

"Cody, honey," Mother said, in a grievous murmur. Her arm, reaching toward him, was trembling.

Dad pushed back from the table. His jaw had hardened. "Get to your room," he hissed, his lips barely parted. "It's time I tended to you, once and for all."

Cody gave a snide laugh. "What are you going to do, spank me?"

Dad blinked his eyes, slowly. His pale, stubbled face had flushed a dull brick-red. When I heard Mother take a quick breath, I looked over. She'd grabbed the edge of the table, her face tensed in fear. Then she winced, and in the same instant I heard the loud cracking blow and looked back in time to see Cody sprawling backwards to the floor, one arm upraised. Dad stood rubbing his hand. He looked angry and confused.

It was the first time I'd seen him hit anyone. He'd always said, in a peculiar boasting way, that he didn't believe in corporal punishment. "But what about capital punishment?" a neighbor had asked him one day, grinning. "Well, naturally I believe in *that*," Dad had said, mock-serious. Then he'd winked at Cody and me.

That clever, joking father seemed gone forever, replaced by the swaying, malodorous man who stood rubbing his fist above his fallen son. Several seconds passed, which seemed a small eternity to me. All four of us had frozen in place, as though awaiting a script for our next words and gestures. The blood was beating in my ears, a muffled sensation like drums in the far distance.

Then Cody came to life, scuttling backward across the linoleum in a clumsy, crablike fashion, getting to his feet as he reached the back door. His blue eyes had clouded with hate. His breath coming fast, he panted his next words: "I'm leaving this house. I'll never come back here!" He hit the screen door with his elbow and vanished into the yard.

My parents' reaction was predictable enough. Dad retreated into the den and Mother swerved quickly into denial, going about her kitchen work as though nothing had happened. Mentally I had fled out the door with Cody, and it wasn't long before I was standing out back, feeling helpless and bewildered—feeling invisible, almost—as I watched his progress up through the branches. I didn't know where I fit into this sudden rearrangement of our family: should I retreat back into the small, stuffy rooms of my parents' house? Should I follow Cody up into the trees, into perilous freedom? Neither possibility seemed attractive and I stood caught between them, uncertain.

When Cody stopped climbing, and had settled into the crook of two large branches a dozen feet above my head, I called up feebly: "Hey Cody, what about our tree house? We've still got some daylight left—why don't we go and get that lumber?"

Cody stared down, solemn as an owl.

"Don't need a tree house," he said shortly. "I'm just an ape, remember? All I need are the trees."

I tried to ignore this, asking more questions in a cheerful, little-brother's voice, using my mother's strategy of pretending that nothing was wrong. But my brother just sat there, imperturbable, gazing past our roof to the horizon. I knew he would not speak to me again.

As the days passed, I began hoping that Dad would do something. He'd become a silent, fierce-browed presence at the dinner table, grunting one-syllable replies to my mother's casual remarks. From my end of the table, opposite him, I could detect the heavy, sweetish odor of the Manhattans he'd consumed during the day. (The only sound I ever heard from the den, where he spent almost all his time—he slept on the Naugahyde couch and snacked out of a half-size refrigerator tucked into the bar area—was the clinking of ice cubes as he dropped them into a glass.) I watched covertly as he shoved forkfuls of Mother's meatloaf and scalloped potatoes into his mouth. I could never really tell how drunk he was. Approaching or leaving the dinner table, he might stumble briefly, grabbing at a chair-back, but otherwise he seemed fully in control. There were no outbursts of rage or hilarity. The whites of his eyes were clear, and his hand seemed perfectly steady as he shoveled down the food. If anything, his long days of drinking seemed not to relax but to stiffen him, giving his limbs the cold rigidity of a marionette's, as if their human suppleness and warmth had drained away.

By the fourth or fifth evening, I'd begun to assume that he wouldn't do anything about Cody. Whenever my mother mentioned him—in her airy, jokey way, as if this were just a clever prank that Cody was playing—Dad's eyelids would close for a moment, in contemptuous weariness or disgust. I'd begun getting tired, too, and understood by now that I couldn't force Cody down from the trees. One day I'd decided simply to stop delivering his food and water; I shoved his breakfast and lunch into the space under the back steps, casting a smirk over my shoulder as I went back inside the house. But coming out that evening I heard my brother coughing—a painful, hacking cough—and my resolve melted at once. I ran with the food and plastic water bottle, jamming everything inside the basket. Cody waited a few minutes before hauling it up, to show that he could have survived without the water. It occurred to me that Cody's stubborn pride was such that even if I *had* stopped delivering the meals, he wouldn't have capitulated until the instant his dead body tumbled out of the trees.

What bothered me most was that Cody seemed more cheerful and energetic than ever. He moved nimbly among the branches; he tossed down candy wrappers and banana peels over his head, as if they were basketballs; he watched intently as, every morning, hurried and shamefaced, I used several paper towels to grab at the pile of excrement that waited at the base of the tree trunk. Often I'd hear that insidious chuckling, *huck-huck-huck,* as he perched overhead, like some prankish spirit enjoying the clumsy travails of the human world.

A week had passed. On the eighth and final morning of Cody's life among the trees, I had what I considered a brilliant notion. Dad had come to the kitchen for breakfast, which he seldom did; he and Mother sat silently drinking coffee as they glanced through the paper. By now I felt that Cody would never come inside, our family would never get back to normal, unless I did something to break the stalemate. My sudden idea seemed so inevitable and right that I blurted out the words impulsively, not subjecting them to my usual deliberation. I wasn't the type of kid who told lies, but I felt driven to desperate measures.

"Guess what," I said casually, glancing at Dad. "Guess what Cody said this morning, when I took his breakfast out."

Mother dropped her newspaper, startled. "He said something?" she asked eagerly. "He addressed you directly?"

Her cheerfulness had abated in the past day or two, but now it returned in full force; she'd needed only the barest scrap of good news. But Dad was a different story. He didn't look up from the article he was reading. He was usually hung over and disgruntled in the mornings, and I could tell by his chalk-white skin and slack jaw that he felt worse than ever. But it was too late to change my mind.

"Come on, Scottie, what was it?" Mother cried. "What did your brother say?"

I was still looking at Dad. "He said he would come down," I said slowly, "if Dad would come out and ask him to."

I glimpsed a brief spasm in my father's cheek, but otherwise he didn't react. It was Mother who finally provoked him.

"Did you hear that, Jake?" she said. "All you have to do is run out and ask him, did you hear? That's a reasonable request, don't you think? Please go out, sweetheart—I'm worried sick about Cody, I want so badly for him to—"

My father pounded the table, just as Cody had done before he'd left the kitchen that final time. The gesture silenced Mother, and now her breathless rush of words echoed pitifully in the room. Dad glared at her.

"Well that's what I'm here for, isn't it?" he said, between gritted teeth. "To provide for all your goddamn wants? Isn't that right, Ellie?"

His tone was so hateful that Mother's eyes filled at once. Whenever she cried, her face suffered an ugly collapse, crumpling and reddening; you had to glance away.

"I just want my son back," she sobbed, her head bent forward. "My son and my—my family," she added, pawing at her cheeks with a napkin.

I understood that we'd reached a crisis; there was nothing to do but keep nudging Dad into action.

"You've got to do something," I told him. "All he wants is for you to come outside."

"Oh, is *that* all he wants? Is that it?"

I caught the whiff of bourbon on his breath. Only then did I understand that I'd made a mistake.

"Dad, listen—" I began, but it was too late. His chair scraped the floor as he bolted upwards; he lurched toward the back door, mumbling a few words I couldn't make out. For a brief, treasonous moment I considered the possibility of just sitting there, passive and helpless like Mother, who sat staring at Dad's empty chair. But only for a moment: then I hurried out back, stopping near the bottom of the steps. I stood watching, my arms hanging useless at my sides.

Dad had detached the basket from Cody's rope and now started tossing the rope in the air. He was aiming for the long, high branch on which Cody was perched, glaring down at him. He'd been on one of his arboreal explorations, evidently; several times I'd watched him climb out dangerously far onto the highest branches, as though testing the tree's loyalty. This morning Cody was about twenty feet from the ground, and had climbed out six or seven feet from the trunk. He was on the side of the mimosa farthest from the elm, and even on the mimosa there were no branches in reaching distance. He seemed to understand at once what Dad wanted to do. He glanced toward the trunk, as if calculating how long it would take to retreat back from the limb, but then he froze, his shoulders hunched, eyes narrowed. That's when he gripped the branch beneath him with both hands, his face a mask of stubborn resistance.

After several tries, Dad succeeded in looping the rope over the branch, halfway between the trunk and where Cody sat. Cody eyed the rope and made a tentative grab for it, but the branch was already trembling. Again he gripped the branch with both hands, easing himself into a straddle, his legs dangling. The loose end of the rope had fallen within a few feet of Dad's head, and now Dad grabbed at it, with a little jump that nearly made him lose his balance. But he didn't look drunk, just coldly determined. Holding both ends of the rope, he started to pull: gently and rhythmically at first, then much faster. Neither he nor Cody had spoken a word.

Behind me, I could hear Mother at the back door, sobbing. A lump had risen in my own throat, but I couldn't move, as if I knew that what was happening could not be stopped but could only be witnessed, and perhaps remembered, in this paralysis of dread.

Now Dad was yanking hard on the rope, in a lunging, violent rhythm. Once or twice I saw his knees bend, his feet leave the ground. Up in the tree, Cody had become a blur of clinging arms and legs. He readjusted his position with each lunge of the branch, losing one handhold or foothold only to flail about desperately for another. My father kept pulling fiercely, doggedly. His face was clenched, masklike, whereas Cody's features had become a smear of agonized effort. Now and then I could glimpse the terrified whites of his eyes.

Though it seemed that Dad shook the tree for half an hour, it was probably less than a minute before Cody's hands slipped from the smooth bark and he fell headfirst to the ground. He dove straight down, not even grazing one of the lower branches that might have broken his fall. Only when he lay motionless on the grass could Mother and I begin to move. We rushed toward him, gently turning him onto his back, then peering into his face. "Cody? Honey?" my mother whispered. "Can you hear me?" But Cody's eyes were closed, his cheeks pale. Taking some deep breaths, I pulled myself away and ran toward the house to call an ambulance. When I came inside the kitchen I could hear Dad in the hall, speaking into the phone, repeating our address in a calm and courteous voice.

At the hospital, a tall young doctor with shadows under his eyes found us in the waiting room. His first words, "You're very lucky," brought a sigh of relief from Mother. She sank down into the vinyl sofa. I stood beside Dad, who had brushed his teeth and changed into a clean shirt before we followed the ambulance to the hospital. He stood there smiling gratefully while the doctor described Cody's condition. Though he'd fallen on his head, he seemed to have suffered only a concussion; they expected him to regain consciousness very soon. Preliminary x-rays showed no damage to his neck or spine. The doctor repeated that we were lucky, very lucky, and at that point Dad made one of his clever jokes, winking at Mother and me: "Well, we've always said he's hard-headed, haven't we?"

The doctor smiled—a mere nervous twitch of his mouth—and left the room.

Every morning, the three of us went to the hospital, Dad dressed in the blue suit he'd once worn to work; he'd taken some shirts to the cleaners on the day after Cody's accident. Mother wore one of her Sunday dresses, lipstick, and some cologne I'd given her last Christmas. Despite her weight, I thought she'd made herself very pretty, and I wasn't surprised that her usual good cheer had returned. After all, we were on the verge of a happy ending.

My parents stood on one side of Cody's bed, but I always went around to the other. Although my brother had awakened, he stayed very groggy and never seemed to recognize who we were. Mother fussed over him, as usual, adjusting his feeding tube or his bedding, speaking in a fond, slightly reproving voice—as if his being in the hospital, and causing so much trouble, were only another bit of mischief. To the nurses who came and went briskly during our visits, I'm sure that she seemed a model of motherly solicitude and care. Only I could glimpse the occasional slip of her public mask, the craven terror beneath her wobbly smile.

I tried to ignore both my parents and to focus on Cody, mentally willing him to give his familiar grin, a conspiratorial wink. But his eyes remained dull, glassy, and the skin beneath them was puffy and bruised, as if he'd gotten on the losing end of a fist fight. The doctor had said his black eyes meant nothing and would fade away soon. What the doctor couldn't see was that the Cody we knew—energetic, willful, unpredictable—bore little resemblance to this pale, bedridden stranger. Each morning I gripped his hand, ran my thumbnail against his palm or the sole of his foot; but there was only an instinctive twitching in response.

"Scott, quit tormenting your brother," Dad laughed, one morning when the doctor was there.

"Just give him time," the doctor said. "It takes them awhile to come around." Winking, he squeezed my shoulder and left the room.

Several days passed, and Cody did show improvement. He seemed to listen when we addressed him, and he'd begun to grunt a few unintelligible words. But when, early one morning, the doctor intercepted us as we got off the elevator, then reported in a hushed monotone that there had been "complications," I don't believe either of my parents were surprised. Mother's face crumpled as she dropped into a nearby chair, one hand across her eyes. Dad and the doctor kept a meager dialogue going: "Most likely a burst vessel in the brain, completely unexpected . . . was there anything that could have been . . . no, nothing, or I promise you that we would have . . . but will he get better, will his speech improve, and what about his memory . . . well, the brain tests suggest the likelihood of permanent disability, though you never know for sure. I'm afraid he'll require constant care but he isn't suffering, at least. I mean he doesn't *know* he's disabled . . . well *that's* something, at least . . . yes, you're absolutely right. That's something. . . ."

They droned on and on, as I stood thinking, *Lies. Nothing but lies.*

But I said nothing, one hand resting on Mother's shoulder while she sobbed in her chair.

We hadn't told any of the hospital staff what had really happened, only that Cody had fallen while climbing a tree. In the days after we brought him home from the hospital, I could sense that Dad was watching me, monitoring my emotional temperature, deciding whether I could be trusted not to blurt out the truth. Even if he'd asked, of course I couldn't have told him.

Slowly, we adjusted to our new life. We cared for Cody, carted him to and from the hospital, gradually developed a routine that kept us constantly busy. Though Cody failed to improve, the rest of us stayed in surprisingly good spirits. It appeared that Dad had stopped drinking, for he'd found another job and no longer retreated into the den when he was home. Dad's new job was a good one, and in August he moved us into a better neighborhood, a bigger house. Cody's disability hadn't caused a financial burden, since Dad had kept up the health policy from his previous job and all Cody's expenses were covered. The new house was spacious and sunny. My mother was relieved, she said, that she no longer had to keep all the rear blinds drawn, to avoid any glimpses of that mimosa tree.

After that, we never referred to what had happened, not in any of the months or years that followed. There were fond references to Cody's life, recollections of things he'd said or done, but never a word about his fall from the tree. These were the years before the concept of "child abuse" had entered the general awareness, so we were never questioned by the authorities. The story my parents had told to the doctors, and to our relatives and neighbors—the story of his tragic accident—became so real in our minds that as time passed it seemed an authentic memory, as good a version of what had happened as any other.

Nor were the next couple of years a sorrowful period for me. I spent more time with Cody than I'd ever enjoyed in the past: I wheeled him around the neighborhood sidewalks, earning kind remarks and smiling glances from people we met along the way (in this new, affluent neighborhood, no one had known us before Cody's fall), and sometimes, feeling jaunty and powerful, I even raced him along, making cheerful engine noises ("budden budden!") until I could hear the *buck-buck* of pleasure Cody made in the back of his throat, one of the few remnants of the kid he'd once been. Cody and I watched TV together in the family room (how much Cody understood was debatable, but I'd decided to stay optimistic), and I would wheel him into my bedroom just for company while I did homework or talked on the phone with friends from school. Cody sat there with an amiable, grateful look on his face, as though he were *my* little brother. Occasionally he made stray, enthusiastic, indecipherable sounds, but I learned (as did my parents) not to pay much attention. As time passed, I felt a strange happiness, and by the time I turned thirteen, and knew myself fully in the midst of that long-feared adventure known as "puberty," I saw that my worries had been pointless. I'd grown taller, slimmed down, become more outgoing; the kids who'd once ignored Cody's "fat-assed" little brother now invited me to their houses, included me in weekend ball games, and chatted with me on the phone—using my last name, "Stuart," instead of the childish "Scottie." I remembered that these same kids had once called Cody "Stuart," and I often had the eerie feeling that I'd quietly taken Cody's place. While spending time outside the house, with other kids, I never referred to my brother, and neither did they.

Sometimes I wondered what would happen if Cody regained speech and memory, or if my father lost his job, or if my mother collapsed one day in an unsightly heap of delayed, hysterical remorse. But none of these things happened. Never again did we become the tense, unhappy family we'd been in the days before Cody's accident. By the time I entered high school I knew that we were home free, and I'd already decided that I would study hard and graduate with honors, that I'd go to college and law school, that I'd be successful and get married and have a contented family of my own someday. And I knew that at some far-off, predictable time, when one of my sons asked about my boyhood, or about their grandparents (whom they never got to meet—my parents died six months apart, shortly after I got married), or about their uncle (now tucked comfortably into a well-regarded institution but who'd shown such promise when he was a kid) . . . well, I really wouldn't mind telling them. It would just be another story, after all—a story as solid and unshakable as the roof above our heads.

Hemingway's Cats

I

WHEN, on the first morning of their honeymoon, Antonia opened their door to let in some fresh air, an enormous cat sprang into the room. Mottled orange and gold, very quick despite its size, the cat leapt onto a chair beside the dresser and then toward Antonia, who recoiled and nearly fell backward, crying out in alarm. Next it went for the bed, bounding onto Antonia's dented pillow and into Robbie's lap, where it curled promptly into a ball and closed its eyes. Propped against his own pillow, half-sitting so he could see Antonia better—watching her dress, watching her move gracefully about the room—Robbie laughed hysterically at the sight of his wife crying out, jumping back into the room's dimmest corner. "Hey—hey, it's only a cat," he managed, but he could hardly speak for laughing, and certainly Antonia could not speak. In fact, Antonia could not move. For what seemed half an hour but was probably only two or three minutes, she stayed back, trembling, while her husband laughed and the cat slept.

Yet Robbie looked guilty, climbing out of the bed. The cat made a small disgruntled noise, then rearranged itself on Antonia's pillow.

"Honey, you're all right, aren't you?" Robbie said, in the solicitous bridegroom's voice he'd tried all during the night. Naked, he came toward her with arms outstretched. "I didn't mean to laugh, it's just that you looked so—so damn *funny*," he said, and he dropped his arms and started laughing again. "I'm sorry," he said. "It's just that squeal you let out, and that little jump backward—"

"I've got the picture," she said, though not bitterly, for seeing the incident through Robbie somehow helped. She felt her body loosen, and when Robbie embraced her, she felt again the wave of pleasurable emotion—gratitude? relief?—that had swept her into this marriage and changed her life so profoundly, in a dreamlike swift few months; had changed *her*, as she liked to think. (For she had lived a meager life, cramped and embarrassed and afraid. It was like her, she thought, to be afraid of an ordinary cat.)

"Don't be mad," Robbie said, rubbing her shoulders.

"I'm not mad," she said carefully. "I'm embarrassed, that's all. For acting like such a fool."

"You were just startled," Robbie said, "it's nothing to be embarrassed about," and he turned back toward the bed, clapping his hands. "Shoo!" he cried, and the cat's tail stiffened with alarm, and in an instant it had leapt off the bed and out the door. The room was still.

"I don't like surprises," Antonia said, from her place in the corner.

"Don't worry about it, it's nothing," Robbie said cheerfully, heading for the bathroom. "It's something to tell Dad—you know, an anecdote. When we get home."

Robbie's father, Vincent, was paying for this honeymoon in Key West. He'd spent his own honeymoon here, in the mid-sixties, and every few years he went back again, telling his wife and children and friends that the island was "another world"—not exactly paradise, he'd say, but as close as *he'd* ever get. Vincent was a large, bearish man with a blunt, square face and quick-moving eyes, ice-blue. Antonia had met him only a few times, and he frightened her in a pleasant way; from the beginning she'd felt that Vincent liked her—which was, of course, very important to Robbie—and on the flight down from Atlanta, her husband had delivered the final judgment, in the off-hand manner Antonia knew he had copied from Vincent. "By the way," he'd said, turning a page of his magazine, "at the reception Dad drew me aside. He thinks you're terrific—that you're 'perfect' for me, in fact." He'd given a brief laugh; Antonia had felt that anything she said might sound tactless, so she murmured agreeably, gazing out the small blurry window. Down her arms and back went that shiver of apprehension she felt whenever Vincent's name was mentioned. She knew that he was, in his son's eyes, a colossus—a decorated Vietnam vet, a self-made businessman, an autodidact who knew several languages and liked to quote Nietzsche, an expert sailor and marksman. In short, any boy's hero. Learning that he thought well of her, Antonia had felt the permanence of her marriage far more acutely than at the moment she and Robbie had said, both of them quite meekly, "I do."

By the time Robbie came out of the bathroom, she'd made the bed and opened their drapes to a flood of sunlight. As she expected, Robbie kidded her for straightening the room—they were on vacation, for heaven's sake, the maid would be arriving any minute!—but she liked to keep busy; she'd never been the type to just sit. Nor did she enjoy waiting around for slower people, though of course she hadn't mentioned that to Robbie. Her mind worked quickly, her senses were keen, but if Robbie was a bit lethargic and had not quite mastered the details of everyday life, maybe that was an advantage: Antonia would have that much more to do, her days would be filled to bursting. Robbie was Vincent's oldest son but the last to get married, and had there been some tacit hope on Vincent's part that Antonia would assume the role of looking after him, keeping him on track? If so, maybe that only meant that Antonia had found herself; or, at the very least, had found a sort of refuge.

Man and wife, they went out into the cool morning air. Vincent had made a list of things they must not miss—not only tourist attractions, but restaurants and bars Vincent liked, little shops where they were to be sure to give the proprietor Vincent's best regards—and now, out in the sunlight, Robbie unfolded the list and stared at it, bewildered. "Dad's handwriting," he said, apologetically. "Somehow I've never been able to . . ." Antonia felt that he wasn't really talking to her, but she said pleasantly: "Here, let me try." Robbie gave her the list and immediately began fiddling with his camera. Antonia felt an obscure pleasure that she could read, and quite easily, Vincent's tiny, crabbed handwriting, which looked at first glance like some other language.

Now her eye paused over one of the items on the list—"the Hemingway house." The address was across the street from their guest cottage, and looking up Antonia saw an enormous yellow-painted house, complete with columns and verandas, several outbuildings, a yard shaded by lime and banyan trees, and a red-brick wall separating the compound, in its dim-shaded serenity, from the sunlit noisy street. Squinting, Antonia saw that there were several cats perched along the wall, as though standing guard.

"Look, it's where Hemingway lived," she told Robbie. "We're right across the street." She didn't know why the fact should please her—she had never read a word of Hemingway—but somehow it did. She felt it might have been some clever signal from Vincent, who had arranged their Key West accommodations.

"Is that right? Hemingway?" Robbie said vaguely, pushing his glasses up his nose, lifting his camera. He snapped a picture of the house.

When they reached the front gate, Antonia thought she saw their intruder on the corner gate-post, stretched indolently on his side, eyes half-closed in the sun. Tawny-gold, tawny-orange, and really quite fat. Antonia had the impulse to lunge toward the cat, to frighten it, but perhaps the cat would not be startled. Perhaps it would not even move, and she would look foolish once again, and Robbie would start laughing uncontrollably. In any case, she resisted the impulse and followed her husband toward the house.

The cats, it turned out, had actually belonged to Hemingway. Every half hour there was a tour of the writer's house; and their guide—a tiny, angry-looking black woman in her forties—paused before one of the dining room windows, where a dainty tan-and-black kitten had perched on the sill. All the forty-odd cats on the property, she said, were descendants of Hemingway's own cats, and if anyone looked closely he would see that each cat's paw had six toes. They're all related, the woman repeated, all descended from Hemingway's cats. She spoke in a bored, precise voice. A man near Antonia and Robbie raised his hand to ask a question, but the woman was already leading them upstairs. Here they saw the writer's bedroom, though the bed itself had been roped off and could not be touched. The room had a musty, oaken smell. Spread out on the bed were several rare books and manuscripts of Hemingway's. The woman was reciting an anecdote about the friendship between Hemingway and Fidel Castro, but Antonia only half-listened—she had glimpsed something under the bed, a slender black cat hunkered down as though ready to spring, its huge gleaming eyes fastened on Antonia. Once again, Antonia froze. Now the other tourists were shuffling out, the guide's voice was fading down the stairs, and Robbie touched her arm: "This is pretty interesting, huh? The room where Hemingway slept, somebody famous like that?" Antonia smiled thinly. She could not take her eyes from the cat, which had not moved, had not even blinked. . . . But Robbie took her forearm and pulled her away, mumbling something about lunch. Downstairs, it occurred to Antonia that she had actually become involved in a staring contest with a cat—a little black orphan of a cat that no one else in the room had even seen. Even worse, the cat had won.

Yet somehow the incident cleared the air between her and Robbie, or perhaps cleared a space in her own mind. She laughed to herself about the cat under Hemingway's bed, and then she could laugh about the first cat, which had frightened her so badly. One o'clock of her first full day as Mrs. Robert Kendall, and a great tension had been relieved in her. She and Robbie found an outdoor cafe right on Duval Street, they had margaritas and sandwiches made with pita bread, they talked and laughed for more than an hour. When their food arrived, Robbie had continued the theme that everyone in his family loved Antonia—literally everyone, and Vincent above all.

"The others take their lead from Dad," Robbie said comfortably. "If *he* likes you, then everyone does."

"But you just found out yesterday?" Antonia asked. She kept her tone light, flirtatious. "Before the reception, you didn't know—"

"If he *hadn't* liked you, I'd have known," Robbie said. "In fact, there wouldn't have been any reception."

Antonia sat for a moment, not eating or speaking.

"But wait, I didn't mean—" Robbie dropped his sandwich on the plate, swallowed his mouthful without chewing. "What I meant is, Dad wouldn't have sprung for everything if he hadn't approved. So it would have been a much smaller affair."

"The wedding, you mean."

"Of course I mean the wedding. What else would I mean?"

Smiling, Antonia took a tiny bite of her sandwich, her jaws nearly motionless as she chewed. Abruptly, Robbie laughed. He lunged for the camera, snapping the shutter before Antonia could duck away.

"I never know when you're kidding!" he cried, delighted.

"I told you," Antonia said, fixing him with a keen, motionless gaze, "*no* pictures. Not today, not ever. Now give me the camera."

Antonia's hand darted out, but Robbie had lunged again, pulling the camera onto his lap; she swatted him several times, making little grabs for the camera, and Robbie hunched over, giggling and jerking from side to side, almost upsetting the table. From the other tables, several older couples looked over and smiled. A pair of young, playful newlyweds, they might have thought. Lighthearted. Carefree.

"Dad *did* mention that," Robbie said, facetiously protecting the camera with both his arms. "'She won't allow a single photograph?' he wanted to know. 'On her wedding day?' . . . He seemed suspicious," her husband laughed, "but I told him to send the photographer home. I said"—and Robbie doubled over, nearly hysterical—"I said that you were wanted dead or alive in twelve states, and to forget about the society page."

"The society page?" Antonia said faintly. "But I thought Vincent—I thought your father scorned that kind of thing." She pawed at Robbie's lap a few more times, but half-heartedly; she didn't really want the camera. If she decided to destroy the film later, she could.

"Oh, that's just a line of his. Actually, he gets quite a kick out of it. They plastered Tod's wedding all over the *Journal-Constitution*," and here his voice lowered, "but then he and Karen had twice the wedding we did. Not that I'm complaining, of course. It makes sense when you consider that Karen's parents—"

Robbie broke off, perhaps catching the implied comparison of Antonia to Karen, perhaps censoring what might sound like criticism—however mild, however indirect—of his father. Stuffing the rest of the pita bread into his mouth, he chewed somberly for a while. Quite often he went into these boyish reveries, as though bewildered by the sinuous windings and sudden pitfalls of even the most ordinary conversations. Delicately Antonia licked the salt around the rim of her margarita, not really alarmed. During these past months she had negotiated her way among the Kendalls as best she could, generally steering clear of Vincent, sending him from a distance the kind of demure but enigmatic smiles that appealed to such men. Brusque and theatrical, with a braying voice meant for whole rooms to overhear, Vincent had few enough occasions to draw her aside, and she had been careful not to create any real opening. His shrewd and watchful true self, she knew, was in many ways a slave to his persona, and after his booming queries received answers that were intelligent but so mild as to lead nowhere, he'd had little choice but to move along, or else to begin one of his monologues that soon had many others gathered around. The other Kendall wives were also intelligent, beautiful, and mild, though naturally rather than carefully so; and she lacked their sleek blonde beauty, not to mention their patrician carelessness. Yet gradually she had felt that she'd won Vincent over; Robbie's comments on the plane hadn't really been much of a surprise. Antonia's eerie containment, her expressionless dark eyes and the dark fine hair that curved along her jaw identically on either side, and of course the graceful but alert silence, if not vigilance, that she had developed throughout her adult years and that had charmed more than a few men—all this had snagged Vincent's interest, perhaps even more than his interest. She discounted Robbie's remark about the society page, after all. The real energies of such men lay elsewhere.

After the waitress brought their Key Lime pie, Robbie blurted out, this time not bothering to swallow, "I'm sorry, honey, I mean about suggesting that Karen— You know I don't *care* about that."

Antonia detested sweets, but she forked off a bite of her own pie. "I know," she said. "I don't care, either." As Antonia well knew, Karen had descended from Atlanta's higher social echelons to marry that upstart Vincent Kendall's youngest boy; soon enough, of course, he'd be far richer than any of Karen's family. "Actually," she said, "I sort of like Karen."

"I don't want to live like that," Robbie went on, not hearing. "I can't stand all the parties, and the pretentious house, and all the talk about their last vacation, their next vacation . . . I want something simpler, I really do."

Antonia laughed. "You've made a fine start, haven't you?" she said.

They spent most of the day following Vincent's list, checking off the items one by one. They bought T-shirts at Fast Buck Freddie's, stopped for a drink at Sloppy Joe's ("Hemingway's favorite bar," Vincent had scrawled), and rented bicycles and pedaled down to the beach, stopping at "the Southernmost tip of the United States," as a sign proclaimed, and gazing out at the calm, rather colorless sea. "Now I know why people love this place—why Dad does," Robbie said, shading his eyes against the sun-dazzled water, his mouth opened in delight. "It's so peaceful here, don't you think? So quiet and relaxed, with the palm trees and the warm weather, and nobody dressed up, nobody in a hurry . . ." Antonia had looked down, a bit self-conscious in her white linen dress and matching low-heeled shoes. Already she'd perceived that she was overdressed for this place, at least for the daytime, and vowed that tomorrow she would wear the T-shirt and pair of blue jeans she'd brought for lounging in their room. She didn't want to stand out, after all. She wanted to be part of all this. As they rode about the island, she'd paid less attention to the scenery than to her husband, watching him from the corner of her eye. Amazing that he seemed so comfortable, she thought, that *he* didn't notice if his wife were overdressed, her white straw purse dangling awkwardly from the handlebars; that *he* didn't keep checking to see was this real, was she really there, were they man and wife forever. He rode with his eyes squinted happily, tongue darting out the side of his mouth, pointing to a lighthouse in one direction—*look, Antonia!*—and a baroque church steeple in the other, *look at that!* Yet he didn't glance at her, and she felt that, yes, they were married, they were irrevocably bound together. Her calves had tensed with a sudden bright energy, and all at once she didn't care how she looked: "Try and catch me!" she cried, pulling her weight hard against the handlebars, and Robbie let out a whoop and began the chase, a wild, laughing pursuit, not of Antonia but of his wife.

She led him all the way to the bike shop and looked over her shoulder, head cocked, as he coasted into the shade where she had stopped, near the entrance. He was panting heavily, shaking his head from side to side; Antonia saw droplets of sweat flying off around him. "You're amazing," he said. "I'm practically worn out, and you haven't even broken a sweat. Your legs must be—your legs are great," he got out, still panting. "Thank you," she said, with a little mock bow, but in truth she *had* begun sweating; a thin film coated her face and neck, even her slender pale arms. For some reason she lifted her wrist and touched her tongue to it, remembering instantly the salt around her margarita at lunch, and she said, "Hey, what does a girl do to get a drink around here," and Robbie raised his eyebrows in a villainous leer.

"Look," Antonia said, "they're selling fruit drinks across the street—go get us one, will you?"

Her husband trotted off, while Antonia carefully parked the bikes, then took her compact out of the purse. Startled, she saw a mussed version of herself in the tiny mirror, her hair plastered against her throat on one side, sweat glistening along her upper lip like delicate whiskers. Quickly she daubed at her face with Kleenex, freshened her tawny-orange lipstick, brushed her hair in place with a few deft strokes. Then Robbie appeared beside her, panting, bearing two styrofoam cups with *Fruit Smoothie* printed diagonally along their sides; the cups held a frozen ruby-colored substance, ruby-colored straws. "Hey, there's a tour bus right down the street," he said excitedly, "it's just loading up. Let's go, Antonia! That way, we're sure to see everything!"

"A tour bus?" she said, and her first thought was how Vincent would disapprove—why follow the herd, why not strike out on your own? But Robbie looked so eager, shifting his weight back and forth like an overgrown kid, smiling. Her husband was past thirty, but Antonia knew he would always look boyish and that Vincent never had: his army pictures showed a stalwart, glaring youth of nineteen, ready to do battle with life. She could imagine him spitting the words out the side of his mouth—"oh by all means, *a tour bus*"—and then grinning or even laughing, but his eyes staying cold, contemptuous. After only four months, could it be that she knew Vincent better than his oldest son ever had?

But she said, "Good idea," and as they boarded the bus—which was actually an open-air trolley, several cars long, crowded with chattering, brightly dressed tourists—Antonia felt glad to do anything; that energy she'd felt when they were on the bikes kept returning in great ecstatic waves. She could hardly sit still, and when the tour guide maneuvered their attention from one side of the street to the other, Antonia moved her head quickly, obediently, as though watching a tennis match. Though really she could not have remembered what she saw. Much of the route she and Robbie had already covered on their bikes, and when they turned into a quiet, tree-shaded street, her legs tensed before she quite understood where they were. Then, just as she'd spotted the compound of detached cottages where they were staying, the tour guide reported through the microphone, with histrionic enthusiasm, "And here on our right is Ernest Hemingway's house, where he lived during the years 1931 to 1938, writing such works as *For Whom the Bell Tolls* and *Death in the Afternoon.* At that time Hemingway was married to Pauline Pfeiffer, a wealthy woman who enjoyed gracious living and who . . . " But Antonia stopped listening, her eyes narrowed as they surveyed the house, the spreading banyan trees, the red-bricked wall. As usual, several of the cats had placed themselves along the wall at random, cats of varying colors in varying positions. None was looking at Antonia. As the trolley passed, one of the cats jumped off the wall abruptly, and in her seat Antonia gave a little jump, too; but the cat had leapt in the other direction, toward the house. Now the trolley was in the next block; the tour guide was pointing out something else. Antonia sat back.

"Honey, is something wrong?" Robbie asked.

"No, nothing," said Antonia. "I'm just restless, that's all. I wish we could get off."

"Then we *will* get off," and before she could stop him Robbie was moving up the aisle, bending to the tour guide's ear. The trolley stopped at the next corner, and on the sidewalk Robbie said, bowing gallantly, "What now?"

She had to laugh. "I hope we didn't offend him," she said, sorting through her purse for Vincent's list. "But it occurred to me that Vincent wouldn't have approved—" The words were out before she could stop herself. She saw the flash of hurt in Robbie's eyes.

"But I thought—"

"Never mind," she said, looking from the scrap of paper to her watch. "Look, it's after six. Let's walk around a bit more, then go down to the Pier House for the sunset. Your father says it's not to be missed. Then we'll have dinner somewhere."

Briefly he'd lapsed into one of his daydreams, but he recovered quickly and soon they were back on Duval Street, pausing at art galleries and souvenir shops and open-air bars where folk musicians were playing. Already the air was cooler, the street atmosphere changing slowly from afternoon to evening. Now there were fewer children, fewer dogs; there were more young couples like Antonia and Robbie, some of them dressed casually for dinner after a day at the beach. Antonia felt relieved, her spirits lightened, and once again Robbie had the eager, slavish energy of a spaniel, loping inside a cafe to get ice water when Antonia said the fruit drink had made her thirsty, fetching a newspaper and postcards from a corner Rexall, then going back again when Antonia discovered she hadn't brought a pen or stamps. She wanted to send a card to the Lassiters, she told Robbie, and of course to Robbie's parents. Though perhaps *he* should write that card . . . ? And what about Robbie's brothers, and his grandmother out in Scottsdale? Since she hadn't been able to make the wedding, perhaps they should—

"Hold on!" Robbie laughed. "I only bought a couple of cards." He reached out and pinched her cheek, lightly. "Let's just write to our parents," he said. "That's enough, don't you think?"

So they went to the Pier House, finding a table at the edge of the sunset deck; they sat to write their cards. Or rather, Robbie studied his for a moment, then thrust it at Antonia and asked if she didn't mind. "Your wifely duty, after all," he said happily, sitting back and opening the newspaper. Antonia stared down at the cards. She sipped at the milky-looking drink Robbie had ordered her—a piña colada?—and addressed the cards in her girlish, rounded handwriting. *Mr. and Mrs. Vincent Kendall. Dr. and Mrs. William Lassiter.* Though her adoptive parents had missed the wedding—her father had pleaded an important medical convention, her mother refused to travel alone—she knew they would want to hear from her. After she'd left Birmingham seven years ago, only weeks after her eighteenth birthday, there had been a good deal of friction over Antonia's disinclination to write, to let them know where she had settled. Yet she never *had* settled, really, moving from Birmingham to New Orleans to Dallas; then back to New Orleans; then to Atlanta; then to Nashville and back to Atlanta again—working for a series of powerful men. "Assistant" to a state senator, "staff coordinator" for an agribusiness tycoon . . . She'd done well in these jobs, even if she'd been little more, really, than a glorified receptionist. A punctual, attractive presence in the morning; close-mouthed but alert all during the day, which her employers seemed greatly to appreciate without taking *her* very seriously; on occasion, a sympathetic listener at night, non-judging, non-committal. Yet she seldom stayed anywhere for more than a year, having a keen sense of when she was wanted, when she was not—the orphan's legacy. She did not want anyone saying she'd outstayed her welcome; there was always another city, another man who needed her. Another opportunity, as she liked to think.

Once her mother had shouted after her, *Go on then! I guess you can take care of yourself!* Mrs. Lassiter was sickly, a professional invalid; in a rare loss of temper, Antonia had remarked how much sense it made, her having married a doctor. The Lassiters had been a childless couple in their forties when they adopted the six-year-old Antonia; and now she thought, staring at the postcard, that she might never—was it possible?—see them again. When Dr. Lassiter had not been too busy, he had sometimes smiled at Antonia as though from a great distance, a rueful smile as though to apologize, to acknowledge that a mistake had been made, he hoped she would forgive them . . . ? When she turned eighteen, he informed her that there would be little money, perhaps no money; it would all be channeled into a research foundation, established in the Lassiter name. This time he *had* apologized, not quite meeting her eyes. By now, his daughter being a very mature eighteen, his wife's shouted accusation must have seemed the one absolute truth about Antonia—that she could take care of herself; that she would always "land on her feet," as one of her bosses would later remark.

I understand, of course, she'd said, lowering her eyes. You've given me so much already.

Now she wrote, in letters a bit larger than usual, *Having a wonderful time!* and then wrote the same message on the card to the Kendalls. She signed both her and Robbie's names and quickly stamped the cards and thrust them in her purse.

"Done?" Robbie asked, not looking up from the paper.

"Done," she said.

She tried to pay attention to the lowering sun—an enormous orange ball, poised above the watery dark horizon—but her gaze had returned to her husband's bent head. It intrigued her, the way her attention kept snagging on Robbie; the way she kept thinking *husband,* rubbing the word along her tongue as though testing its meaning, its relevance to herself. As though feeling her attention—for how closely, how strangely she was watching him!—Robbie looked up, giving her a quick boyish smile, both happy and fearful.

He stretched his arm across the table, the hand upturned. "Antonia?" he said. "Is something—?"

Her heart had filled, and she felt a sudden catch in her throat, a loss of poise. Confused, she put out her own hand and Robbie grasped it, hard.

Off to the side, there was a sudden burst of applause and the clicking of cameras.

Startled, Antonia and Robbie looked over. A crowd of perhaps forty or fifty, many of them photographers, had gathered along the deck; the couple followed the crowd's attention out to sea, where the sun had just dipped below the horizon, sending brilliant orange and pink trails into the sky.

"The sunset," Robbie said, and quickly he and Antonia exchanged glances, and just as quickly broke into laughter.

"And I thought—" But Antonia didn't dare finish: the idea was so absurd.

"Me too," Robbie said, and they laughed again.

When the waiter approached and asked if they cared for another drink, Antonia was remembering the cat that had burst into their room that morning: so quick, insistent, full of life. She remembered how fearful she had been, her cartoonish alarm that Robbie had found so hilarious. Evidently the cat was one of Hemingway's, and evidently its paws had six toes; but the cat, after all, did not understand. The cat had not meant to frighten anyone. She remembered the way it had curled into Robbie's lap and gone to sleep, uncaring, as Antonia cringed against the wall.

I don't like surprises, Antonia had said.

Now the table was jostled, nearly upsetting Antonia's drink. When she looked up, she saw that Robbie had leapt toward the waiter and begun embracing him. "Hold on! Hold on!" the waiter laughed, pulling back from Robbie's ecstatic greeting. As Antonia watched, her husband kissed the waiter's cheek, the side of his neck; good-naturedly, the waiter kept pushing him away.

Then Antonia saw that the "waiter" was Vincent.

He had commandeered an empty tray, and one of the little red aprons; had approached their table with his head lowered and voice disguised, was there anything they needed, would they care for another drink . . . ?

An elaborate, funny ruse: very typical. His skill in making himself the center of attention, delighting his son, disarming criticism: very typical indeed. Antonia felt light-headed, though she was hardly surprised. Now Vincent winked at her, slyly, over Robbie's bobbing shoulder, as if they were conspirators. Oh yes, very typical: funny and charming, mischievous, certainly beyond criticism.

For Robbie, of course, this was the high point of the trip.

"Dad, you joker!" he cried in delight, falling back into his chair as Vincent took the seat next to Antonia. "When did you get here, anyway? Were you here for the sunset? We've been following that list you made out, all day long, but we never dreamed—Gosh, this is great! Isn't this great, Antonia!"

She gazed across at Vincent, her head lighter than air, feeling dazed in a half-pleasant way; but no, she felt no surprise, no alarm. She felt nothing. "Yes, this is great," she said without irony, not that Robbie was listening. He kept reaching across to cuff his father on the shoulder; he kept hitting the table happily, so that the glasses and silverware rattled.

"Now settle down, everybody," Vincent laughed, watching Antonia. He looked sunburnt, authoritative, his eyes a bright, sharp blue; he wore a tan polo shirt that stretched tight across his massive chest, and a tan nylon windbreaker, and white tennis shoes without socks. Dressed so casually, boyishly, he looked like a sportsman of some kind—an amateur sailor, perhaps. Out in the water, a few minutes ago, Antonia had glimpsed a sailboat going past, the sail billowing, tinted pink by the lowering sun. Now she glanced out to the horizon, but the sailboat was gone and the water had turned dark, choppy; dusk had fallen quickly, she thought, and craning her neck she saw that the crowd had dispersed from along the deck; most everyone had gone off to dinner, to their plans for the evening. . . . Antonia remembered that burst of applause, how it had startled both her and Robbie—the newlyweds, the lovers—and how they had laughed, embarrassed and pleased to discover that no one had noticed, after all; that really no one cared. They were part of the world, she thought, and why should anyone mind if they loved, or failed to love?

Watching Vincent and Robbie, their heads bent close in conversation, Antonia understood that her life was over.

II

There are no surprises, she thought. After all.

The next few hours passed swiftly, or very slowly—she could not be sure. It was true, she thought, that in dying you flung open a door to your past life, your past lives; and again you lived them, quickly. Or slowly. There are no surprises, she thought, because everything is connected, leading in a zigzag chain back from the present moment; leading back, finally, rather than forward. Attuned very lightly to "the present moment," her expression blank, stunned, neutral—vaguely she heard the scraping of chairs, vaguely she understood that Robbie and Vincent were leaving, Vincent's arm across his son's shoulders, their heads bent close together—she sat remembering the cat from that morning, understanding how everything was connected, knowing with a pitiless thrill of certainty that there were no surprises, after all. Only errors in perception.

Though the knowledge arrived, as knowledge usually did, too late.

When someone spoke, using the name "Antonia," she looked up. She fixed her eyes on Vincent settling back in his chair, Vincent drawing something from the pocket of his windbreaker—a yellowed newspaper clipping, a bulky white envelope—and Vincent finally gazing back at her, his eyes a cold blue but not unfriendly, not really, just frank and forthright. Now that Robbie was gone.

Instantly she knew the contents of both the clipping and the envelope.

"Another drink?" Vincent asked, almost gently.

She shook her head, *no*.

"I sent Robbie back to the room, Antonia."

And she nodded, *yes*.

She said, "But the key— I have the key, here in my purse. . . . "

"Don't worry, Antonia, he'll get the key from the manager. He can handle that much, don't you think?"

Vincent smiled, though his eyes didn't smile.

"Yes. Yes, of course."

But someone else was speaking in Antonia's place; someone else sat here prim and pale, hands folded around the icy drink as though anchoring her body to this table, this world.

"How did—how did you find out," she said, faintly.

She'd been afraid, for a while, that somehow her boss had found out, but he was a pathetic man, gossipy and embittered, and soon enough she'd dismissed him as a meddler. Those were satisfying days, after all, with the eldest Kendall son paying her such lavish attention, sending roses to her desk each morning, taking her to the same exclusive restaurants where her own boss took his clients. The owner of an accounting firm that had seen better days, her boss had two-thirds of his office space leased out from under him by the Kendalls and he spent much of his time gossiping about Vincent—that "heartless opportunist"—within hearing range of Antonia's desk, never failing to mention the two younger sons who were "sharks, just like their father," and that oldest boy who did well to find his desk in the morning. . . . Hearing this, Antonia smiled thinly; she signed for her flowers, she blocked two hours off her calendar for lunch. Why should she be afraid, after all? She'd never enjoyed such self-possession, such eerie poise. She'd never held such power.

Powerless, she sat watching Vincent as he examined the palms of his hands.

"I almost didn't," he said, trying to sound casual, trying to spare her, "and the man I had, um, looking into you, I'd paid him off the day before the wedding. He's an old gumshoe type, a real digger, and he seemed disappointed that he hadn't found anything. So he kept on, without my knowing—I guess he figured there'd be quite a bonus, if he could uncover . . . " Vincent was almost whispering.

He pushed the newspaper clipping to the middle of the table.

So she let her eyelids fall, let her eyes skim across the headline, ONE OF 'DAWSON'S GIRLS' KILLS SELF, DAUGHTER FOUND IN LOCKED CLOSET, but she said nothing. She felt nothing.

She remembered her own closet, back home. A locked closet.

She remembered how Mrs. Lassiter complained all during Antonia's high school years, why wouldn't she go out, why wouldn't she come downstairs when one of those nice young men dropped by, didn't she want to be popular, did she want people to think she was *odd*? There was no reason for this, absolutely no reason—she was so pretty, after all! Sometimes Antonia locked the door against her, she turned up the stereo or buried her head in a book, she felt her skin drawing tight along her bones, *no, no,* and soon enough the boys stopped coming around. Soon enough, her mother stopped worrying that Antonia would not go out at night, would not accept dates, would not lead the "normal" life of a high school girl. Dr. Lassiter took her side, saying to leave her alone; he'd always despised the slavish conformity of most teenagers; why shouldn't they admire Antonia's independence? Occasionally he would give her a twenty-dollar bill, or a fifty, which Antonia stored away. For the future. By her eighteenth birthday she had nearly three thousand dollars locked in her closet, in a shoebox thrust back into the closet's dimmest corner. Possibly the money would come in handy someday, for who knew what the future held, who knew?

"This is very awkward, of course, for someone like me," Vincent told her, "someone who has been brought up to respect women, to understand their needs. . . . " He nudged the envelope a bit further in her direction, and obligingly she picked it up, gauging its thickness with her sensitive fingers, as though taking the measure of Vincent's grief, or embarrassment, or pride.

"Yes, of course," she whispered.

"I want the best for my family, I really insist on that," Vincent said mournfully. "It's more than just money, you know. It's a name they can be proud of, proud to give their own children, and their grandchildren. . . . If there were some kind of blight, at this early stage—" Out of tact, he stopped himself. He gave her a pleading look.

"I understand," she told him.

Do you understand? Father Callahan kept asking, and Antonia knew she must say yes, always yes, and especially to this tall silver-haired priest to whom Mrs. Lassiter had presented her new child, her dark-haired lovely child, for instruction in the faith. Eventually the Lassiters had become "lapsed Catholics," and when they stopped attending Mass, Antonia stopped; but at six she had received the sacrament of baptism, followed the next year by her First Holy Communion, Antonia only one of a giggling horde of little girls in white dresses and veils, interchangeable. She remembered feeling happy, that day. She remembered feeling a vague sort of joy.

"Mrs. Kendall is very devout, of course," Vincent was saying, "but an annulment won't be difficult, I'm told, and we have a story—a rather carefully detailed story—which it would help a great deal if you didn't contradict. Not to anyone. Not ever. I'd be very grateful, Antonia. If you'll send your new address to my office, preferably an out-of-state address, I'll see that you're taken care of. This is *my* mistake as much as anyone's, and I don't intend for you to suffer for—" Again, he stopped himself. He nudged the envelope a little closer. "This," he said, "is only for now. I think you know that I'm a responsible man. You know that, don't you? So there's no reason for you to be angry or to feel—well, vengeful."

"Yes," she said, mechanically. "I mean, no."

And finally she'd answered Mama's question—What do you say to Mr. Jones, sweetie, what do you say?—and Antonia stammered Yes, I mean no, and while Mama and Mr. Jones laughed—she hadn't known him as "Mr. Dawson" then, much less as "Senator Dawson"—while they laughed she gripped her mother's leg, pressed her flaming cheeks against the warm fleshy thigh. What, you don't like me? Mr. Jones said again, grabbing Antonia's sides and hauling her into the air. Is that it, huh?—but the question confused her, she didn't understand, she winced at the smell of his cologne and his breath reeking of cigars and his eyes a bright hard blue in the fatty ridges of his face. Is that it, Antonia? Well, next time I'll have to bring you something, won't I? Maybe some jelly babies, how about that?—or a doll, one of those new-fangled dolls that wets and everything? Or I could take your picture, eh?—why should your Mama get all the attention? Thinking yes, I mean no, she'd only nodded, and Mr. Jones and Mama laughed again, and again they hugged each other in that slow way, and Mama said in her husky voice, She'd rather have money, she's just like me, and they laughed once more before he left. Mama was so pretty then! And after he left they always hugged in the real way, tight and wild and crazy, and Antonia said, What do I say, Mama, I never know what to say, and Mama said, Honey, it doesn't matter. They don't listen anyhow.

"Antonia, I wish you'd say something," Vincent went on, returning the clipping to his pocket. Ready to leave, but wanting something more. "Listen," he said, "if it's any comfort, I think it's a shame what they did, letting that Dawson off, sending him back to Washington with a slap on the wrist . . . I was a young man then, and I remember thinking how unfair it was, how badly the system had failed. . . . What could be more sickening, all those girls stashed here and there, half of them on drugs, and just because some oversexed buffoon . . . Well, I shouldn't be bringing this up, but I wanted you to know—"

She reached across and took his hand; squeezed her fingers along his wrist, his forearm.

"Maybe it's not too late?" she said, hoarsely, her eyes vacant. "Maybe we can work out some kind of . . . arrangement?" she said. She smiled, thinly. "You like me, don't you? Robbie said you did."

"Yes—I mean, no," Vincent said, the first time she'd ever seen him stammering and confused; his eyes swerved away. "I'm sorry, but no," he said, taking a deep breath. He recovered. " . . . You look a little pale, why don't you sit here by the water, have a nice dinner," he said, and quickly enough the waiter was summoned, the order given; her food arrived only minutes after Vincent left.

Calmly, Antonia picked at the red snapper.

She picked at the roll and butter.

You're so pale, Mr. Jones said, taking off the seersucker jacket. Doesn't your Mama ever let you play outside? Not waiting for an answer he stalked around the little trailer, identical to the one on the other side of the park where Mama's friend Rita lived, Rita who had hung around all the time after Daddy left, bragging about how she never had to work, how modern these little trailers were, complete with little stoves and little bathrooms and even a closet for your clothes! And a TV. And a stereo. Rita hung around her trailer all day reading magazines and smoking Kools and taking little pills Mr. Jones gave her that made her feel airy and weightless, and happier than she'd ever felt in her life. C'mon, you've got to meet him, Rita said, and later Mama had bent to Antonia and said, It's only for a little while, honey, till we get back on our feet, OK? There was a little curtain to pull across Antonia's sofa-bed, for when Mr. Jones came to visit, or Rita came with a bottle of Early Times to sit gossiping all night with Mama, or even when Mama was home and Antonia just wanted to shut out everything: she could draw the curtain, pretend she wasn't there. But she couldn't pretend with Mr. Jones's heavy presence in the room, his weight jostling the trailer as he stalked up and down, looking into drawers, rifling through Mama's little closet. Where is your Mama, anyway? he asked. Does she always go out when she's not expecting me?—I'll bet she does, I'll bet she *does*, but Antonia remembered not to answer; she just sat on the sofa-bed with hands folded in her lap and waited, waited. When he got close enough she could smell his breath, the same as Rita's when she brought the Early Times, and he sat beside her and gave her a wobbly smile and said, How old are you, anyway? Eight or nine by now, eh? Antonia waited. She stared at the camera Mr. Jones had brought out of the closet. What's the matter, kid, cat got your tongue? he said, and something in his voice told her to answer and so she said, No sir—I'm six, and for some reason Mr. Jones found that funny and asked how long her mother would be gone, and Antonia said she didn't know.

"Dessert, ma'am?"

"No," she said. "Nothing else."

Calmly she opened the envelope, extracted a twenty and put it beside the check. Touched her napkin to one corner of her mouth, then the other. Outside the Pier House she headed toward a taxi but then hesitated, turned, moved out along the street instead. A mild, fragrant night. All the shops and restaurants and bars were still open; music drifted onto the air; people were strolling, laughing, in no hurry. Antonia herself walked slowly, in no hurry. When she did reach the cottage, the door was unlocked, and first she checked the closet to see that Robbie's clothes were gone but hers were not. She went to the window.

She heard someone opening the door, she heard footsteps just behind her, and she tried to ignore her heart—it had begun to beat fast, as though she had raced all the way home. Willing herself to stay calm, she gazed out the window. She gazed across the street.

The windows in the trailer were too high, and she could not get to them; Mr. Jones was holding her down. In any case, there were no streets outside, no lights, nothing at all to help her. Only a few darkened trailers, placed about at random. It was quite late, Mama had gone with Rita and another friend to the movies, a double-feature, she had made Antonia promise not to go outside and *not* to answer the door, and to get in bed before ten o'clock. Of course, Mr. Jones had his own key. Of course, Mr. Jones had the habit of doing whatever he wanted, and now Antonia simply lay on her mother's bed, her legs twitching despite herself, pretending she was behind that curtain and fast asleep in her own bed, and then pretending she was outside, running, running, darting this way, that way! She did not feel the probing fingers, she did not hear the camera's clicking or see the dazzling flashes. She wasn't there, exactly, so how could she make a noise? But when she heard Mama's key in the lock (they decided not to stay for the second feature, Rita would say later: thank God for that, at least), she screamed and screamed. The other woman ran off, and then Mama started screaming, and Mr. Jones struck her across the mouth, but she kept screaming, and then she was crying, and by the time the police arrived Mr. Jones was crying, on his knees and crying, begging forgiveness. He came toward Antonia on his knees, begging, pleading, where she lay very still on the bed. And later, when her mother started screaming again, taking handfuls of pills and screaming at people not in the room at all, Antonia did not object when she opened the closet and said, Just for a little while, I promise—till Mama feels a little better. She went out for a moment—to the phone at the corner, it turned out—and rushed back in, sobbing, and Antonia heard more pills rattling out, and all was still until the giant yellow-haired policeman unlocked the closet door and said, Good Lord—

Motionless, she stared out the window and across the street. Her heart had calmed. Her legs had relaxed. Every minute or two she touched her cheeks with the palm of her hand. Robbie had spoken a few times, but had fallen quiet at last. He sat on the bed, behind her; or on the chair. He didn't know what to do, he'd wept—whether to go or stay. "Antonia, what should I do? I feel like I'm nothing inside, like I'm dead, I don't know. . . . Can't you speak, Antonia? Honey?" Outside, a car had honked: several quick impatient beeps.

She didn't answer. She would like to comfort him, she thought, but it was not in her nature; she hated emotional displays. In any case, she couldn't pay attention to Robbie. Her eye was drawn out of this room, to the house nestled in darkness across the street. She stared, stared. Yes, it was Hemingway's house, and along the brick wall she could make out soft dark clumps in the moonlight, the cats perched at random, vigilant, eternal. They were everywhere, she thought, covering the walls and the grounds and the house itself, guarding everything that was not theirs.

Robbie tried again. "Antonia," he wept, "I'll die if I lose you, don't you understand? Already I feel like I'm dying, like I'm nothing inside . . . you understand, don't you? Antonia?"

Outside, the car horn blared. Or was it one of those cats, sending its wail into the night?

"I don't mean to be cruel," she said at last, "but Robbie, you really won't. You really *won't* die."

Uncle Vic

WHEN Uncle Vic got out of the hospital, early that summer, Mama said he'd be staying at our house for a while. Daddy was dead-set against it, and so was my older brother, Ronnie, but since she did all the housework and bought the food, Mama said, they had no right to complain. And besides that, she told Daddy, she'd have thought *he,* of all people, would understand how awful it was to be an invalid, and Daddy shot back that he wasn't an invalid, not any more, and that Uncle Vic sure the hell never had been. After that everybody got quiet for a while, but you could tell that Mama had won.

Daddy was hurt in Vietnam when he was twenty and had disability, but now he worked at the V.A. hospital down on Clairmont Road, organizing "recreation"—games and crafts and such—for vets worse off than he was. (Daddy had chronic back pain and a limp from shrapnel in the left thigh, but some vets he knew had lost limbs and even their eyes.) It was a volunteer job but he took it serious, worked nine to five just like he got paid, and would fuss like hell at Ronnie if he got him there five minutes late. Ronnie had gone down to the Winn-Dixie on his sixteenth birthday, the week before Uncle Vic showed up, and got a job unloading food trucks and stocking shelves. That same day, Daddy spent one of his disability checks on a beat-up Ford Fairlane for Ronnie, and Ronnie was paying him twenty-five a week and having to chauffeur Daddy around, as Ronnie put it, which he hadn't figured was part of the deal. They were always coming and going now, Ronnie and Daddy, fussing at each other about gas money and the best way to get places and the jillion other things you can fight over when you have one car with two people inside it. Mama said they sounded just like an old married couple.

It was Mama who supported the family and, in general, ran things. When she was full of herself, she'd stand at the stove and sing the song from that TV commercial—"I can bring home the bacon, fry it up in the pan"—and twitch her hips a little. I would laugh, and even Ronnie, but Daddy would get up and leave the room. Mama had managed a wallpaper outlet over on Howell Mill Road since before she and Daddy got married, so she handled the money and gave me an allowance every Sunday—ten dollars, which was enough since I was only fourteen and stuck at home for the summer—and couldn't understand why Daddy and Ronnie were so hateful about Uncle Vic, her baby brother, who'd had so many troubles in his life, who was a gentle soul, and who just needed some kindness and understanding until he got back on his feet. Mornings after Ronnie and Daddy were gone and while Uncle Vic was still sleeping, she'd use me as her "sounding board," hurrying around the kitchen and cleaning up the breakfast dishes before leaving for the store, arguing with Daddy and Ronnie even though they weren't there, and asking questions out loud like "Didn't you have to help out family, no matter what? Did they just expect her to turn Uncle Vic out on his ear, with no prospects for a job and no money for food and rent, never mind his medications? Could she live with herself, if she did such a thing?"

I didn't answer. About Uncle Vic as on most touchy subjects in the family, I stayed neutral. One time Mama said I should be one of those guards over in England with the red uniforms and big black woolly helmets who stand outside the palace and never bat an eye, even if you scream bloody murder right in front of them; another time she said I must be Swiss, though there was no Swiss blood in our family. Daddy said he thought they'd had a Swiss milkman, once, and that time it was Mama who left the room. Ronnie asked what being Swiss meant and what a milkman was, but nobody answered him.

There was one bad thing: I was stuck alone with Uncle Vic during the day. Not that I didn't like him, or that he wasn't nice or whatever, but it would've been so much better to watch TV in the den or shoot baskets out in the driveway without wondering if he might be standing back in a shadow somewhere, watching me. If I saw him, he'd come up and say, "Whatcha doing," not the most brilliant thing to ask a person sitting in front of a TV set, or he'd ask some jerky question like when did school start and what grade would I be in, the type of thing clueless adults ask teenagers when they don't know what else to say. One morning he even tried to make a joke, shambling up behind the sofa where I was sprawled in my Braves T-shirt and cut-off jeans, changing channels with the clicker but not finding much.

He said, "Hey Jimmy, heard anything lately from the ball and chain?"

He meant my girlfriend, Becky, who was gone with her parents on a car trip out west—the Painted Desert, the Grand Canyon, crappy places like that—for three solid weeks. This was a sore subject, since in the last few days I hadn't gotten even a postcard, much less one of the long, syrupy letters she'd sent the first week, on motel stationery from towns like Meridian, Mississippi and Texarkana, Texas. *I miss you so much, Jimmy, I don't know why my parents made me come on this stupid ridiculous trip,* etc., etc., with lots of X's and O's at the end. Now I figured she'd gotten into the trip and was having a good time and had forgotten me.

"Nope," I said, staring at a woman with long pink fingernails, holding up a gold chain on the Shopping Channel. I had the "mute" button on, but she seemed to be excited and happy about the chain.

I didn't say anything else. If you gave one-word answers to Uncle Vic, I'd discovered, there was a good chance he would shamble off again. Most days he didn't crawl out of bed before noon. Mama said his medications made him sleep a lot, Daddy said he was a layabout, but I didn't care which it was. I wished he'd sleep all day. When I first heard him stumbling around in the bedroom, I'd usually go outside and start shooting baskets—Uncle Vic never came out there—or even take my bicycle out and ride around the neighborhood like a smaller kid. Sooner or later, though, I'd have to deal with him. When I came inside, he'd approach me with this nice, expectant look on his face, as if somehow I were in charge of planning our time together, so I avoided eye contact as much as I could decently do. Besides, although Uncle Vic was otherwise an ordinary-looking guy—about forty, slender build, with receding auburn hair the same shade as my mother's—I didn't like his eyes. They were a bright, clear blue, like a little kid's, and they bugged out slightly, as though someone had just surprised the hell out of him. One day I heard Daddy mutter something about "old owl-eyes," and Mama hushed him quick, saying they'd given Uncle Vic shock treatment in the hospital and she'd think Daddy, of all people, would understand about making fun of people over things they can't help. Daddy had said nobody knew what "shock" was about until they'd been to war, but I didn't want to hear him start yammering about that so I left the room.

Sometimes I'd break down and play cards with Uncle Vic—he taught me Gin Rummy and Hearts, which are pretty moronic games but at least they passed the time—or board games like Checkers and Pokeno. Uncle Vic had brought these with him from the hospital, and when I thought about his time there I must admit I felt pretty bad for him. He concentrated hard on the games, hunched forward over the table with his jawbone clenched and his eyes glazed with effort. This meant that we didn't have to make conversation while we were playing—another reason I went along with the games, and sometimes even suggested them—and it even made me like him a bit more, I guess; he tried so hard, yet he always seemed just as happy when I won as when he did. Sometimes we kept track of how many hands of Gin or Checker games we'd won by using matches, and on the last go-round we'd usually go all or nothing. One day, when he'd won, he cupped all the matches in his clean smooth hands and pulled them toward his chest, saying with a grin, "To the victor go the spoils"—you know, making a play on his name, which was something he did quite a bit. In the hospital I guess there isn't much to do but play games and hope you'll win, maybe to help you forget the real world thinks you're a loser.

Just before he got here, Mama had arched one eyebrow and told us that her brother was "highly intelligent, and sensitive, and creative," and that was the reason he'd had so many problems in his life. This was at dinner, when she'd fixed Daddy and Ronnie's favorite meal—meatloaf smothered in tomatoes and onions—and they were too busy forking it down to make a fuss. I wasn't even sure they were listening. Sometimes when she talked about my dead grandparents or her only sibling she'd address herself just to me, putting that pleasant, musical lilt in her voice that I'd heard her use on customers down at the store. I guess I had this way of listening without looking hostile or bored. Sometimes I'd even ask her a question or two, just to keep things moving along, and peaceful, and she would answer in the same polite, "intelligent" voice, talking in complete sentences and using words that Ronnie and maybe even Daddy wouldn't know. "That's often been the case, you know, throughout history," she said. "The most gifted people often have a psychological malaise of one kind or another."

At that point, Daddy did glance up with a narrowed, smirking look, but his mouth was full so he didn't bother. At the time I didn't know what *malaise* meant, either, but I nodded like I understood and pretty much agreed.

"So I want you all to be nice to Vic," she'd said, in a voice that sounded both scolding and fearful. "Don't forget, this is a man with a degree in political science"—and she went on to narrate the familiar story of how Uncle Vic not only sailed through college but had gotten into his last year at Emory Law School before having some type of breakdown. This was evidently related to his being sensitive and creative though Mama was never too specific on this, and she never told us what he'd created, if anything. Then he'd moved up north for a while, to Illinois, where he'd worked in a bank for a couple of years, and after getting promoted to bank manager had started having problems again. That time he'd gone into the hospital, and soon afterwards came back to Atlanta, where he got another job—in a restaurant, bussing tables. But there was some sort of fracas evidently caused by Vic, since Mama always rushed by this part, and he was sent off to Milledgeville when I was about five years old. He'd been there ever since. All through the years Mama would drive down and visit him, and keep in touch with the doctors, and fill out Uncle Vic's disability forms, and do whatever else needed doing, all in the hope that he'd get out someday. So, she'd told us, her little brother's homecoming was a big deal to her, and he wouldn't have to stay here long: only until he got used to being out, Mama said, and "readjusted to society." Daddy did stop chewing long enough to ask what about society getting readjusted to *him*, but Mama had pretended not to hear. By the end of the summer, she said, she would find him a little apartment or duplex, maybe over in northwest Atlanta, near the store, where she could check on him during her lunch break and after work. Uncle Vic had told her, she claimed, that he didn't want to be a bother, and she'd assured him that he wouldn't be, and she reminded us all that if we couldn't be nice to a member of our family then there was probably no hope for peace in the world.

Ronnie asked where was the peach cobbler she'd promised for dessert. Nobody spoke of Uncle Vic again until the next week, when Mama drove down to Milledgeville and got him.

There were times, like I said, when I got mopey about being stuck with him during the day. I'd have traded places with Ronnie in a second, even though he complained about his job, coming home with bruises on his arms, and even on his face; he called them his "battle scars." He and the other guys, unloading the heavy boxes and crates down at Winn-Dixie, liked to throw the boxes at each other when they weren't looking, and that's why they got so banged up. Mama and Daddy's jobs didn't seem like much fun, either, since who'd want to deal with sad-eyed vets all day or persnickety old ladies trying to pick out wallpaper, but at least they got out of the house, and ate hamburgers with their friends at lunchtime, and came home more often than not all revved up and full of themselves. Whereas I was feeling low, spending all day with my lunatic uncle, and had gotten pretty tired of seeing my face in the mirror. What a dweeb, I thought. What a loser. Even my best friend Roy had stopped calling. He was a year older than me and had his license now and had started spending time with his tenth-grade friends who could drive, and have cars and part-time jobs, and now Becky had stopped writing as if she could sense, all the way from Arizona or wherever the hell, that I was no longer much of a prize. Sometimes I wondered if Uncle Vic, who supposedly had tried to off himself a few times when he was younger, hadn't had the right idea.

And it gets worse, believe me. But before I go into that I want to say a little more about Uncle Vic—on the plus side. There were times, I have to admit, when I was almost glad to have him around. For instance, some days at lunchtime Mama would drive all the way home just to eat with us. Since our house was in east Atlanta, a fifties-style neighborhood off Flat Shoals Road, she had a pretty long, trafficky drive from the store, about twenty minutes each way, and on top of that she'd usually stop at Picadilly Cafeteria or Fellini's Pizza and bring lunch for the three of us. Uncle Vic just couldn't get over that. He thought Mama was a saint or something, and when he knew she was coming he'd get up by eleven and have the house all tidy, and once even hiked down to the corner store and got a bouquet of flowers to give her when she walked in the door. "Here she is—Queen for a Day!" he said, giving her a little bow, and when Mama started to get tearful and I asked what "Queen for a Day" meant, they explained that when they were kids there was a TV show where every day the show picked some poor, deprived housewife and proclaimed her Queen and granted all her wishes. Mama said, wiping her eyes, that having her sweet little brother home, getting her family back together, was the only real wish she had in life, and all of a sudden I thought I was going to choke up, too. But then Mama, in the way she does, turned on her heel and got busy with the lunch, so I caught hold of myself.

It occurred to me that before Uncle Vic came, I'd never seen Mama cry except when she was frustrated with Daddy or Ronnie; I'd never seen "happy" tears from her, in other words. But lately she'd seemed full of energy, telling us about her plans to reorganize the displays down at the store, and asking Daddy what he thought of their having the house repainted and maybe building a redwood deck out back. When Daddy said he didn't think much of it, she didn't seem to hear. It was almost like Daddy and Ronnie both had lost their power, had turned into a couple of boarders or something. They drove off together in the mornings and later, as usual, crabbed at each other all through dinner, but they were no longer the center of Mama's attention. Uncle Vic was that—and I guess I was, too—and somehow, for this brief while, the house was a pleasanter and more peaceful place to be. Granted, a little boring in the daytime, but without as much tension and yelling as we'd had in the past.

It occurred to me, too, that I was losing my neutrality, though I don't think anybody noticed.

I had to give Uncle Vic his due, in other words, even though I didn't think he'd really tried to make any sort of difference, or even knew that he had. In fact, he seemed to go out of his way *not* to make waves, and sometimes this got on my nerves a little bit. "Sorry," he'd say, coming through the den after dinner, on his way back to the kitchen. I'd be watching TV with Mama and Daddy, and I'd wonder to myself why the hell he had to apologize. We'd invited him to sit with us a hundred times, but he almost always spent the evenings by himself, playing solitaire or reading old magazines in his room. He'd come out to get some cookies, or a glass of tea, and then he'd scurry back again. "Just pretend I'm not here," he'd say, hunching down his shoulders and glancing sideways at Daddy.

All my life I'd heard that my uncle was not "all there"—a phrase Daddy liked to use, pointing to his head—but now I wondered if the words didn't have another meaning. For Uncle Vic was the quietest and most nondescript person I'd ever met. He wore white, polyester-and-cotton dress shirts—he had seven of these identical shirts in his closet, all hanging in a row—and ordinary black pants, and since he seldom went outside he had a pale, mealy complexion that made his buggy blue eyes stand out all the more. For his birthday, shortly after he got here, Mama had bought him a couple of plaid sport shirts, but two months later they were still all folded and pinned in his drawer, the price tags attached. Uncle Vic claimed he was saving them for a special occasion, but Mama said something strange to me one morning, talking half to herself while waiting for the toast to pop up; she said he was *afraid* to wear them, for some reason, and though I couldn't understand this to save my soul, I knew that she was right.

Early on, when Daddy noticed that Uncle Vic was timid and shy to a fault, he'd tried one morning at breakfast to encourage him, man to man.

"There's a whole world out there, Victor!" he'd said, in between bites of his Cheerios.

He had that excited, happy look in his eyes, and the attitude that there's no problem in creation that can't be solved in five minutes, so I knew he'd taken one of his pain pills before breakfast.

"What you need to do," he said, shaking his spoon at Uncle Vic in a friendly way, "is stop moping around this house and—get out there!"

He gestured vaguely toward the kitchen window, in the direction of I-20.

"Yeah, you've had some troubles in the past, but that's over now. You need to get out there and make your mark. It's never too late, you know. Do whatever it takes, Vic—introduce yourself to people, join a club, go out drinking—hell, get a girl pregnant!"

At this, Ronnie looked up and laughed. "Rich, for heaven's sake!" Mama hissed at him, while Uncle Vic turned red and smiled and stared down at his plate.

"How come you never gave me no advice like that?" Ronnie said to Daddy, grinning.

But soon after that Daddy got disgusted with Uncle Vic, and the attention Mama paid him, and said again that her brother was just mooching off us, for no reason. I kept my own opinions to myself, as usual, letting Daddy rail at Mama about the situation in the evenings, during TV commercials, and paying no attention when Ronnie would come in from work, all banged up and with a mean look around his mouth, and stop at my bedroom door and say, "What you two sweethearts been doin' all day, Jimmy? Did you weave a few baskets? Huh?" Then he'd slam the door to his own room and turn on his head-banging music, and I wouldn't see him again until dinner.

Like I said, I'd started to feel sorry for both Uncle Vic and myself, and during the last week he was here, just before everything started going downhill, I even went out of my way to spend time with him. One day we walked down to the corner and took MARTA to South Dekalb mall for an Arnold Schwarzenegger movie. Now I thought it was pretty boring, fights and chases and all that, just kids' stuff, but Uncle Vic really seemed to get into it; his eyes bugged out even more than usual as he sat there, mechanically stuffing popcorn into his mouth, not looking away once during the whole movie. "You know the last movie I saw?" he asked, during the bus ride home. "*The Sound of Music*. They played that in the hospital, last Christmas. The year before that, it was *The Wizard of Oz*." Then he added, in a quieter voice, "Like we were a bunch of kids. It made me pretty mad, I tell you."

I looked over at him, surprised. It was hard to imagine Uncle Vic getting mad about anything, much less a harmless movie at Christmas time. So I said, "Well, this Christmas you'll probably spend with us. I mean, by then you'll have your own place and all, but you can come over."

He looked at me, and one side of his mouth twitched upwards, but I couldn't tell if he was pleased or a little annoyed. Then something else took his attention: a little kid, a baby, looking at us from a few seats up. He was staring over his mother's shoulder, with a pacifier in his mouth, grinning. After a minute the kid held up two fingers, like he was answering the question we would surely ask him if we got the chance.

"Pretty cute, huh," I said. "I guess he's two years old."

Uncle Vic didn't answer. He raised his own hand, with two fingers pointing neatly upwards in a little V. I'd heard Mama call this the "peace sign." He was answering the kid, I guess, but for some reason I thought, "V is for Victor," and then the bus slowed down and I realized it was our stop.

* * *

That same night, when Ronnie got home, he was in a worse mood than usual. He'd gotten off early, but that meant he'd had to hang around the V.A. hospital waiting for Daddy, and it was clear they'd found something to fuss about all the way home. Mama was working late at the store, doing inventory, but she'd reminded us that morning about the leftover lasagna she'd made from scratch the night before. All we'd need to do was heat it up. So the three of us were shuffling around in the kitchen, getting the food and glasses and silverware together. We were making a respectable mess, as usual, when Ronnie noticed a flat cardboard box sticking out of the trash. He pulled it out far enough to read the lettering along the edge.

"What's this, from Fellini's Pizza?" he asked, whirling toward me. "What'd you and Vic do, have your goddamn lunch delivered?"

"Hey, watch your language," Daddy said. He was already getting settled at the kitchen table, buttering his bread. When Mama wasn't home, we always ate in the kitchen.

"No, Mama brought it for us," I said, feeling awkward and vulnerable in my cut-offs and bare feet. Ronnie was wearing his Guns'n'Roses T-shirt, and his ripped blue jeans were stuffed inside his favorite black boots. They came almost to his knees and weren't the cowboy kind, but almost like military boots. Mama complained they made marks on the kitchen floor, but Ronnie wouldn't wear anything else.

"See?" he said, turning on Daddy. He was so furious, his eyes seemed to turn red. "She can bring home lunch for these lazy jerks, but we work all day long and then have to make our own."

"She's doing inventory, remember?" I said. "They always do it after the store closes."

Daddy was bent over his plate, chowing down; he never waited for us. "Inventory, huh," he said, sopping up tomato sauce with his piece of bread. "Big deal." Then he looked at me. "By the way, where's Mr. Excitement? Getting his beauty rest?"

"He's in his room," I said, starting for the doorway. "He's reading or something. I'll go get him—"

"Hell no!" Ronnie said roughly, reaching into the refrigerator for the tea pitcher. "Let's eat in peace for once, without that sorry fool watching us."

"Oh, hell, he's got to eat dinner," Daddy said. "Go get him, Jimmy."

"Let the bastard starve," said Ronnie. "Just let him!"

Then my brother did something that amazed me. He was holding his plate in one hand, his glass of tea in the other, and was just about to come to the table. But his hands were trembling, and all at once he slammed the plate down on the counter so hard that some tomato sauce spewed out onto the floor. It looked like a splash of blood.

"I'm sick of this goddamn house!" he said with his teeth clenched, more to himself than to us. His eyes were redder still, and wet-looking. He glanced at Daddy and then me, like he would be happy to strangle either one of us, and then he ran out of the kitchen and slammed the door to his room. A few seconds later, one of his heavy-metal CDs started blaring.

Daddy just lifted his eyebrows and finished chewing. "Looks like somebody got up on the wrong side of the bed," he said, winking at me.

Mama had once said that Ronnie had inherited Daddy's looks but not his sense of humor, and I had to agree. After Daddy's joke, the cold, sickish feeling in my stomach eased up, and I went in and called Uncle Vic and the three of us had a pleasant meal. We practically had to yell to be heard over Ronnie's music, but at least we could be pretty sure that Ronnie would stay in his room for the rest of the night.

A year or two ago, I might have been more upset about the way my brother acted, since we still did things together then, and even had a civil conversation once in a while. Ronnie hadn't ever done that well in school, and was always getting into fights, but otherwise he hadn't been such a bad kid. When he got to high school, though, he'd started hanging around with some long-haired, head-banging types, and Mama was scared to death he'd start taking drugs. I didn't think he had, but something had sure gotten into him. For one thing, he no longer seemed to like the ordinary kids he'd grown up with—they all drove pick-ups now, and had girlfriends. Once when we saw an old buddy from his junior-high football team driving along I-20, wearing a cowboy hat, Ronnie mumbled something about "that stupid redneck" out the side of his mouth. Now that he had the job at Winn-Dixie—thank God for that, at least, Mama would say—he'd stopped playing sports or doing anything at all with the family, including going to church. When he wasn't out carousing with his friends, he stayed in his room and listened to music. He didn't have a girlfriend, and not long ago had stopped at my bedroom door to tell me that Becky was a "little simp," as far as he was concerned. He might have turned into an asshole, but Ronnie could still hurt my feelings. Though I hadn't said anything back, it was hard to take Mama's advice and just ignore him.

After that night when Ronnie threw his fit in the kitchen, I made the mistake of thinking that everything would be okay. Daddy started being a little nicer to Uncle Vic, as if to show that we weren't a totally crappy family, and that same week Mama announced that she intended to find him an apartment by Labor Day. For his part, Uncle Vic was starting to come out of his shell, just a little, asking Daddy about his work at the V.A. and volunteering to help Mama down at the store. When she said she'd love to hire him but couldn't afford it, Uncle Vic said he'd work for free—but Mama said that would be taking advantage. When he said something about room and board, she said you didn't take money from family. But she did start handing him the classified section at breakfast, and after everybody left for work Uncle Vic would sit at the kitchen table, reading the ads and making little, precise circles with a red pen, concentrating just as hard as if he were playing checkers.

After that, everything happened so fast and crazy that it reminds me, looking back on it, of one of those stock market charts they show on TV, where it looks like the company is doing just fine, thank you, but then all of a sudden something happens and the line starts zigzagging, first down, then maybe back up for a while, but then plunging straight down again like it's falling off a cliff. That's the way it happened with our family—and there I was, smack dab in the middle of it, but not able to do a thing. Like some dweeby stockbroker who can't do anything but shrug his shoulders and try to figure out what the hell went wrong.

First off, something went right: Uncle Vic got a job. Or rather, Mama got him one. A customer from the store, some older guy who said he was a doctor, was setting up an office over in midtown, and he'd stopped by to get some wallpaper for the waiting room. He and Mama got to talking, and it turned out that the guy was a head doctor—a shrink—and I guess Mama had decided to start blabbing about her poor little brother. Well, one thing led to another, and it turned out the guy needed somebody to answer his phone and do his bookkeeping; he was just starting out and could only pay eight bucks an hour, but with Uncle Vic's education he thought it might be the perfect "starter" job for him. Plus, Mama said, she felt sure the doctor would keep an eye on Vic, and make sure he took his medicine, and so forth, so before we knew it, she had Uncle Vic down there meeting the doctor, and it was all a done deal. He would start on Monday.

Now, you'd have thought that Daddy and Ronnie both would have been glad to hear that Uncle Vic had a job, and would appreciate his saying that he intended to hand over part of his check for the first few weeks, to pay back what he owed us. (Mama said she'd die before she'd take that money, but I figured that Daddy would take it.) And you'd have thought they'd be glad that Mama had found Uncle Vic a garage apartment not far from the doctor's office, and that he'd be gone within a week. But, as Daddy liked to say, "That's what you get for thinking." During that last week before Uncle Vic started his job, Ronnie was more hateful than ever at mealtimes, and wouldn't even look at Uncle Vic when he said something. One side of his mouth would move upward, in a kind of snarl I guess you'd call it, and even when Mama asked him a question, Ronnie would only give answers like "Yeh," or "Naw," or "How should I know?" Daddy's behavior wasn't too princely, either. He'd started complaining that his leg was hurting him and that the pain pills didn't work any more, and when he'd snap at Mama and she'd snap back that the leg wasn't *her* fault and to give her a break, he'd mutter something like "I'll give you a break, all right," and Ronnie would snicker, and Uncle Vic would glance up from his plate with that scared-rabbit look of his. So, to keep it short, the tension was worse than ever, and it was uncomfortable as hell, and I didn't understand what was going on. I thought that once Uncle Vic was gone, maybe that would be the end of it—but that's what you get for thinking, like Daddy said.

Anyway, I guess it's time for the gory details. It was Sunday, the day before Uncle Vic was supposed to start working, and after we got back from church (except for Ronnie, who was working at the store), Mama said something during lunch—she always cooked a big lunch on Sundays—about how high the grass was. Daddy made a face like she'd poked him in the side with a stick. He said that she knew darn well his back was hurting, and she knew there was a Braves game starting in thirty minutes, and *he* knew that's why she'd picked this particular time to ask him to cut the grass.

Now his tone of voice—kind of whiney and mean at the same time, just like Ronnie's—made her mad, as Daddy probably knew it would.

"All right, forget it!" she said, and then she closed her eyes for a second, as if reminding herself that this was Sunday and we'd just heard a sermon about family values. She took a deep breath and said in a tight, calm voice, "I'll put on my blue jeans and do it myself, then. Might as well—I do everything else around here."

"I could do it," I put in. "I don't care."

"No, honey," Mama said, in a sweet voice like I was four years old. (But she was still looking at Daddy.) "You know what would happen, Jimmy, with your allergies—you'd be sneezing for a week."

"No, I won't," I said. "I'll wear my nose pinchers, like I did that other time."

I was talking about that stupid rubbery contraption I had to wear when I went swimming, to keep the chlorine out of my nose. Since I'd met Becky, I hadn't worn it; I preferred choking, coughing, and the possibility of a watery death to the way I looked in those pinchers, with the little white stripe they made across my nose.

"No, honey, you know you look ridiculous when you wear those things. And I need the exercise, anyway," she said, trying to make a joke of it. "My thighs—"

"For heaven's sake, Vivian, *I* can cut the grass for you. I'm not totally useless, you know."

Everybody looked over in surprise at Uncle Vic, even Daddy. He spoke up so seldom, much less to interrupt, that we all wondered if we were hearing things.

"Oh, honey, you need to rest up," Mama said. "You start your new job tomorrow."

Daddy shot his eyes toward the ceiling and made a whistling noise with his teeth. He was about to make some ugly remark, but Uncle Vic spoke first.

"If you'd just help me get it started, Rich," he said to Daddy. "I think I could use the exercise myself."

"But Vic, honey, are you sure?"

"But Vic, honey, are you sure?" Daddy mimicked, in a screechy voice that sounded exactly like her, I have to admit. Then he turned to Vic; I saw the cold light in his eyes, but I could tell he'd decided to cooperate.

"Sure, Vic," he said. "There's nothing to it."

It was settled. Mama was so pissed about the way Daddy imitated her, she didn't say anything else for the rest of the meal. Soon as she finished eating, she started carrying bowls back to the kitchen, and Uncle Vic excused himself, too, saying he needed to change into some old clothes before doing the yard. That left me and Daddy alone at the table.

"Want me to show him?" I asked. "The game's about to start. You ought to go back to the den and get comfortable."

Daddy was cleaning his plate, as usual, sopping up leftover gravy with his dinner roll. But he wasn't watching what he was doing; his eyes had a sad, empty look, and his voice sounded far away.

"No, I'll do it," he said. "I reckon that's one thing I can do."

Needless to say, Daddy and Uncle Vic disagreed over how to cut the grass. I'd gone into the kitchen to help Mama finish up the dishes, and we could see them from the window over the sink. Everything seemed okay while Daddy showed him about checking the gas tank, and setting the throttle, and cranking the mower up. It was when Uncle Vic actually started mowing that things started to happen. Daddy couldn't leave it alone, of course, but had to stand and watch Uncle Vic while he started mowing along the chain-link fence. Daddy stood on the edge of the patio, hands on his hips and already shaking his head, like he should have known he ought to do the job himself. "I wish he'd just come on in," Mama said under her breath. "Want me to go out and get him?" I said, drying off the gravy boat she'd handed me. "The game's probably started by now." But before she could answer, Daddy had already stalked out across the yard toward Uncle Vic. It made my heart clutch a little to see him, because his leg was making him limp a little. Daddy had been a stocky, athletic type of guy when he was young, and he was still muscular in his chest and shoulders, so it pained me to see him limping like that.

Of course, Mama and I both knew what the problem was. Uncle Vic does everything in a kind of slow, finicky way, and it had taken him at least five minutes to cut about a six-foot ribbon of grass along the fence. See, he kept backing up and going at the fence from all angles, making sure he got every little blade, and anything he couldn't cut with the mower, he'd stop and walk around and pull by hand. At this rate, I figured he'd finish the yard by sundown on Tuesday, but at the same time I thought he wasn't doing any harm and why not let him alone? Of course, Daddy didn't see it that way. He poked at Uncle Vic's shoulder with his forefinger and gestured him aside, then took the mower and moved off along the fence, leaving Uncle Vic staring after him. Daddy finished one side and went along the rear, came up the other side and along the house, and came full circle back to where he'd started in less time than it had taken Uncle Vic to do that one tiny strip.

Then Daddy went up and cupped his mouth and yelled something to Uncle Vic over the roar of the engine. Uncle Vic cupped his own mouth and said something back, and whatever he said must have irritated Daddy, because Daddy gestured him toward the house and went back to the mower like he was going to finish the job himself. But Uncle Vic followed him, and they both grabbed onto the handle, and then Mama and I were treated to the sorry, ridiculous sight of two grown men fighting over a lawn mower.

We had to laugh, at first.

"Our very own Laurel and Hardy," Mama said, shaking her head. "Sometimes I think they haven't got a lick of sense, either one of them."

"Yeah," I added. "Too bad Ronnie's working today, or else we could send him out there to help. Then we'd have—"

"The Three Stooges!"

We both said it at the same time. The two of us had always thought alike, and now we looked at each other and started laughing. It was one of those things that catches you by surprise and seems so funny that you can't laugh enough. We laughed so hard our eyes started to water, and Mama pulled her sudsy hands out of the sink and wiped at her eyes with the sides of her wrist. As for me, I stood half bent over, with one hand on my stomach. After everything that happened in the last few weeks, I figured we needed and deserved a good laugh and that's why I let myself go, which normally wasn't like me.

The next thing we heard was the screaming. We'd both paused for breath at the same minute, Mama giving a little hiccup as she tried to stop laughing, and then the mower had stopped and Daddy was out there yelling at the top of his voice. We looked out the window and saw him laying flat out in the grass, holding onto one of his legs with both hands. It wasn't the leg that got hurt in the war, but the other one. The bottom part of his jeans was a mess of blood and wet grass, and the blood was still spurting everywhere—up onto Daddy's shirt, onto the overturned mower, and even onto Uncle Vic, who stood there pale and still and not doing a damn thing but staring down at Daddy.

While Mama ran out back, I called 911, and the ambulance came pretty quick and took Daddy to Dekalb General. We followed them, with Mama driving, and I was surprised and impressed by how calm she was. I sat in the front seat, staying pretty calm myself, while Uncle Vic sat in the back with a glazed-over look in his eyes. Like a moron, I thought—like a killer moron. I was thinking this because I was mad as hell, and hoped the police would come to the hospital and escort Uncle Vic back to Milledgeville. Of course, I wasn't thinking straight, but that's the kind of thing that churns through your head at such a time.

After a couple of hours, they had Daddy in a hospital bed and the doctor told us, just like on TV, that Daddy had been lucky. (The doctor could have played on TV, in fact; he was tall, with a full head of silver hair, and he had that sincere, crinkly-eyed look that appeals to women like Mama, who was smiling up at him like a teenager.) With the blood and all, the doctor went on, the accident had looked worse than it was. We were all clumped around the foot of Daddy's bed, looking sideways at him while the doctor talked. They'd given him a pain shot that had put him to sleep, they'd stuffed him into one of those little pale-blue hospital gowns, and they had his leg bandaged and elevated. But the mower blades had mostly just grazed his flesh, the doctor said, and it didn't look like any muscle or tissue had been damaged. He'd lost some blood, and the doctor wanted to check him in the morning, but after that Daddy could probably go home.

The doctor put one hand on Mama's shoulder, squeezing. This guy was a real pro.

"He'll be mad," Mama laughed, "that we didn't take him to the V.A. He works over there, you know, and he's—"

"He can go home in the morning," the doctor said, turning up the wattage on his smile. "That ought to make him feel better."

So we were left alone with Daddy, who apart from the leg looked pretty comfortable. He had a half-smile on his face and had even started to snore a little bit.

The doctor said he'd probably sleep all day, so Mama decided to take me and Uncle Vic home, get Daddy's pajamas and some toiletries, and come back to spend the night with him. On the way home, Uncle Vic seemed to come out of his trance. He started saying how terrible he felt, and how he would move out that day and never bother us again, and Mama kept telling him to hush, that it wasn't his fault. "It's Rich's temper," she said, with a little sigh, while we were sitting at a red light. "It's going to be the end of him, one of these days."

Now I didn't think this was fair to Daddy, but I didn't say anything. I turned my head halfway around, not looking at him, and said to Uncle Vic, "We weren't looking when it happened. What *did* happen, exactly?"

Uncle Vic's answer sounded pretty straightforward, I have to admit. It didn't sound like he was making a story up off the top of his head. While they were arguing over who should mow the lawn, he said, the mower had started coughing, like the blades were clogged up with grass. Daddy was already red-faced and mad, and this made him madder, so he jerked up one side of the mower and kicked at the blades. Well, this unstuck the blades so fast that he couldn't get his leg back in time, and the next thing Uncle Vic knew Daddy was down on the ground, shimmying back like a crab from the mower, and yelling.

"That sounds like one of his stunts," Mama said. "Imagine, kicking at the mower blades! Without turning off the engine!"

"He was impatient with me," Uncle Vic said meekly. "It was my fault, I was going too slow—"

"It was *not* your fault," Mama said, and I decided there was no point in arguing.

When we got home, though, I made a mistake. While Mama was getting Daddy's things together and Uncle Vic was in his room, I used the kitchen phone and called up Ronnie at the store. He was a member of this family, I reasoned, and had a right to know that his daddy had almost lost his leg to a lawn mower. I planned to tell him what happened in a calm, reasonable voice, but when he came on the line, I blurted out, "You won't believe what that lunatic did to Daddy!"

"Jimmy, is that you? What the hell—?"

He sounded like he'd been asleep, but once I'd told him what happened I knew I'd messed up. Before I could finish, Ronnie started howling a bunch of questions at me, like he didn't know whether to cry or to piss.

"Is Daddy gonna be all right? Why didn't you call me soon's it happened? Why the hell isn't Vic in jail? Put that fucking asshole on the phone!"

I switched the receiver to my other ear. My hand was shaking.

"Hey Ronnie, calm down," I said feebly, wishing there was some way you could unmake a phone call. "Mama said it wasn't his fault, so maybe—"

"You little faggot!—you little fuck! I don't believe this! He practically kills Daddy and—"

I could picture Ronnie jumping up and down in his white grocery apron, his eyes red-hot with fury. I said, panicked, "Just meet us at the hospital, we're leaving in a minute," and I hung up the phone.

Mama was back in her and Daddy's little bathroom, banging drawers shut and mumbling to herself like she does when she's trying to get organized, so I knew she hadn't overheard me calling Ronnie. But Uncle Vic had, I guess, because when I came into the hall he came out of his room and stood at his doorway, watching me. He had this kind of sad, baleful look, and I figured that if I apologized for calling him a lunatic he'd probably insist that he deserved it. But as it happened, we didn't exchange any words at all. He just held up his hand and made that "V" with his two fingers again—that little peace sign. I nodded, and tried to smile, but I guess my effort was pretty feeble compared to that grinning doctor back at the hospital. Anyway, I eased past Uncle Vic and went back to try and speed things along with Mama's packing.

We weren't quick enough, though. We'd made it into the kitchen, where Mama was hunting around for her car keys, when I heard Ronnie's Fairlane come rumbling up the driveway.

"Oh, shit," I said, and Mama whirled around at me. I guess she'd never heard me cuss before. "Look," I told her, "I should have waited, but I called Ronnie at the store and he's mad as hell. You'd better not let him in."

We could already hear Ronnie hollering as he came through the front yard. Mama had turned white, and since I rarely saw her get scared, this got me even more scared. In half a second I decided what to do.

"Lock all the doors and hide," I said. "You too, Uncle Vic." By now, he'd come into the kitchen and just stood there bug-eyed and silent, as usual. I added, "I'll go out the front and head him off."

Which I did. Locking the front door behind me, I made it to the porch just as Ronnie hit the sidewalk. He had both fists clenched at his sides and the meanest look in his eyes I'd ever seen—and for Ronnie, that's saying something.

"Out of my way," he said. "I'm gonna kill that loony bastard."

"He—he's not in there," I said. "He went out to the garage. He heard you coming and he—he's hiding."

I kept my voice steady, and fortunately Ronnie is so stupid that he believed me. He veered off right away, heading back toward the driveway and our detached garage sitting at the end of it. I figured while he was back there, we'd all have time to get in the car and get the hell away. But that didn't happen, of course. I'd locked myself out of the house, and by the time I got Mama to open the door—I was calling her in a sort of loud whisper, so Ronnie couldn't hear but Mama could—Ronnie had already made it to the garage and figured out I was lying. We could hear him yelling and cussing out there, and by the time I got to the dining room window, the only one you could see the garage from, Ronnie was already fuming back up the driveway, looking madder than before. Worse yet, he had a crowbar in his hands.

"Mama," I called over my shoulder, "you'd best call for help," but she was one step ahead of me. I could hear her in the kitchen, on the same phone I'd used to call Ronnie.

Now, thanks to me, Ronnie was at the back door, ramming his fist against the wood, and yelling.

"Mama, Jimmy, you'd better let me in this goddamn house! It's my goddamn house, too, and I'm gonna kill that sorry motherfucker!"

He'd started that hoarse, throaty screaming again, like he'd done on the phone, and I knew that was the most dangerous kind because it meant he was about to cry.

"Nobody's gonna put my daddy in the hospital and get away with it!" he yelled. "You hear? Now open this goddamn door!"

The three of us were huddled in the kitchen, just watching the door. It was double-locked, but I knew it was only a matter of time before he started beating it in with the crowbar. I kept hoping I'd hear the police sirens in the distance before that happened. I figured if worse came to worst, we could all run back and lock ourselves in the bathroom, to buy a little more time. I decided I'd throw myself on top of Uncle Vic if I had to, so Ronnie wouldn't kill him. Of course, I wasn't sure he wouldn't kill me, too, and hoped I wouldn't have to find out.

Instead of beating the door down, though, Ronnie went back around the house. As we learned later, he stopped in front of the living room, deciding to come in through the big picture window. He steadied himself in front of the glass, lifted the crowbar, and started swinging.

From the kitchen, it sounded like the world was ending. I ran with Mama and Vic back to the bathroom, where we locked the door and I motioned

Mama and Uncle Vic to get in the tub, behind the shower curtain. I know that was pointless, but I couldn't think of what else to do. I stayed with my ear to the door, figuring we had five minutes at the most, since the bathroom door wouldn't give him much more difficulty than the picture window had. When the glass stopped flying, though, and I heard Ronnie jump inside the room, I also heard the sirens coming up behind him. A minute later Ronnie was shouting it out with some Dekalb County officers—they were all three crunching around in the living room, on the broken glass—and that took the heat off us.

So, I knew what would happen—Uncle Vic would move out, just like he'd said, and Daddy would come home from the hospital, and Mama would be jolted into seeing that Ronnie had some major problems and they'd better get him some help or something really bad would happen. I couldn't see Ronnie becoming an "A" student, or getting voted the "Most Likely to Succeed" when he graduated high school, but I figured we'd be doing good if we could keep him out of jail.

As for me, it was that last few minutes, locked in the bathroom with Mama and Uncle Vic, that taught me a thing or two, and long after things had quieted down I kept thinking back to that. This was a hell of a mess, after all—Daddy in the hospital, doped and bandaged up like a vet, and us barricaded in our house, and Ronnie and then the police crashing through the living room window. And I kept recalling poor, pale, sick Uncle Vic at the door of his room, giving me that little peace sign, or victory sign, or whatever the hell it was. Sure enough it did seem like we were having a war of some kind. My phone call to Ronnie had almost gotten Uncle Vic killed, and I learned once and for all what happens if you get mad and let things run away with you, and start taking sides. From now on, it was a sure thing I'd be staying neutral, lonely and comfortless as that could often be. I figured it was the smartest thing you could do in a war, if you couldn't win.

Evening at Home

WHEN the accident happened, June stood in the middle of her garden kitchen thinking that she looked like one of those newspaper ads the subdivision had been running. A happy homemaker at Windrover Estates, the caption might read, never mind that she had a good job—she made more money than Roy—and never mind that their sparkling beige stucco four-bedroom, with its sleek surfaces of cool white tile and glaring chrome, still felt nothing like home. Returning after work she sometimes felt that she'd stumbled onto a TV sound-stage; that Bill Cosby might appear in a doorway, in one of his ugly expensive sweaters. Nonetheless here she stood, at her "convenience island," making a garden salad—chopping at radishes with one of the ultrasharp knives her parents had sent from Fort Worth, knives in graduated sizes all tamed and nestled into a red-velvet-lined case like some sort of valentine. The knives had arrived UPS three days ago. June was thinking (because of her name, she had a lifelong sensitivity to months of the year), But this is September, not February, and wondering at the sudden pump-pump of anger from her heart. That's when she sliced open the tip of her thumb.

She wailed, holding her left hand aloft and grabbing a dishtowel off the refrigerator handle. Roy heard her—he was sitting out by the opened garage door, whittling, a boyhood activity that soothed him when he was nervous—and came running in.

"June?" he cried. "What on earth?"

She'd returned to the island and now leaned against it, holding her thumb straight up like one of those movie critics she couldn't stand; she felt ridiculous. She'd wrapped the towel around it three or four times, so it appeared to wear a grotesque green-and-white striped turban. June stared at the towel, waiting for blood to begin staining the cloth like some insidious blossom. She didn't look at Roy, but she'd heard the distress in his voice.

"It's okay, hon—I just cut myself. Run up to the medicine cabinet and get me a bandage, would you? One of those thick gauze ones—the lower left-hand side, I think."

While he was gone—she heard his clomping footsteps above her head—June gingerly unwrapped the towel. No blood had seeped through, and she felt a peculiar breathless curiosity about the wound. She lifted the last layer of towel just long enough to see the plush-white ball of her thumb, contoured by a neat rounded slit so exiguous and perfectly shaped that it might have been a surgical incision. Then the slit gaped open, as though emitting a small cry of outrage. The dead-white skin became empurpled and swollen, giving way to a little geyser of blood before June, her breath coming in quick pants, wound the towel back around the thumb. It began to throb, with an oddly moist and pleasant sort of pain. But she'd done the wrapping less neatly this time and now the turban looked comically disheveled. June felt tears springing to her eyes just as Roy came back in, undoing the bandage.

"Poor baby," he murmured, but when she saw that he wasn't having much luck with the little red string along the bandage wrapper, June grabbed one edge with her right hand—fortunately she'd wounded her left—and held it while he tore the string. Together they unwound the towel—"Have the bandage ready," she said, "it's a real bleeder"—and then Roy slapped on the bandage before that mean little slit had the chance to reopen. June had glimpsed the skin around it, though—all stained with blood. She had seen the whorls of her reddened thumb and thought of her thumbprint in red instead of black, her unique print, hers, *her.* She felt lightheaded, as though she'd lost a quart of blood instead of a spoonful. When he finished the bandaging Roy kissed her cheek and smiled as though she were a child, which struck June because he was seven years younger than she and in many ways a childlike type of man.

"Clumsy," he said.

Then he noticed the tears—one had started out from her left eye-corner and began following the bony contour of her cheek—and he wiped at the tears gently, with the sides of his own healthy thumbs.

"Hey, are you okay?" he said.

"Sure—I'm just a little nervous." But she couldn't look up. Roy had a large open childlike face—artless blue eyes, ruddy cheeks—and the sight of him might set her to bawling.

"Want me to finish this?" he said. She looked with him around the kitchen—pans on the stove, water measured into them for rice and steamed beans; casserole dish Pammed and ready beside the fridge; all the dessert makings, cooking chocolate and sugar and cream, stacked neatly next to her biggest mixing bowl; the four salad bowls in a rectangle on the island, alongside the separate little plates heaped with the vegetables she'd been chopping. She loved Roy to death, but he couldn't finish all this if you gave him three days.

"I'm okay," she said. Now she did glance over, smiling with one side of her mouth. "You could set the table, though."

"Sure thing," Roy said, turning aside. He'd given one last look at the bandaged thumb, as at a piece of handiwork done well. Now the thumb looked, to June, like a tiny doll's pillow, so thick and white that no pinprick of blood—still less the billowing red blossom that flooded June's imagination—had much of a chance.

Her parents, driving in from Fort Worth, were due in an hour. They were on their way to Florida, where June's mother had a great aunt dying slowly of pancreatic cancer. "It's our last chance to see poor Bitsy," her mother had said last week, calling with her alarming news about the visit. June had lived in Atlanta for more than a decade, ever since coming here to college, but her parents had never visited together before. June's father wouldn't fly and her mother, a gregarious woman, claimed she couldn't sit still for long car trips. Several times her mother had flown out alone, and they'd done some mother-daughter things—shopping and matinees and expensive lunches out—but even she hadn't visited since June and Roy's surprise elopement three years ago. "Don't want to butt in," her mother would say brightly into the phone. She was the one who'd kept using that word, *elopement*. To June and Roy, what they'd done was just go down to the courthouse and get married, with Roy's widowed mother and June's best friend Sherry as witnesses. Both Roy and June went back to work the next day as though nothing had happened. They'd been living together for eight months, though they hadn't mentioned this to June's parents. Soon after the marriage they'd taken a quick trip out to Fort Worth so her parents could meet Roy, and the visit went well enough. June's mother had bought a paperback book on the etymology of names, and had told Roy that his name meant "king." June's mother had laughed, "So that means you're king of the castle." Though Roy had glanced nervously at June's father (but June had not), he'd blushed with pleasure. That night in their room, June's childhood room, Roy had said what a nice lady June's mother was.

During the past week Roy had repeated this compliment several times, as if reminding himself. He kept telling June that he looked forward to her parents' visit, but she could hear the boyish anxiety in his voice. She knew it wasn't her mother who concerned Roy, but her father, who'd said very little during their visit in Fort Worth and who, unlike Roy, never picked up an extension during one of June's phone conversations with her mother. One time Roy had made the mistake, near the end of one of these three-way chats, of asking about Mr. Caldwell. "Is he home?" Roy had said, with his country boy's friendly forthrightness. "Can he get on the phone, too?" June had lapsed instantly into silence, her breath coming fast. The question had reminded her that Roy was still an outsider, with minimal knowledge of her family's habits—for June's father was always home—and even her mother had succumbed to an awkward pause. "Oh, he's . . . out in his workroom, doing *some*thing," she'd said, with even more strenuous good cheer than usual. June had tried to breathe quietly, evenly, counting the breaths. Roy had said, puzzled, "Well, tell him hello, okay?" And June's mother had said quickly, "Sure will, sweetie," and then had changed the subject.

When the doorbell rang, Roy wiped his palms on the side of his jeans and grinned across the table at June. "C'mon," he said, "let's answer it together." He stood, looming above her, and for a moment June felt that he would bend down to help her, as though she were an invalid. She knew she must look fragile, drained. She held her good hand cupped around the wounded thumb as though concealing or protecting it. Above her, Roy looked impossibly large and healthy in his starched white shirt and new Levi's; they'd had a glass of wine together, waiting, and now Roy seemed eager rather than anxious, his ruddy face a bit flushed, blue eyes crinkled at their corners. June's friend Sherry had claimed for years not to understand why June preferred the boyish type—I like *men*, not boys, Sherry would say with a wink—but now Roy seemed formidable as any man, his body solidly muscled under the new clothes, his skin exuding a fleshy male heat. When he did bend down, not to lift her but to take the wounded hand with exaggerated tenderness and bring it toward his lips—"Kiss it and make it better?" he murmured, smiling—she jerked the hand back before she understood what she was doing. "I—I'm sorry," she said, "I'm just—"

The doorbell's second ring interrupted her.

"It'll be okay," Roy said huskily, not quite meeting her eyes. She could see the hurt and perplexity in that sideways glance. "Guess we'd better get the door," he said, turning away, and June had no choice but to follow.

There had been the typical exclamations from June's mother: how pretty the house was! how beautiful Junie looked! what an exhausting drive it had been, and how she could *kill* for a glass of that wine! From the foyer, Mrs. Caldwell had glimpsed the dining room table, neatly set for four, with candles and flowers, and the two half-empty wine glasses where June and Roy had been sitting.

"Coming right up," Roy said jovially. He hesitated for a second, but then said, "The same for you, Mr. Caldwell? Or I've got some Bud. And some of the hard stuff, too."

June's father had waited outside the doorway, in the shadowy September dusk, while his wife exchanged greetings and hugs under the small cone of light cast down by the foyer chandelier. Now, as Roy's question echoed awkwardly in silence, he and June stepped forward at the same moment, pressed their cheeks together briefly, then parted. "Hi Dad," June said.

"Come on back to the kitchen, both of you, and we'll get you something to drink." Roy was already headed that way, followed by Mrs. Caldwell, who exclaimed over the table as she passed. "Junie, I told you not to make any fuss!" she cried, but it was just something to say, not requiring any answer. Standing in the foyer with her father June felt lost, stranded. Yet she wasn't afraid. She looked at him and smiled, and as if by reflex he smiled back. People had always said they looked alike: the same deep-set eyes, stubborn jaw, slender build. Once their hair had been the same shade of tawny-red, too, but when June started perming hers out a few years ago, she'd had it lightened, while her father's had turned a deep auburn, tinged at the crown and sides with gray. In the past few years he'd filled out a bit—his cheeks less gaunt, a roll of fat above his belt. Though he looked tired, and clearly hadn't shaved in a few days, his smile seemed sincere, though it held nothing of guilt or apology.

"I guess I could use something," he said. "It's been a long drive. Your mother . . . "

But he stopped, presumably out of tact. June felt her own smile aching at the corners and said quickly, "I made you some veal—that's still your favorite, isn't it?"

His eyes had grazed down her body, slowly, and now he was staring at her hand. "What happened?" he said.

She lifted her thumb quickly, holding it up as if to ridicule it; at once it began throbbing with pain. "Oh, just a stupid accident," she laughed. "I was cutting some vegetables—it's nothing."

Her father smiled woefully. "Well, accidents happen," he said.

Dinner proceeded with a predictable but bearable awkwardness. After some preliminary chatting in the kitchen—more of Mrs. Caldwell's enthused observations about the house, along with her anecdotes (which she called "horror stories") about some renovations they were doing to their home in Fort Worth—June eased the others, drinks in hand, into the dining room. Roy took his usual place at the head of the table, but at the last minute, with a loud-voiced bonhomie that touched June, he insisted that he and her father should switch chairs. "You're the man of the house, now," Roy said, winking, taking hold of Mr. Caldwell's chair back, so that her father had no choice but to smile wanly, get up, and shuffle over to Roy's vacated chair. June saw that

Roy's face had flushed a darker red; he'd finished a second glass of wine and had poured himself a third. Again June understood that he was anxious, since excepting a few beers during Sunday football games on television, Roy seldom drank. Of the four of them, only June's mother drank much; alcohol was part of her various activities—the weekly poker games and bowling league and her Friday nights out "with the girls." Roy had poured her a fresh glass of wine, too, and had offered a second drink to Mr. Caldwell, who had merely pointed to his still-full glass and smiled. Like June, her father was a sparing drinker.

Meanwhile June's mother was exclaiming over the lovely appearance and delicious aromas of the platters and bowls of food June had placed on the table. Once June had sat down, and saw with relief her family's heads bent appreciatively over their first bites, she told herself again that all would be well. Her mother and Roy were both talkers, after all, and the extra glasses of wine would lubricate the conversation nicely. After dessert, when her mother would announce that she was exhausted, June would show them to the guest bedroom—at the opposite end of the house from the master suite—and in the morning there would be a quick breakfast before Roy went to work and her parents left for Florida. On the phone, her mother had insisted that they wouldn't be "in her hair" any longer than that; they needed to get down to Bitsy as quickly as they could, and anyway she knew that Roy and June were both very busy with their jobs.

And that's what they talked about first: their jobs. Soon after their marriage, June had learned through her mother that Roy's line of work—he was a construction foreman—was a sore point with Mr. Caldwell, who reportedly worried that some young stranger (he hadn't known Roy, then) might be trying to take advantage of June. For June, focused on work rather than romance all through her twenties, had risen swiftly through the ranks of her consulting firm; the year before she and Roy married, she'd been promoted to manager at the unprecedented age (for this company, for a woman) of twenty-eight, and now, four years later, she was the prime candidate for a vice-president's slot that would soon come open. Though Roy was doing well, too, she still made more than twice what he did. Mr. Caldwell had also been unhappy (so her mother had reported, in a quick embarrassed voice) that this new husband was seven years younger than his daughter. Yet June, in her quietly determined way, had managed the conflict well—it was her profession to manage things well, after all—and her father had never expressed any disapproval directly to her. By now, she sensed that he actually liked Roy, though of course he would never say that, either. He'd always been a silent man, but now in his quietness she sensed resignation, not anger. While the others talked, he listened to each of them in turn with the same studied, polite attention, but then turned back to his food, as if he were alone, whenever an awkward silence fell.

Thanks to June's mother, the silences were few. "We always knew Junie'd do well," she said to Roy, touching his forearm. June had always liked this about her mother: she had to touch, especially when she addressed you. "Why, on parent-teacher nights at school, the teachers were constantly drawing me aside. 'Mrs. Caldwell,' they'd say, 'we wish the other kids were *half* as serious and hardworking as your daughter. She's so grown up for her age.'"

June remembered those parent-teacher nights: her mother went alone, while her father stayed home with June. By the time June was eleven, both her brothers were already off at college; she was still too young, her parents both said, to stay home by herself.

"How old was she, then?" Roy asked. "I mean, when they said that?" He'd reddened with pleasure at Mrs. Caldwell's words, as though June's childhood industry reflected well on him. Taking a deep breath, June had to smile, for she understood what was behind Roy's question: he was forever trying to synchronize the events of his and June's lives before they'd met. Early in their marriage, after much calculation, he'd deduced that when he'd caught the glorious winning pass at his high school football championship, one Friday night in 1985, June was alone in her apartment, watching the 11:00 news, and she *could* have seen the tape of the winning pass during the sports segment, a tape that had been played on all the Atlanta channels. (June hadn't the heart to tell him that she always flicked off the set when the sports began.) He'd discovered, too, that he'd starred in his fifth-grade operetta on *the same day* (for they'd both saved memorabilia from their school years) that June, a high school senior, had played Margot in her school's production of *The Diary of Anne Frank.* These synchronicities tickled Roy as much as they secretly depressed June.

"How old?" Mrs. Caldwell said, perplexed. "Why, they *always* said it. All the way through school."

"Oh," Roy said, crestfallen.

"But what about you, sweetie?" Mrs. Caldwell asked him. "How does it feel to be a *fore*man?"

"Well, it's been six months now," Roy said, his voice deepening. He'd sat back, squaring his shoulders as he did when feeling self-conscious or embarrassed. June had often noticed how natural modesty and a boyish pride in his accomplishments contended in her husband; such private observations were among her delights in living with Roy.

"But it's going okay," he added. "We're framing up a big place now, over in Sandy Springs. Eight thousand feet. And we're pouring slab on a couple of others next week, if the weather holds up."

"Eight thousand feet!" Mrs. Caldwell cried. "It must be a huge family."

"Nope," Roy said, "just a doctor and his wife, and one grown daughter. Retarded," he added somberly.

Mrs. Caldwell swallowed her mouthful of salad and then clicked her tongue. "Goodness, that's sad," she murmured. June glimpsed the sheen of moisture in her mother's eyes and quickly dropped her own. Her mother had always been one to empathize instantly with the plights of strangers. She couldn't pass a street person without digging in her purse for change; she ran the Christmas food drive every year at her church, and was always dunning her poker and bowling girlfriends to donate canned goods and bake holiday cookies. Still staring at her plate, June felt a blurring in her vision, as in some helpless mockery of her mother's quick tears. Her bandaged thumb, held carefully out of sight in her lap, throbbed mildly but persistently, as though the pain were a mockery, too.

"The odd thing is," Roy went on, "their plan is set up like three separate houses. There's one side for the daughter, with its own separate kitchen and sitting room, and a room for the live-in nurse. And on the other side of the house, there are *two* master suites, and they both have a sitting room, too. It's the weirdest plan I've ever seen. They'll never be able to resell it."

"Well—a doctor," Mrs. Caldwell said. "He probably doesn't care."

Now June's father spoke, for the first time since they'd sat down. "Sounds like they're hoping not to run into each other," he said, with a short laugh.

June looked up, startled.

"Goodness, it's really sad," her mother said again.

June glanced around at the plates and asked if anyone wanted seconds.

That's when she noticed that her mother hadn't touched the veal: she was eating all around it. June's tasted all right, and she saw with relief that Roy and her father were both eating theirs, but still . . . June remembered that her mother had praised the salad, and the homemade hollandaise covering the broccoli, but she'd said nothing about the veal. Mrs. Caldwell, from a working-class Louisiana family, nonetheless had the Southern gentlewoman's aversion to rudeness, and June knew that at one of her friends' houses she'd have eaten the veal, oohing and aahing, even if it were rancid. Her mother had that gift: she could keep her high spirits if anything went wrong. As June watched, her mother moved back and forth eagerly between the salad and the new potatoes, talking busily, stopping long enough to chew and give vehement nods to Roy as he replied to her incessant questions. June marveled at how well her mother looked. Tonight she'd worn a red-and-blue plaid "peasant" dress, with gathered short sleeves and a full skirt; large plastic teardrops, a bright blood-red, dangled from her ears and swung manically as she chatted and ate. June knew that for a car trip her mother would have preferred blue jeans and an old oxford cloth shirt of her husband's, but she'd dressed up for this visit, and June supposed she should feel touched and mildly grateful. Instead, she had lost her appetite altogether. She could not stop staring at her mother's large but thin-lipped mouth, painted a blaring red that matched the earrings.

Mrs. Caldwell had worked through the retarded daughter's sadness quickly enough.

"She's lucky, really," she said to Roy. Occasionally Mrs. Caldwell would glance at her husband and June, politely including them, but it was clear that she preferred to address her son-in-law. "Her parents are keeping a nice roof over her head, after all, when they could have shipped her off to an institution. And a live-in companion! Heck, I wouldn't mind trading places with her!" Mrs. Caldwell threw her head back for a raucous laugh, hollandaise gleaming at one side of her mouth, and Roy laughed along. June felt her father glance up, sharply, but at once he bent his head back to his plate. Nervously June eyed her mother's empty wineglass.

"And I'll bet if you asked that doctor, he'd say that he's thankful for *any* daughter. I mean, what would they have without her? Anything is better than nothing, right?"

That's when Roy said an unexpected thing. What most soothed June about her husband was his good-natured predictability, but after all he'd had a bit of wine, too, and this "special occasion" had enlivened him.

He murmured, glancing at June, "I hope *we'll* have a daughter someday, or a son—I don't care which." His smile faltered when he saw June's strained expression. "That is, if June wants to."

Mrs. Caldwell glanced her way, too, but with a mischievous grimace.

"These career women don't know what they're missing, if you ask me," she said. "Now honey, don't mind your loud-mouthed old mother"—for Mrs. Caldwell had seen June's expression, too—"but that biological clock isn't going to slow down, you know. Granted you're just thirty-two, but for a first baby that's already kind of late."

June tried to smile, glancing down, cutting her veal methodically into tiny bites even though her stomach was writhing.

"Well, we've got plenty of time," Roy said, in a worried voice.

"One of these days," her mother said, "you'll have to sabotage her pill box—put in some sugar pills or something." She was stage-whispering, in a throaty conspiratorial voice. "After all, accidents do happen!" she added cheerfully. "Why, our boys were half-grown when Junie came along. We wouldn't have missed you for the world, Junie Moon," and her mother touched June's forearm, "but we certainly didn't expect you! Did we, hon?" she asked her husband.

Mr. Caldwell glanced up, smiling wanly, but didn't reply.

"We're not quite ready yet," Roy said uneasily. "But one of these days . . ."

June knew she should come to Roy's aid, but somehow she couldn't speak. She inhaled, exhaled; she had finished cutting the veal and now moved onto the broccoli. She tried to make all the bites the same size, exactly, as though she were cutting the food for a very small child. As she worked, her mother moved along to another topic while June kept hearing that phrase, *Junie Moon,* echoing again and again in her head. It had been years since her mother had used June's childhood nickname, one which sounded innocuous enough but whose open rhyming vowels were like hammer-blows against June's heart. *Why the moony little face, Miss Junie Moon,* came her mother's sing-song voice. *Poor little Junie Moon* . . . She remembered that in grade school she'd felt such relief when the kids played their own word games—*Loony June, June the Baboon*—and even laughed along with them; compared to the other, the taunts of her classmates were like mere insect bites, like a sharp sandy wind against her skin, the outermost surface of her being by which they identified her as *Junie Caldwell* and by which she fooled them into believing that's who she was. In her high school years, Junie had become June, and she corrected her occasional date if he tried using her little-girl's name. Now, at the office, her oversized pink-marble desk plate ("It looks like a grave marker!" her friend Sherry had laughed) read *June C. Bynum, Manager.* If she got the vice president's job, she imagined having her marker read *J. C. Bynum,* but she supposed that would be ostentatious. Whenever a salesman visited her office and asked, in that new defensive way of younger men, "Should I call you—is it Mrs. Bynum? Or—?" she tried to put him at ease. "Mrs. Bynum, or June," she would say. "Whatever makes you comfortable."

For that was June's way, wasn't it? she thought in scorn. Make everyone comfortable. Keep things running smoothly. *Manage* things—schedules, other people, above all herself. Cut up your food efficiently, she thought, even when reaching a perilous stage of nausea.

June put down her knife and fork; her hands were trembling, but she noticed that her wounded thumb no longer hurt. She put the bandaged hand back in her lap, but then brought it out, placed it on the table as though for display. What difference did it make? she thought. Her father had already noticed the hand and her mother would refuse to notice.

"Mom," June said, as evenly as she could, "is something wrong with your veal?"

By now, Mrs. Caldwell had almost finished her salad, vegetables, bread; the untouched piece of meat sat on her plate like a little pale-brown island. Both men glanced at the plate—they'd finished their veal some time ago—and Mrs. Caldwell, caught off guard, flushed a crimson almost as lurid as her lipstick. She pushed the plate forward and laid her napkin on top, smiling awkwardly. "I'm sorry, honey, I hoped you wouldn't notice, but—"

She gazed plaintively across the table to her husband, who, of all people, tried to lighten the moment. He glanced at June, with a doleful smile.

"It's another of her 'causes,' I'm afraid."

"Not eating meat?" Roy said anxiously, looking from June to her mother. "You mean you're a vegetarian, Mrs. Caldwell? Shoot, you should have just told us and we'd have been glad to—"

"Not exactly," June's mother said. Her flush had died away, and now she gave a crinkly sad-eyed look to her daughter. "It's just—it's just that I can't eat veal," she said. "I'm sure you don't know about it, honey, but the reason veal is so tender, what they do to those poor baby calves—"

She stopped, a catch in her throat.

"She read a magazine article," June's father said dryly. "One article."

"Not only that, I've seen pictures," Mrs. Caldwell said. She seemed near the point of tears, yet June watched her coldly. "They force these little calves to live *standing up,* and to make them fat and tender they give them a diet that causes diarrhea, and there the little things are, trapped for their short lives and hardly able to move, and then while they're still babies they're led off to the slaughter. It's just—well, I don't believe in torturing animals," she said summarily, with a quick sniff. She grabbed her napkin and poked briefly at each of her eyes.

"It's okay, Mrs. Caldwell," Roy murmured.

But June's mother had recovered rapidly from her distress and now glanced around at all of them. "Sorry, folks," she said. "I don't believe in imposing my beliefs on others, please understand that. You can't control what other people do. And Junie, honey, I *do* appreciate all the work that went into this meal. I'm afraid your old mom is just one of those bleeding hearts. . . . " She laughed, thinly. Again she picked up her napkin and dabbed at her eyes.

By now, June had pushed her plate away, too, discreetly covering the tiny uneaten bites with her own napkin. Her hands had stopped trembling. Her breathing had calmed.

"Don't worry, Mom," she said. "I don't know why I decided to cook, anyway. Roy offered to take us all out to dinner, and I should have let him. You could have seen a bit more of the city."

"Nonsense!" Mrs. Caldwell cried. "Why, we can eat out anytime, Junie. What we wanted was to see the house, visit with you and Roy, just have an old-fashioned evening at home. Isn't that right, Wilton?" she asked her husband.

"That's what you told me," Mr. Caldwell said. "Although it's not much like you—wanting to stay home."

He looked at June, winking. This was an old joke in the family, especially when June's two older brothers were around. When June was small and her brothers were in high school, they would kid their dad for staying home on weekend nights while their mother, as she herself phrased it, went "gallivanting around." Even back then she'd had her poker and bowling nights, her

Friday nights of bar-hopping with friends from her old job at the phone company—a job she'd had to quit when June was born. Mr. Caldwell, on the other hand, had few friends; he put in his eight hours and came home. June's own evenings at home, at ages ten, eleven, twelve, had been punctuated by the arrivals and leave-takings of her parents. Her brothers were almost always gone (they had jobs, girlfriends), and after her father arrived home from work Mrs. Caldwell would put together a quick supper before bathing, putting on her pedal-pushers, her colorful blouses and jewelry, and her slightly excessive makeup—the rouge in particular was too heavy, June had thought as a child, observing the reddish smears along the tops of her mother's sharp-boned cheeks. Then her mother, smelling of Chanel No. 5, would give June a peck on each cheek and blow a kiss to her husband. Already jangling her keys, already snapping her spearmint gum between her back teeth. She was out the door by seven o'clock, and June and her father would be left alone.

And then while they're still babies they're led off to the slaughter. . . .

June pushed back her chair, just a few inches, but this was the signal they'd all been awaiting. Roy, rising, said something about brandy to June's father, and her mother asked for directions to the powder room. "But don't *touch* those plates," she said chidingly, as June reached down to the table. "I want to help with the cleaning up, honey. It's the least I can do."

Only June's father stayed at the table, while June followed Roy into the kitchen. As soon as her mother had left the room, they'd both gathered up an armful of dishes. June took hers immediately to the sink and stood there, gripping the edge of the counter. Behind her, Roy was scraping plates into the trash—she still hadn't trained him to use the garbage disposal—and talking idly about how good the food had been. When, after a minute or so, he noticed that June wasn't answering, he came over and eased his arms around her waist.

"June, are you—" He stopped, peering around at her. "What's wrong, baby, why are you crying?"

She could scarcely bear the tenderness in his voice, yet she didn't want to pull away; his arms seemed impossibly strong and pleasurable, applying just the right amount of pressure, not confining her but gently anchoring her in place. Tears leaked of their own volition from her eyes. Without moving or thinking, she held up the bandaged hand.

"It hurts," she told him.

"My goodness, why didn't you—it must be infected or something. Maybe we should—"

"No, listen, I'll just go into the bathroom and get some ointment. That, plus a fresh bandage, and I should be good as new." She wiped her eyes with a dishtowel, giving him the same sad wet-eyed expression (as she was uncomfortably aware) that her mother had used in the dining room. Now she did turn around, gently pushing him away.

"Well, if you're sure," Roy said.

"I'm sure," she said. "Just help Mom, get the clean-up started, and I'll be back in a flash."

"Use that new stuff we bought," Roy called after her. "It's got some painkiller in it."

Avoiding the dining room, where she could hear her mother chattering, clanking dishes together, June went down a short hallway that led from the laundry area to the powder room her mother had used. From the doorway, she stared down the darkened longer hall to the dining room door, the sliver of light beneath it showing the quick shadowy movement of her mother's footsteps. The movement seemed miles away, she thought. Years away. In the bathroom, once she'd locked herself in, she could smell traces of her mother's perfume, a thick sweetish scent that resembled honeysuckle. She flipped on the fan, thinking it would help kill the smell and also cover her noise if she needed to cry again, and then she opened the medicine cabinet above the sink. She was looking for the ointment Roy had mentioned, but then she remembered it was in the other bathroom, the one adjoining their master suite. Here in the powder room, she stored supplies that she sometimes bought in quantities on sale: economy bottles of aspirin, boxes of toothpaste, packets of Roy's razor blades. Roy disdained cartridge blades, preferring the old-fashioned kind of blades and shaver his father had used, and now June, wanting for something to do, took a little tin packet and slipped one of the blades out the side; she closed the medicine cabinet door and stared into the mirror.

It occurred to her that she no longer needed to cry. Instead she wanted to take this razor blade and slice a tip off her other thumb and each of her eight fingers. She decided to do this, and her hands became slender pale faucets of blood. With a dazed happy smile she lifted her splayed fingers and drew them down along the medicine cabinet mirror, trailing wavy stripes of blood and leaving her pale triumphant face to stare outward from what looked like a prison cell enclosed by jagged red bars.

No, she would never do this—melodrama wasn't June C. Bynum's style—but it felt good to think about it. Her heart had begun racing, as if feeding that imaginary flow of blood and her own bitter joy. She blinked her eyes, as though to make that vision of the red bars reappear. She took a deep breath. Fortunately there was also a supply of gauze bandages and Band-Aids in the medicine cabinet and now she opened the mirrored door again, quickly removed her old bandage and replaced it with a new one, dispensing with the ointment. She didn't need it, for she had lied to Roy; the wound had stayed numb, there was no pain at all.

She told herself that the rest of the evening would be predictable enough, manageable enough, but when she opened the bathroom door she cried out when she saw her father's pale haggard-looking face looming out of the darkened hall. "Oh, it's you," June gasped, "—you startled me—" He stood there, gazing back at her. "Sorry," he said. "I didn't mean to." Again her breath came in quick shallow pants. She moved to one side and he moved to the other, in the awkwardness of such moments, and finally he was in the doorway and she stood in the hall. "No, it's all right," she said, "I just didn't expect—" Again his steady gaze broke off her words. She stood mesmerized, helpless, but he decided to be merciful, giving that practiced wan smile. "I'll just be a minute," he said, "then I'll come out and help." She shrugged quickly and said, "Oh, don't hurry, I'll just—" but then he closed the door and she stood there alone.

If it hadn't been for that thin crack of light beneath the dining room door, she might not have known which way to move—the house was still new, she still found herself making wrong turns when she came out of a room—but she saw the light and she heard Roy's voice, just on the other side of it. "I think she'll be fine," he was saying. "She's just a little . . . " but she didn't need to hear any more. She focused on the voice—its kind and virile certainty, its innocence of pain—and followed it out of the darkness.

Scene of the Crime

"YOU know how Daddy feels about shopping, don't you?" Mrs. Goodman says.

She fans her red-nailed fingers above the wheel, awaiting her daughter's reply. They're stopped at a traffic light, not far from the mall entrance.

Edie knows her next line, of course; it's just a matter of her delivery. She stares out her window and for some reason presses her nose to the glass, like a child.

She says, but not hearing herself, "No, how does Daddy *feel*."

Mrs. Goodman says rapidly, "He feels that shopping is our privilege and our right. Nay, our solemn duty."

Edie knows that her mother isn't smiling. It's part of Mrs. Goodman's humorous persona—the Marsha Goodman whom her bridge-party acquaintances consider "outrageous," "hysterical," etc.—that she almost never smiles.

It's a technique, of sorts.

"Is that so," Edie says back. "My, my."

Her father: the last person on earth she cares to think about.

Thank God, there's a parking place right in front of Saks. Mrs. Goodman complains mightily if she has to park more than a few steps from the stores. Lately Edie has noticed that Phipps Plaza—always Atlanta's ritziest mall, and now renovated and expanded—has begun attracting larger and larger crowds. The mall has Lord & Taylor, Tiffany's, Gucci, and Mrs. Goodman's favorite, the deliciously expensive Saks with its salmon-carpeted, curving staircase and unctuous sales clerks; and there are assorted smaller stores like Skippy Musket (antique jewelry) and La Bottega (imported handbags), which are equally expensive. Mrs. Goodman approves all the stores in Phipps Plaza and is a familiar sight in here: busy, prepossessing, overdressed, a heavily made-up blond Jewish lady, one eyebrow arched, her blank-looking daughter in tow. But most people can't afford this kind of shopping, after all. Not long ago Edie suggested, just for a change, that they go to Lenox Square, the much larger mall just across Peachtree Road. "You know," Edie had said, in a mock-petulant voice, "where the people are—the *normal* people?" But Mrs. Goodman had pretended to be shocked, her red-glossed lips forming a horrified O.

"Are you my daughter, truly?" she'd asked. "You know that Daddy prefers the better stores. You know that Daddy is very particular about our shopping."

Now mother and daughter maneuver themselves out of Mrs. Goodman's year-old burgundy Seville, a challenging task because both are rather plump inside their bulky fur-trimmed coats. The Cadillac's velvet upholstery is so luxuriously thick that it seems to retard their progress, urging them to stay seated, stay inside this beautiful car forever. . . . So Edie's sardonic thoughts run, in any case, as she opens the heavy car door, with a grunt of resigned effort, then stands and pushes it shut. She glares over the car's roof at Mrs. Goodman—a petite woman in her ash-blond wig (only one of her several dozen wigs), her thick powder and makeup that today include bold black eyeliner and violet shadow, and her famous wet-looking cherry-red lipstick. As she often does, Edie imagines that her mother is another woman, a stranger. Watching Mrs. Goodman gather her dark-red coat around her, fluffing the ranch mink collar along her jaw, Edie thinks yes, oh yes definitely: a stranger.

At such moments does Edie drift gently into lurid fantasies of escape and betrayal. Shall she simply turn and walk in the opposite direction from Mrs. Goodman, heading for Peachtree Road and Lenox Square instead of Saks, while her mother gapes after her? Or, inside Mrs. Goodman's favorite store, should Edie pick a fight over nothing, over a necklace or a pair of gloves, screaming shrill obscenities in front of the clerks and well-dressed customers while Mrs. Goodman stares in disbelief? Or, more covertly, will Edie scrutinize the other middle-aged women in the store as though shopping for a replacement mother? And when she finds a likely prospect, does she simply walk off with her, take hold of the woman's arm, chatter in her ear of inconsequential things?

Yes, Edie supposes dreamily that she might do any of these things—or all of them!—but instead she follows her mother into the mall.

It's eleven o'clock, a weekday in early January: out of the thin frothy sunlight, and into the open luxurious spaces of Phipps Plaza. Mrs. Goodman heads for the escalator, talking and gesturing, while Edie tries vainly to keep up. Inevitably she falls a few paces behind, her eyes downcast, and at such moments the fantasies intrude again: for what if she stopped, abruptly, and allowed her mother to continue up the moving stairs, chattering busily to herself? What if she ducked into a store and strode purposefully toward one of the outside exits? What then, what then? But, getting off the escalator, Mrs. Goodman pauses, waiting until Edie trudges up to her mother's side.

Her eyes blank as a statue's, Edie thinks, *Maybe we should start off with . . .*

"Maybe we should start off with a little drinkie," Mrs. Goodman says, eyeing the entrance to the Peasant Uptown, her favorite restaurant. "After all, it's almost lunchtime," she adds, as if convincing herself.

Edie thinks, *Then we'll be fortified, won't we . . .*

"Then we'll be fortified, won't we, for a bit of shopping. And then we can get ourselves a bite of lunch."

Edie stays silent, so Mrs. Goodman stares at her.

"Right, honey?" she says.

"By all means, let's fortify ourselves," Edie mutters, following her mother inside. An effusive, hectically smiling hostess leads them to their table and, not needing to ask, a deft young waiter quickly brings a double martini with two olives for Mrs. Goodman and a diet cola for Edie.

"Good morning, ladies," he says with a little bow.

But it's almost . . .

"But it's almost afternoon, so we're allowed," Mrs. Goodman says primly, and now it's Edie's turn to stare.

"Honey, is something wrong?" her mother asks, when the waiter is gone. "You look so—so—" She gives a little shudder.

Edie ponders the ultimate sacrilege, then decides against it, then thinks why not, just why the hell not?

She settles her level, hard look upon Mrs. Goodman's eyes (which are really quite tiny and frightened-looking, inside all the mess of paint and goop), and says in her best droll manner: "Mother, I've been meaning to ask you something. What is the point—could you tell me, please—of all this shopping?"

Of course, her mother's beak is already inserted into the martini, her small eyes darting busily around the restaurant. Of course, her mother hasn't heard.

"Ah, thank you," Edie says under her breath. And she takes up her own glass. She drinks.

My goodness, there aren't many . . .

"My goodness, there aren't many people out this morning," her mother says, in her fake-disappointed voice.

"Oh, but *we* are," Edie replies.

During that busy, hectic time between Thanksgiving and Christmas, Dr. Goodman had finally left them.

Or, as Mrs. Goodman prefers to say, airily, he had "decamped," leaving them the big house on Haversham Road and all the furnishings—including some priceless antiques and paintings inherited from his parents—and both Cadillacs and the bulk, by far, of his stock and bond holdings. And his bank accounts. And those big chunks of Buckhead real estate he'd been quietly acquiring through the years. Two sets of lawyers had been in the house during those last weeks—Edie would pause at the base of the stairway, listening to their dark murmurous voices from the library-den where Dr. and Mrs. Goodman conducted their business—and the upshot had been that

Mrs. Goodman could have everything, or almost everything. Dr. Goodman had kept the small stone-and-redwood house up at Lake Lanier, and his beloved little Porsche Carrera, and perhaps half a million in cash and securities: he wouldn't need any more, he told Mrs. Goodman, for the kind of modest retirement he wanted. As for the rest—worth four million? six million?—Mrs. Goodman could do her worst: she could fling wads of bills from the top of the IBM building, she could slurp Dom Perignon from morning to night, she could shop till her plump little legs wore down to nubs.

Or rather, Edie imagined that *she* might have said such things, in her father's position.

In truth, she could not put herself in her father's position, for she no longer knew him, really. Dr. Goodman no longer came home early from the office to take Edie on meandering strolls around the neighborhood, as he'd done when she was nine or ten. (Mrs. Goodman never accompanied them: she had her headaches, she was "indisposed." Mrs. Goodman hated any kind of exercise unrelated to shopping.) No longer did he take his "little girl" on impulsive Saturday trips to Six Flags, or to the lake house where they fished from the motorboat or tramped gaily through the woods, Dr. Goodman looking funny and boisterous in his short pants and sneakers, his portly frame moving nimbly over tree roots and puddles, his plump womanish legs gleaming mushroom-white in the dank gloom of the woods. . . . Yes, Edie had adored her father. People said they looked alike, which at that time Edie hadn't yet heard as a veiled rebuke or a sorrowful prediction. She and her father were short, squat, pale-complected, and both moved along with a "duck's waddle," as Mrs. Goodman laughingly said. (Rather heavy herself, Mrs. Goodman nonetheless walked with the bold and purposeful strides of a huntress. Following along, waddling along, Edie did her best to keep up, feeling by comparison that she was hardly "walking" at all.) Nonetheless Edie and her father had been inseparable, back then. Whenever Edie was taunted at school about her weight, or called "frog legs" by the prettier girls, she'd simply close her eyes and think of Daddy who called her his "little princess," his "little ballerina," and even (somehow, this was Edie's favorite nickname) his "little whatchamacallit."

But that had changed. By the time Edie was twelve or thirteen, her father spent much less time at home. Sometimes, late at night, they'd bump into each other in the upstairs hall, and he'd say "Oops, sorry" in the oddly formal voice one uses with a stranger, an *adult* stranger, or else he'd say nothing at all, just cup her face for a moment in his hands, as if she were one of his plastic surgery patients and he were asking himself was there hope, was there anything he could do. On one such night he bent down to kiss her forehead before shuffling down the hall to his room—by now, he slept in the spare room alone, while Mrs. Goodman stayed in the master suite with a black sleeping mask over her eyes—and Edie would be left to return to her own room, where she had the habit of standing before a full-length mirror (stolid, dour-faced, her eyes dark and sad and impenetrable) for long silent minutes before climbing into bed. That time, a Friday night about six months ago, she'd felt her father's kiss still moist and clammy on her forehead, but she thought: Nope, not a little princess, still a frog. She thought: And tomorrow, I'll get dragged to the mall by Mother, to shop for some frog clothes. She was tempted to give herself a little frog-croak in the mirror, but these days she'd begun losing even her humor, no longer quite seeing the point.

So she didn't respond to her mother's occasional late-night tirades about "that other woman"; she didn't look twice when, some mornings, Mrs. Goodman came down to breakfast without makeup, her face doughy-pale and unformed, and sometimes even without a wig, her colorless hair floating in thin dry wisps about her head. But Edie noticed that the woman's eyes were pink, like a rabbit's eyes, and she thought: The rabbit and the frog, having breakfast together. She thought: I hope she croaks, too, ha ha. But she said nothing.

So the months passed and the divorce happened and Mrs. Goodman has seemingly become obsessed with spending every penny of her ex-husband's money before she finally does croak, but Edie still follows along numbly—waddling, friendless, doomed—and knowing she still looks like a smaller version of her father, even with her chunky body wrapped in this bulky wool coat with its fur collar. But unlike him, she isn't able to cut herself off, get free, simply turn and waddle away. Unlike him, she's only fifteen years old.

Half an hour for her mother's two martinis, then an hour for their lunch—lobster crepes plus a third martini for Mrs. Goodman, Caesar salad and a club soda for Edie—so it's past one o'clock before their shopping really begins. Today, Edie has been thinking, as her mother chatters endlessly over her lunch about the divorce of one of her bridge partners ("Poor Brenda," Mrs. Goodman said, "everyone saw it coming but *her*"), today there is one good thing: Mrs. Goodman is shopping for herself instead of for Edie. One of her mother's New Year's resolutions, repeated endlessly to Edie around the house, was her plan to become more sociable: to accept invitations when they came her way, whether invitations of "the male or female persuasion." Yesterday she received one of the male persuasion—oddly, he was one of Dr. Goodman's divorce lawyers, a man likewise divorced, portly, good-natured—so it's important that Mrs. Goodman find a dress. Tonight they're going to the ballet, or the symphony—Mrs. Goodman can't remember which, she was so flustered and pleased by the offer. "Your father never took me anywhere," Mrs. Goodman told Edie, "so I've got to find something new—maybe a lovely white winter wool? Or should I get a new black frock, something sleek and 'slimming,' as they say? What do *you* think, Edie?" But of course she didn't wait for a reply. Of course she wouldn't have appreciated the reply, had her daughter dared to utter it.

So today Edie's merely a sidekick, a tag-a-long. She has no particular function, except as the receiver of her mother's queries, complaints, exclamations. First they go to Lord & Taylor, since it's closest to the restaurant, but this is just a warm-up, Edie knows. Recently Mrs. Goodman informed her that she doesn't "take Lord & Taylor seriously, not any more," since she no longer considers the store stylish enough. Nonetheless she tries on a bright-gold silk jacket, with shoulder pads, and a matching skirt; then a burgundy velvet dress that shows Mrs. Goodman's pot belly so clearly that she shrieks the instant she steps before the triple mirrors; then a blue-and-black sequined jacket with black chiffon harem pants, an outfit that makes her look even shorter and dumpier than she is. "Oh well," she sighs, standing before the mirrors in this last outfit—she appears almost to be kneeling, Edie thinks cruelly—"I'm afraid that Lord & Taylor has failed us, once again."

The saleswoman who has been helping them comes up with two more outfits draped over her arm, asking would Mrs. Goodman care to try these, but Edie's mother says brusquely, "No, I certainly would *not*." And, winking at Edie, hurries back behind the curtains.

Edie hasn't winked back, but now the saleswoman stands gaping at her, as if awaiting an explanation. Edie feels the words forming on her tongue: Don't mind my mother, she's just your garden-variety psychotic, but of course Edie doesn't say these words. Or any words. She gives her best blank look until the woman, smiling feebly, shrugs and gives up and goes away.

At last, they're headed toward Saks, where her mother is sure to buy something: where her mother has never *not* bought something. Ah, the lovely muted colors and delicious aromas of Saks!—even Edie likes coming here, knowing that nothing really bad can happen, that even the most profound embarrassments are here diffused by the lilting background music and the perfumed, gently circulating air and by the smiles of the saleswomen, who are so impeccably groomed and dressed that at first glance Edie will often mistake one of them for a mannequin. . . . Now, as Mrs. Goodman veers toward an alcove marked "After 5," already talking to the woman who has hurried forth to greet her, Edie dawdles nearby at the glove counter. She picks up some soft brown gloves, brushing the fragrant cool leather against her cheek—the price tag reads $75—then drops them and picks up another pair, an irresistible vanilla suede so incredibly soft and supple that suddenly she is moved to gather up several pairs and thrust her face into them, inhaling with her eyes closed, and for a moment she's transported somewhere else altogether. . . . Then a woman behind the counter approaches: "Help you, dear . . . ?" She is smiling indulgently, knowing well the power of those exquisite gloves, but quickly Edie straightens, drops all but one pair, and asks, "How much are these?" The price tag is plainly visible, attached to a small plastic security device that would trigger an alarm if Edie tried to shoplift the gloves; nonetheless the woman bends over the tag, frowning. "Let's see, those are $125. And so lovely, aren't they? Shall I check for a pair in your size?"

Edie hears herself say: "Yes, please. Size seven."

When the woman hands the gloves across the counter, Edie takes them reverently, works her plump fingers into them one by one.

"May I take them over there? Show them to my mother?" Edie says, not quite meeting the woman's eyes.

"Of course, of course!" the woman says, with a pleased glance in the direction of Mrs. Goodman. "I'm sure she'll want you to have them."

"Yes, um—thank you," Edie says, contorting her mouth into a feeble approximation of the woman's relentless smile, and then she backs off, in that dreamy, slow-motion way of experienced shoppers, her eye still grazing the glass shelves heaped with gloves. Then she steps across the aisle and joins her mother.

"Well, what do you think?" Mrs. Goodman says at once, holding up a black beaded cocktail dress with a deep-cut bodice and flaring skirt. When Edie stares at the dress but doesn't answer—she is picturing her mother's pale, dimpled cleavage, shoved upwards by that bodice—the saleswoman says quickly, "That one's so versatile—a perfect foil for your lovely skin, or a special piece of jewelry. Would you like to try it on . . . ?"

"Yeah, maybe," Mrs. Goodman mutters, still plowing through the rack. She snaps each dress into view with an expert flick of her hand, stares for several seconds, goes to the next one. She pauses at a yellow silk with puffed sleeves, then slowly lifts it from the rack.

"*That* one's lovely, too," the saleswoman says. "With your hair color, especially, it would be simply—"

"Edie, what do you think?" Mrs. Goodman says. Her daughter stands there looking doleful, the suede gloves drooping from her clenched fist. With her other hand, she touches the shoulder of the dress—a meaningless gesture. "It's nice, I guess," she says neutrally. "The color is . . . I guess yellow would be . . . "

"Okay, I'll try these," Mrs. Goodman tells the woman.

While her mother is changing, Edie sits in the waiting area in a big overstuffed chair and endures the saleswoman's small talk. Helplessly Edie is remembering one Christmas day, many years ago, when Mrs. Goodman had given her husband a beautiful fawn-colored suede jacket. Though they were Jewish, Dr. Goodman had thrown a large "open house" every Christmas during Edie's early childhood, declaring that the spirit of Christmas was available to everyone—and it was the spirit that counted, after all, not anyone's particular religious beliefs. Edie recalls that the year he'd gotten the jacket—she must have been five or six—her father wore it around the house proudly all during the party. *That's* why she remembered the smell, why she picked up those gloves, for she could still feel the thrilling luxury of riding in her father's arms, borne from room to room as he greeted their guests—his medical associates, his pals from the neighborhood and the club, aunts and cousins and other family members whom they saw only once a year, at this huge catered party. Edie was still young enough, that year, that she could ignore the guests, look away shyly when they proclaimed (speaking to her father, not to her) how "cute" she was, though even at that age when all children are cute Edie was, as she now knows, a borderline case: her body chunky and graceless, her face already lumpish, sallow, the same mushroom-white as her legs. But she didn't know, then. She didn't care, then. She felt so protected and privileged in her father's arms!—carried like a princess through the rooms. And didn't he sometimes say, laughing, that "his home was his castle"? He knew it was a cliché, he admitted, but he didn't care—like most clichés it was *so true*. And who had invented the majority of clichés, after all? Shakespeare!

Even that claim, which he repeated often, became something of a cliché for Dr. Goodman. He loved to say things like "Beauty is only skin deep, you know!" Or, pointing his stubby finger at Edie, "Money can't buy happiness, sweetie—it can't buy *love*." Even that Christmas Day as he carried her among the guests, looking pleased and prosperous in his new suede jacket, he told everyone, "It's days like this when we remember what's important in life—am I right?" And he jiggled Edie in his arms, up and down, and people would say with their eyes crinkled half-shut how *cute* she was, and Edie would feel the delicious thrill of ignoring them, simply putting her face to her father's big shoulder and inhaling the expensive fresh aroma of that suede jacket. Surely this was happiness, surely this was the happiest moment of her childhood—though she couldn't know it, then, and indeed its glory lay in not needing to "know" it, or to know anything. In any case, it's a moment Edie must now recall with jealous longing, with an emotion akin to dread. Sitting in this plush overstuffed armchair, in Saks. Waiting for her mother, eternally waiting, the saleswoman chattering brightly into her ear.

Finally her mother emerges, wearing one of the dresses. And minutes later reemerges, wearing another. After trying on six or seven outfits—asking Edie her opinion on each, not listening as Edie mumbles her noncommittal replies—Mrs. Goodman finally decides on two of them. One of which she prefers, but only slightly; the second as a "spare," in case she changes her mind.

Sometimes, when you get them home . . .

All the while Edie sits watching glumly from her chair. She hasn't even unbuttoned her heavy wool coat with its thick mink collar, and she supposes she must be getting warm, overwarm; but really she feels nothing. She imagines that she is a beached whale, enormous, numbed, immovable . . .

and she recalls another cliché her father loved. "It's not a person's appearance that matters—it's what's on the *in*side." Edie wonders if her father repeated this particular cliché to his women patients, who came to his office shopping for expensive new faces. She wonders how he would react if *she* showed up one day and gave him her best impenetrable dull-eyed glare and said, "What about me, Dr. Goodman? Is there anything you can do for *me?*"

Now her mother says emphatically to the saleswoman, handing her both the dresses, "Sometimes, when you get them home, they don't look right after all. Yes, I'd better take them both. I can always use a spare."

So the matter is decided, and now there are shoes to buy, and some new earrings, and perhaps a scarf to drape across one shoulder, that's become such a fashionable look. . . . As her mother makes these various purchases she hands the boxes and sacks to Edie, who has become expert these past few months at shuffling packages from arm to arm, putting smaller sacks inside larger ones, and all the while giving her opinion—"Yeah, well, I guess so"—whenever her mother requires it. In this way do the hours pass. In this way does Edie's life pass. Once or twice she glances at her watch, adjusting the packages so that she can tilt her arm sideways, and she sees that it's past two o'clock—and then it's a quarter to three—and yes this day of shopping is passing quickly like all the others. For, as her father used to say, during their Saturday father-daughter outings together, years ago, "Time does pass quickly, doesn't it?—when you're having fun."

As if reading her mind, Mrs. Goodman now says, "Isn't this fun?" Edie can't tell if she's being ironic or not. They're at the jewelry counter, where Edie's mother has tried on perhaps three thousand pairs of earrings while Edie stands holding the half-dozen packages, long-suffering Edie in her heavy wool coat that's still buttoned up to her throat. Countless bright lights shine down on this counter, to give the gold and diamonds an added sparkle, and Edie is very hot. Yes, she *does* feel the heat, she *does* have a heavy lardish perspiring body, and as she confronts this knowledge she stares down, as if from a great distance, at one of her hands—it doesn't seem to be Edie's hand, quite—and watches it dart inside one of the sacks and then out again. When it comes out, the hand is empty. The palm is sweating, and itching almost unbearably.

"Okay, I guess I'll take these," Mrs. Goodman says, when Edie doesn't answer. Edie feels a gleam of sweat along her forehead and now, as her mother signs the slip, she says, "Mother, would you carry a couple of these? They're getting heavy."

"Sure thing, hon," her mother says, taking the sacks Edie hands her, and Edie feels a glow of satisfaction already pervading her chest, her stomach and limbs . . . oh yes, she definitely feels it.

Well, I guess we've done enough damage . . .

The jewelry salesman thanks Mrs. Goodman profusely, and so here they are, in the middle of a wide aisle on the main floor of Saks, looking unmoored and disconsolate. Edie feels her mother's tiny dark-gleaming eyes brush past hers.

"Well," Mrs. Goodman says, "I guess we've done enough damage for one day."

"Yes," Edie says mildly. "I guess we have."

Her mother turns and heads for the exit—not the mall exit but the one leading directly from the store into the lot where their Seville is parked. As though observing the scene in a dream Edie watches her mother getting farther and farther away, moving with her usual bold strides, confident that her daughter is behind her, that her daughter's legs have not turned gelatinous, then leaden, and then stopped altogether like two clumps of stone. Now Mrs. Goodman is out of sight, and within another five seconds Edie hears it—the security alarm, though in Saks even that sound is muted and almost pleasant, a low static humming—and now she sees a man, wearing a coat and tie, headed in the direction her mother has gone. Her mother, who has just stolen a pair of expensive gloves.

Already the glow of satisfaction in Edie's belly is fading, dissolving, and in its place there is nothing. A blank sensation. An emptiness. *Not a person's appearance that matters—it's what's on the inside . . .* So she returns to the glove counter, the scene of the crime, and to the pile of beautiful vanilla-suede gloves still heaped on the counter, and again Edie takes two enormous handfuls and presses them to her face. She inhales deeply, greedily. When the saleswoman approaches again from behind the counter, asking her something, Edie smiles invisibly into the gloves and doesn't respond: doesn't even hear.

In the Deep Woods

ON that morning, I hadn't wanted to go hunting with my father. At the kitchen door he stood waiting, holding the two guns, and I kept sitting at the table over some cold oatmeal, clutching my stomach and saying I didn't feel well, I didn't want to go.

"Come on," my father said. He pulled the plastic flask from the pocket of his khaki work shirt and took a long draw, wincing. From the opened door, I could smell the damp morning; I could hear the twittering birds.

"I don't want to, Daddy," I said, resting my forehead on the fleshy part of my hand in what I considered the posture of a sick boy.

"Come on, get your jacket," he said, his glassy stare settling on me, in that now-familiar eerie way, so that the exposed part of my face started tingling.

"Daddy—"

"Jared, I said to get your jacket. Now let's go."

I remember looking away for a moment, back toward the bedrooms of that tidy white-frame house where I'd passed my first eleven years, a house that would soon be snatched from under us, and wishing that Mama would come out, weeping or screaming, causing enough distraction to make my father forget what he wanted to do—as sometimes happened. That year he was easily sidetracked, confused; even a child could distract him. But I knew that Mama lay in bed with a real stomachache and that partly my father was angry because they hadn't planned to have another baby. How could they? he had shouted. He'd lost his job and the bills were piling up and what did they want with another kid, anyway?—another goddamned kid. His voice had lowered viciously on the last phrase. From my bed the night before I had listened to them argue, my eyes twitching and excited in the dark.

Now the screen door slammed shut and I heard him calling my name as he stomped out to the truck, so I had no choice but to get my jacket and follow him outside.

Our family life had come undone that winter, but I'd supposed that the worst was over. In December my father lost his job at the fire station, but instead of looking for work he'd kept going to the station every day, taking a flask of bourbon and a deck of cards, spending his time in the firemen's rec room because his boss, Chief Tompkins, didn't have the heart to ask him to leave. Soon I began missing days at school—and I loved school—either because my father wanted my company or because Mama, who'd started looking for work, took me along for moral support. How sharply I remember those cool dove-gray mornings when she would totter around the kitchen in her one pair of high heels, trying to make toast and coffee without spotting her Sunday dress, a blue linen with a wide, stiff white collar spread along her breasts and shoulders like a bib. She wore this dress every day during those three weeks in January she spent looking for work. Her unusual burst of energy, I knew even then, had been motivated not by maternal grit and determination but by that ultimate child's disappointment: a spoiled Christmas. My father, drunk and downcast from mid-December through New Year's, hadn't bought us anything.

"Mama," I remember asking her, one morning, "can't you go by yourself today? Miss Simpson's holding a spelling bee, and you get ten holy cards if you win. And I missed two days last week, didn't I?"

At our parochial school, Miss Simpson was my only lay teacher, an energetic young blonde with upswept hair for whom I'd developed a schoolboy's desperate affection.

"Honey, today's my second interview at Monkey Wards, so they must be interested. Come along and hold Mama's hand, okay? Tomorrow I'll write you a note for Sister Monica." She stood over my plate, buttering a piece of toast with quick, dainty strokes. "Monkey Wards" was her nickname for Montgomery Ward, the department store where she had applied for a job in the lingerie department.

"Why don't you make *him* get a job, Mama? Then you won't have to work."

At that moment my father sat slouched in the living room, staring at our black-and-white Philco though nothing was on but farm reports, and Mama allowed herself a quick wrinkling of her nose, cutting her eyes in that direction; but she wouldn't criticize him in front of me.

"Don't worry yourself about that," she said in her mock-kidding way, touching my nose with the butter knife. "Just eat your toast and let's go."

Out of reflex I obeyed her, washing down my toast with the milk-coffee I'd only lately been allowed to drink. I didn't know enough to feel angry, even though my father sat slumped before the buzzing TV, and my mother looked hopeless in her fancy blue dress, and I sat eating breakfast with a tiny dab of butter perched on my nose. Even much later, remembering, I would not feel angry. I would recall this tableau as though it portrayed some other family—doomed but pitiable, enduring their last days of innocence.

We took the old highway out toward the state park, and I wasn't surprised when my father steered abruptly onto the rutted, sandy lane that led out to Grandma Slater's farm. Though she'd died more than a year before, my father checked the old place every chance he got—peering into sheds, picking up stray trash that blew into the yard, unlocking the back door and treading boldly through the dimmed, musty rooms, whistling or humming as he tested windows, glanced into closets, stopped to check his own reflection in the tarnished bathroom mirror. He claimed to worry about burglars or vandals, since the place had stayed empty for so long, but I felt he was really looking for Grandma, unable still to believe that her abrupt, snappish presence had fled these rooms. Usually I felt uncomfortable, following him, but today I was glad we had stopped. I thought he might get involved in some small repair or other, as often happened, and that he would forget about the hunting. We hadn't hunted since two years before, when Chief Tompkins had taken us out to his cabin by the lake, for some duck hunting. My father had never shown much interest in hunting, himself, and we'd never gone alone.

Now my father veered the truck off the twin ruts of the driveway and alongside the sagging back porch, where we jerked to a stop. He muttered, "Wait here."

"I'll come too," I said. "I can help with—"

"No, I'm just getting some shells. Wait right here."

He opened the door and half climbed, half stumbled down from the cab. When he said "shells" I had a sudden memory, causing my scalp to tighten. The house had a long hallway down the middle, separating a row of small bedrooms from the living room, dining room, and kitchen. At one end of the hall was a narrow glassed-in cabinet where Grandpa Slater had kept his guns and ammunition. Although I had never known Grandpa Slater, I'd often wondered about his death, and now I remembered that he'd used a shotgun, and that he'd driven out to the pine forest adjacent to the state park, going back deep into the woods. It had taken me years to put together even these meager facts; my father didn't talk about Grandpa, and whenever I would ask Mama about what happened and why, she would hesitate a long moment and then say, "You'd better ask your daddy." Around the age of nine I'd stopped asking: the long illness of Grandma Slater (she died of abdominal cancer on the morning of my tenth birthday) eclipsed my ancient curiosity about my grandfather, who seemed less mysterious and less interesting now that Grandma herself was gone.

Not knowing what else to do, I sat in the cab with my hands folded in my lap, as though I were in school. I told myself that I was letting my imagination run away, a trait that my father once said I'd inherited from Mama. Probably my father just wanted to go hunting and forget his troubles for a while, and had brought me along because—as Mama had begun accusing him—he hadn't paid me much attention lately. Not that I really minded that; I just kept hoping that he'd straighten himself up after a time, so our lives could return to normal. Mama thought his behavior since last year was due to something *she'd* done wrong, and I'd watched in dismay as she sat before her little vanity mirror, trying some new hair style or putting more makeup on her face, though I thought the makeup gave her a slightly clownish look. She didn't understand that when Grandma Slater died, something crumbled inside of my father. It was sad to see Mama working so frantically to supply something she figured my father wanted, when what he wanted lay out in the graveyard west of town.

By the time my father came out of the house, twisting the key and letting the screen door slam behind him, I had put my head and folded arms over the side of the window. I gazed for a while at the parched, bumpy back yard. There were two clotheslines with sagging wire and T-shaped supports on either end that had always reminded me of crucifixes; beyond were the massive pecan trees and an ancient, gnarled persimmon tree at the far edge of the yard, just where the desiccated corn fields began. I tried to imagine the days when my father and his two brothers were boys and must have chased one another through those fields.

He had no brothers, now; one had died in Korea and the other had left Georgia even before that, getting work as a logger in the Pacific northwest. He was alive, we presumed, but we never heard from him.

My father had brought a paper bag out of the house; the shells rattled softly when he tossed the bag down onto the seat.

"Why don't you keep them at home, Daddy?" I asked, wanting to make ordinary conversation.

His mouth made a forced, ugly grin. He didn't intend the ugliness toward me, exactly—I'd have sensed that—but rather at something he'd heard inside my words. Not long ago, tucking me in, Mama had whispered: "Be careful what you say to your daddy, he's having a hard time. And he can't help it, either." But the half-snarling twist of his mouth scared me just the same.

"Ain't you heard, Jared? We ain't got one—not any more."

Not long ago, during an argument, my mother had screamed that we no longer had a true home; it was just a house, and at the rate we were going, we'd soon be losing that. I remembered wincing at these words, and wishing she would follow her own advice.

Now I said, "But Mama didn't mean that. She's worried about the rent, that's all. . . . "

And my father said, "Worried. That's a nice word."

I didn't like the way he drove: one arm crooked in the window, the other draped carelessly over the wheel as if he couldn't be bothered to steer properly. He sat with his shoulders slightly hunched, and in the old khaki shirt and week's growth of beard he seemed a much older man. He didn't look handsome like he once did, dressed in a new fireman's uniform or wearing his black wool suit and red tie for Sunday Mass. Though he had a broader face and thinner hair than I'd glimpsed in the old photographs of my grandaddy (coarse black hair, hawkish profile, an Adam's apple like a blunt knife protruding at his throat), my father did have the Slater good looks, the glistening straight teeth and ruddy skin and eyes so blue they made your heart ache, as I'd once heard Mama say. She'd also said he looked like John Gavin, a twinkle-eyed movie star who had figured prominently in her high school scrapbooks, or maybe more like Robert Taylor, she'd once suggested, kidding him, or Clark Gable?—but now he had lost all that.

When my father said "Huh," it usually meant he was sinking into his own thoughts again. I wanted to pull him back.

"We're only two months behind, aren't we?" I said. "That's not so bad. And just see if Mama doesn't land a job soon, quick as that."

I snapped my fingers the same moment we hit a pothole, and my father gave me a sharp look.

"And so will you," I said quickly.

I was talking too much, which wasn't like me, and without much idea of what I was saying. Maybe I was imitating Mama's empty cheerfulness at the breakfast table some mornings, which in any case I disliked. Biting my tongue, I braced myself against the sudden jolts and swerves of the truck. The shells, on the seat between us, rattled together in the old paper sack, making a hissing noise beneath the truck's racket that I could barely stand. I picked up the sack and took out a couple of shells, passing them back and forth in my hands with faked nonchalance.

"Might as well tell you," my father said slowly, as though reading the words from somewhere beyond the windshield. "We're gonna move soon, at least for a while. It's that or the poorhouse."

"Move?" I said. "Move where?"

"Out to your Grandma's," he said, his voice falling softly on the last word. "Just for a while, probably. It's mine now, you know"—he glanced over, his eyes defensive and full of hurt—"and anyway it's free and clear."

I sat still for a moment, so taken aback I couldn't speak. Ever since Grandma Slater died, I'd thought of the old place as a kind of relic; I couldn't picture us living there. There were no other houses nearby, the rooms were drafty and needed paint; I couldn't imagine Mama standing in that big grease-stained kitchen before Grandma Slater's antiquated iron stove. I took a deep breath, remembering how I'd lied about being sick to my stomach. Now I really was.

"Does—does Mama know?" I finally got out.

He grunted. "Oh, she knows. Why do you think she's laid up in the bed this morning? She'll milk this for all it's worth."

"It's not her fault—" I began, but quickly bit my tongue.

He ignored me. We'd turned off the highway and onto the oiled road that led out to the park. I hugged my side of the cab, but kept watching him: I felt my breath coming heavier, seeing the slung look of his jaw and the smug hatefulness in his narrowed eyes.

I wanted to distract him, so I asked, "You're not supposed to hunt in the park woods, are you?"

He blinked, very slowly. "Never mind," he said.

I took another deep breath.

"Which rooms are we taking?" I asked. "Out at Grandma's. And how will I get to school?"

"Your Mama can have her room," he said, and I could tell from his tone that he'd already thought everything out. That surprised me. "And the bunk room's for you," he said. "That's where me and Clint and Billy used to sleep." He stopped as if recalling this. "Things might change by next fall, but if not, the school bus stops just a few blocks south, at the corner of Hedge."

I pictured the house again, unable to believe that we'd be living there. Grandma's room, at the kitchen end of the hall, was the biggest. At the other end, the bunk room had two beds stacked against the inside wall, with a row of bright, thinly curtained windows facing east on the other wall that meant a blinding swath of sunlight hit your eyes soon after dawn; I'd spent the night there a few times, in the months before Grandma Slater died. The room had that ancient, gummy smell typical of rooms long occupied by adolescent boys. I thought of my own cozy, blue-painted room and felt another shiver of disbelief.

My father was driving slowly now, looking off toward the woods as though deciding where to park. From my cracked window I could already smell the lake, the greening trees, and now I looked down at the long smooth-papered shells in my hands. I remembered again.

My father swerved abruptly off the road, bumping out into the foot-high grass and toward the trees. I could hear the grass swishing against the truck's underside, and I looked around for signs of other people. My father had chosen a deserted back section of the woods, away from the lake, away from the "Pine Trail" where the boy scout troops from town sometimes came on Saturdays. We were alone.

I said in a calm, determined voice: "Daddy, I don't feel good. I don't want to go hunting."

He pulled alongside a stand of pines, next to a small clearing. I looked into the cleft and saw the deepening green darkness toward the heart of the woods. I knew that on the other side of the pines, by the lake, there were signs posted about every hundred yards: NO HUNTING. Here there were no signs, but I knew that my father would have ignored such a warning. He was tracking some wilderness inside himself, paying scant attention to the outside world. And that world included me. He gestured roughly and said, "Bring the shells," then climbed down from the cab and went around back for the guns.

For a moment I waited by the truck like a sulky child, watching as he plunged into the woods. He went briskly, blindly. I remember thinking: He's forgotten me. I looked down at the sack full of shells and briefly considered running, but there was nowhere to go; and if it came to that, he didn't need the shells. He also carried my .22 rifle, loaded. When he was almost out of sight I took a few steps forward and then, as he made a sudden turn, a few steps more. I could either stay with him or lose him, I reasoned, so I followed him into the woods.

In the preceding months I'd often felt that I watched my father from a great distance, feeling a genuine but muffled pity. At the dinner table I'd tended to address my conversation to my mother, glancing in the opposite direction only as an afterthought, my face tingling and neck muscles tightening on that side. Sensing his exclusion, my father had started bringing his bottle of Old Granddad to the table; he would sit there pouring small dabs and drinking them and then pouring again, as though he sat alone at a bar. He'd developed the habit of blurting out his words, often delivering outrageous, nasty remarks that left my mother and me gazing downward at our plates. One evening: "Well, I passed that Father Rourke on the way home, sitting like a prince up in that black Cadillac of his. That's what I give my ten percent for, so the priest rides around in a Cadillac?" And another time: "Listen to this, Tompkins brought a friend of his around this morning, he wanted to make an offer on Mama's place. I won't pollute the air by saying how much he offered—that son of a bitch Tompkins, he knew the guy was trying to screw me and he stood there grinning." My mother would give him a cool, dry-eyed look and not bother to point out that Father Rourke drove an Oldsmobile Ninety-Eight, not a Cadillac, and that Chief Tompkins was probably his best friend in the world and was only trying to help.

For a long while, I didn't worry that my father drank and became belligerent, because then my mother would react with that kind of smug, quiet contempt in which I could easily share. But her calm exterior had crumbled during the brief tumultuous weeks when it seemed likely that my father's mind would come apart and that he might pass from our lives altogether. Alone in her room, she would no longer invite me inside or accept the snacks and reading matter I brought her. Instead she hobbled out of bed whenever I approached and urged me back with a vague murmur, then gently but firmly closed the door in my face. I heard her muffled sobbing and went about the house feeling bruised and hollow, summoning my familiar hatred and deciding that my father was a bum, a deadbeat, a criminal. By now, he came home from the fire station before noon—a look of bitter jocularity on his face, his smile tilted and drunken—but my mother scarcely reacted. She had become more detached, as though turning inward; I had already assumed that she was physically unwell, judging by how little she ate and the way she clutched her abdomen while trying to fix our meals and occasionally rushed limping into the bathroom, where she ran water into the tub to cover the sounds of her nausea. But I learned of her pregnancy only by accident, hearing them late one night in the bedroom they still shared in spite of everything.

"Don't even *say* such a thing," my father broke out, in a loud hissing voice. "I won't have that word spoken, not in this house!"

"It's easy for you, isn't it?" my mother said wildly. I imagined her crouching forward from the bed in her soiled pink robe, her teeth bared, as though she'd been waiting to spring on my father the moment he arrived home. "Easy for *you* to be so moral, isn't it, being a Slater boy and having that fine Catholic upbringing of yours! But you're not the one who'd worry over the kind of life it would have, are you? You're not the one to bother yourself about how we'd feed it, for that matter. You're just thinking about how *she* would have reacted, aren't you? That's all you care about, right?"

My father had scarcely responded—he'd lowered his voice, he'd seemed on the verge of tears, and I heard only disconnected phrases like "against the law," and "so shameful," and "for the love of God"—before my mother broke out, bitterly: "I think I'd rather it died, Wayne, than have you for a father!"

For what must have been the first time, he struck her; it sounded like nothing more than a hard slap, but nonetheless he struck her, and neither of them said another word, and on that night a new silence entered the house, without tension, without hope. Sometimes they still fought but I didn't pay attention any longer, my father's drunken self-pity became normal and my mother's fiery sorrow became normal and I spent a great deal of time thinking soberly about that child my mother carried but didn't want, trying to decide for myself whether the child should live or die.

When the trail had narrowed to a footpath and the footpath almost to nothing we entered a small clearing in the woods and my father stopped, then pivoted slowly on his heel. He looked all around, the gun cradled loosely in his arms. We had come so deeply into the woods and my attention had focused so sharply on *him*—his blind plunge through the trees and brambles and vines, the way he slapped at branches with the butt of his gun, his lifting the flask to his lips and grunting words over his shoulder that I could not make out—that I'd paid little attention to where we were going. It didn't matter, I thought; we might have been wandering through the tortuous maze of his thinking, and I knew that for him I wasn't really there. Around us the air had darkened, the high tops of the pines closing above our heads, even the brisk March wind dying off and leaving only the harsh, abrupt crackling of our footsteps. When he turned in that slow dreamlike way and his fuzzy blue gaze settled on me, I took a step backward. My hands tightened around the stock of the .22.

"Ssh," he said, raising one finger to his lips. His eyes fluttered upward a moment so that now I saw the whites underneath. "Don't you hear it?" he said. "Listen, now."

"Hear what," I said.

"The crick," he said in a hushed, almost childish way. "You can hear it if you're quiet."

Straining, I did hear the soft rushing murmur beyond the thick stand of pines at my back.

"C'mon," he said, and without looking back he'd left the vague path and begun stalking off through the trees. I picked my way over stumps and brambles, ducking vines and low-hanging branches. I followed until the woods cleared again around a slow-moving creek, which ambled twenty or thirty yards into the murky distance before it curved out of sight. The air was shady, cool, rank-smelling; the sun had never shone here, I thought. The brownish-green creek water moved sluggishly and had a mucous-like scum along its sides, but nonetheless the mild stench of mud and decay was halfway pleasant, intoxicating. . . . My father moved in a quick side-step down the embankment to the edge of the creek and again looked around him, slowly. In the dim light he cut a handsome figure, dark-haired and pale, his profile—the sharp-angled Slater profile—giving him a look of nobility and cunning. I stood hesitating at the top of the embankment, passing the .22 from one hand to the other.

"We used to come here," my father said in a sudden, clear voice, pointing his gun along the creek bed. "Daddy and me, when I was little," he said. "When we came hunting, he'd bring me down here and we'd follow the crick."

I'd never heard him say "crick" before today and wondered if Grandpa Slater had pronounced the word that way.

"You could hunt in the park woods?" I asked. "Back then?"

"Heck," he said, spitting to one side, pawing vaguely at his shirt pocket. "Wasn't no park, not back then. It was just the woods."

When he tilted his head back to drink from the flask, I stared at the globule of spit where it had landed on the bank, a few yards from my father's muddy boots.

"Grandpa Slater, he liked to shoot?" I asked, and now I came down the embankment cautiously, stopping near a huge, rotted stump. For some reason I started kicking at the stump, as though performing a chore.

"Well, he liked to come out here," my father said. "We'd bring our guns, sure, but we didn't kill much. Except one day—"

He broke off, turning aside to where the creek meandered into the darker woods. The flask had slipped out of his hand, making a soft *plop* as it landed in the mud.

"One day . . . ?" I prompted him.

He lifted his shotgun again and pointed in the direction the creek flowed. "One day," he said, "we came out here and followed the crick, and it led us out into a meadow. We both looked up and there was a couple of chicken hawks, just two of them, and we looked at each other and smiled, and we lifted our guns at the same time and we fired. We brought them down with a single shot, him one and me one. I never saw anything so pretty, the way they dove down through the sky, and I remember Daddy let out this big laugh, and he said, 'Come on, Wayne, what are we waiting on,' and we ran out into the meadow."

My father stood tensely as he spoke, his hands tightening around his own gun, his forefinger caressing the trigger, very gently.

I didn't know how to respond, so I said: "I wish I'd known him."

He turned, focusing in my direction; for that moment or two he'd been lost in the distant past, inside his memory, and I saw how hard it was for him to change from one thought to another, one time to another.

"I wasn't but ten, you know, when your granddaddy died," he said thickly. "Not even your age."

"Yes sir," I said.

"He came out here to die," my father said. "Somewhere out here, Mama would never say exactly where . . . " He gestured vaguely with the gun, holding it up as if prepared to shoot, to force the mysterious past into focus, into clarity.

"I never knew why, but your grandaddy gave up, he died somewhere in these woods. . . . But you can't give up, you know. You just can't."

"No sir," I said.

"You remember that, hear? Remember what I told you."

"Yes sir," I said, and suddenly I wished that something would come along—a jackrabbit, a squirrel. I would lift the .22 and look coolly along the barrel and blast it into nothing.

Now my father's head made a sharp, twitching movement; he had thought of something else.

"C'mon," he said. "This way."

I didn't ask where we were going. We had turned away from the creek and now there was no path at all, there was nothing, only a dark maze of trees and vines and sometimes a tantalizing glimpse of sky through the branches overhead. My father muttered to himself, kicking at the foliage as he went, gesturing sharply with the gun barrel. I remembered that if you walked long enough in the woods you always went in a circle, so you couldn't really get lost because you'd always end up right where you started. Now I had trouble believing this. I couldn't imagine that we would suddenly reach a clearing, and there would be the normal blue sky and the barbed-wire fence and my father's familiar old truck to take us home.

"Daddy?" I said. "Shouldn't we turn back? Maybe we can follow the creek, you said it leads out into a meadow—"

"Hush up," he said. He stopped abruptly, listening. Then I heard the rustling overhead, followed by a sharp, cawing sound.

My father pointed the shotgun up toward the trees and fired.

"Daddy, wait—" I began, but the rustling and squawking overhead blotted out my words. Now he crouched down again and pointed the gun, but I saw that he didn't really aim; I saw the blurred frustration in his eyes as he lifted the barrel and pulled the trigger, hard.

"Sons of bitches," he muttered. "Goddamn sons of bitches."

The noises had stopped and now my father hurried ahead a few yards, trampling through a mass of brambles and what looked like poison oak, moving with exaggerated caution as though he were stalking the birds, as though they hadn't flown away. He muttered something and made a soft grunting noise that resembled laughter. Then he turned, his head at a strange angle. He fired blindly into the woods.

"Daddy, don't!" I said, but I spoke in a soft hopeless murmur, knowing he couldn't hear. Now came the rustling sound again, this time from the ground—a whistling of disturbed brush in the distance. Grunting, my father sent a shotgun blast in that direction, then another, moving the gun a little sideways each time.

"Damn them," he said hoarsely, his voice descending to a whimper, "God damn them to hell," and he reloaded and fired again as the rustling grew louder and even after we heard voices shouting from deep inside the woods.

"Hold your fire!" one of the voices called. "I order you, *hold your fire!*"

The voice had gotten closer, booming loudly from beyond the near curtain of trees, but somehow it didn't seem real. I didn't believe in the voice and I watched hollowly as my father reloaded, his breath coming fast, his hands trembling, and lifted the shotgun another time and fired. I stood maybe six feet behind him, and I waited for the blast of his gun to make the rustling stop, the voices stop. For a moment there was silence, but then:

"Stop shooting, do you hear! *Do not shoot!* You're in our sights, do you understand?—you and the boy, too. Now drop the guns, both of you!"

I'd lifted my .22 to shoulder level, though I hadn't fired. Now I lowered the gun, but I could not drop it; I felt that it had melded with my arms and become one with them.

"Do you hear?" came the voice again, much more threatening and clear, and my father looked wildly in that direction, his eyes twitching in their sockets.

"Do you hear, I said to drop your—"

My father raised his gun and fired, and then came a fury of shots and raised voices, and from that commotion a piece of bark exploded outward and hit the side of my forehead. I felt the sharp hot pain and an instant light trickling of blood, and I raised my hand instinctively and in that moment dropped the gun. I rubbed at my forehead with the back of one hand, then the other, amazed at the sight of blood and dimly aware that my father had fallen and that two men in uniforms had entered the clearing with pistols drawn, their boots crunching on the pine needles as they rushed toward my father.

For a moment they bent over him and I thought they didn't see me; then I understood that I simply wasn't important. I stood watching, one hand to my forehead. My father had moved abruptly and gotten to his knees, moaning, and now I looked at him and saw his deathly-pale face and the faint gleam of tears along his jaw. The bullet had struck his arm, just above the bicep, and I stood trembling, nauseated, watching as my father rose with no expression on his face and stood shakily, supported by the two men.

One of the rangers was tall, big-chested, burly—it was his voice, I knew, that had boomed out at us from the woods—but the other was quite young and had turned as pale as my father. He had a full, smooth face that might never have been shaved; he kept plucking nervously at his ear, shifting his weight from foot to foot.

"Go ahead, Jenks, I've got him," the older man said, and I could tell from his voice that he despised Jenks. "You're sure you can walk?" he said then, addressing my father. "We're a quarter-mile back, maybe a little more. . . ." He jerked his thumb back behind him.

My father didn't answer but stood gaping into the distance, his mouth slack. I kept glancing at his upper arm but there wasn't much blood, just a deep-red gash in his shirt, and a few drops on the gun barrel where it had dropped beside his boots.

"Go ahead, Jenks, get back if you're so damned scared," the burly ranger said now, supporting my father single-handedly and trying to lead him along. "Make yourself useful, for Christ's sake," and now he jerked his free hand in my direction, as an afterthought.

"Go on, Jenks," he said, turning, his arm around my father. "Go over there, why don't you, and tend to that boy."

No sooner had he spoken than I rushed forward, butting in between my father and the ranger. I seized my father's good arm, pulling as though to lead him back to the truck, to safety. For a moment the ranger and I struggled, my father standing groggily in the middle as though caught in some bizarre tug-of-war.

"Whoa now," the ranger said, almost gently. He had grabbed hold of my wrist, struggling to loosen my grip on my father's limp hand. "Now listen, boy," the ranger said, "you don't want to make my job harder, do you?"

My father, his wounded arm held close to his stomach, groaned briefly in pain.

I knew I should let go, but I could not. My breath came fast, ragged. I saw the younger ranger, Jenks, standing a few feet away, his mouth hanging open, I saw the older ranger with his jaw set firmly, trying to pull me off my father, I saw the guns fallen among the pine needles and the perfect stillness of the surrounding woods, a solemn deep green in the half-light—but I couldn't make sense of anything, I couldn't stop struggling, I kept trying to pull my father back, away. Only a few seconds passed, probably, but it seemed much longer: I felt that the ranger and I were paralyzed in the struggle for my father, deadlocked eternally.

"Jenks, you're about as useless as a little girl," the ranger said in an offhand, cheerful voice. Grunting, he pushed his bulky torso between me and my father. He managed to separate my hand from my father's, one finger at a time, and then he squinted down at me, shaking his head as though I'd caused him a good bit of unnecessary trouble.

"Don't hurt him," I said.

The ranger told Jenks to gather up the guns. Slowly, the two men led my father away. I felt that they'd forgotten me but I knew I'd have to follow, if I ever wanted out of these woods.

Little Death

ONE morning in November a man and his daughter arrived at the county hospital, an old red-bricked building that might have been a barracks, or a prison. Most of the hospital's patients came from surrounding farms and the scattering of towns in a thirty-mile radius; more affluent locals preferred hospitals in Atlanta, sixty miles to the south. Phil McCrea often drove his chortling black pickup along this hilly road from the smallest of the nearby towns, where he worked as a mechanic, but usually he was headed for the cemetery, which was separated from the hospital's rear parking lot by a narrow ridge of woods. Local people joked that you arrived at the front door of the hospital but went out the back, though few would have made the joke within earshot of Phil McCrea.

The pickup pulled into the graveled lot and sat there for a minute, idling. Neither McCrea nor his daughter, a strong-looking teenager named Jody, had spoken or glanced at each other during the half hour's ride. Since his wife's death last year, McCrea wasn't used to company: he put in a solid eight hours at the shop but seldom spoke to his co-workers, while at home Jody and her father inhabited separate worlds, like two boarders accidentally sharing a single house. McCrea was a tall big-boned man with thinning red hair, a prominent forehead and jaw, eyes and mouth that seldom smiled. His only child resembled him, though she had her dead mother's straight brown hair, which she parted severely and tied in back with a rubber band. Father and daughter even dressed alike: boots, jeans, and flannel shirts, usually, though today Jody wore a white cotton blouse and a small gold crucifix that had both belonged to her mother. In the truck cab she sat there fingering the tiny cross, gazing through the scarred windshield as though lost inside a trance.

"Reckon it's time," her father said, shutting off the ignition.

Jody's face showed nothing, though she blinked her eyes, slowly, in what might have been contempt.

She said, "I reckon it's about four months too early."

Her father's jaw hardened. "Don't fight me, now. We done been through this."

"Well, *I* been through it," his daughter muttered. She took a breath. "Okay, then."

At the same moment, father and daughter opened their doors and got out.

Inside, they waited for a while, and then they were shepherded into a small ochre-painted waiting room where Jody, her father sitting silent next to her, grunted one-word answers to the nurse's questions and jabbed her initials onto some forms the woman handed her. This nurse—young, blond, and apparently frightened—then led Jody into another, even smaller room and handed her a plastic cup. She pointed to a small adjoining bathroom, while Jody stared at the cup as if she might enjoy crushing it in her hand. Yet the tension went out of her face when the nurse said, breathlessly, "Mr. McCrea, if you'd kindly wait outside . . . ?" He had followed them to the doorway and now stood there looking block-like, immovable. "Well, I reckon I'll go on," he said, and again Jody closed and opened her eyes with deliberate slowness. Whenever you suggested something to Phil McCrea, he would repeat the idea as if he had thought of it. But Jody told herself: It doesn't matter, he's gone. She went into the bathroom, filled the specimen cup, then spent a long moment staring at her pale strong-boned face in the mirror. Even as a young child she was teased, called "horse-face" by the kids at school, and refused to be comforted when her mother said not to worry—she was just a tomboy, this was a phase that many girls went through. Two years ago, when she was fourteen, she'd yelled at her mother during supper, "I ain't a tomboy, I'm just plain homely," an outburst that had brought a rare smile to her father's lips. Her mother, who was pretty but tired-looking, hadn't known how to respond when Jody ran out of the kitchen.

Jody often thought about that night, only because it was her last memory before her mother fell ill with cancer ("female trouble," her father preferred to call it), and after that, the two had talked only of her mother's illness. Her mother had had a kind heart but a weak disposition, Jody thought, and it seemed that for her entire life she might have been preparing for her slow and painful death. Her gaunt face had become strangely beautiful, and instead of fighting the cancer she seemed to thrive on it, often telling Jody that she didn't mind the pain, or any of what was happening; Jody and her father really shouldn't worry. Jody wanted to ask, "Why the hell *don't* you mind," but her anger was mixed up with sorrow and fear and, above all, confusion, for the first weeks of her mother's illness had also been the time when she'd met Lennie. Everything had happened all at once, and she'd never been able to tell her mother. Jody had felt stranded inside her father's realm of silence, where words and love and pain were just symptoms of female trouble, nothing more.

When she came out of the bathroom, the young blond nurse had left and an older, severer woman—she could have passed for Phil McCrea's sister, Jody thought—had taken her place. She was tall, gray-haired, unsmiling, and stood with her arms folded. "Ready?" she said briskly, taking the plastic cup.

For some reason Jody didn't answer, and the woman looked at her.

"I said, are you ready?" she asked.

"Ready for what?" Jody said, in the pert voice of a much younger girl.

The nurse turned and started out of the room. "This way," she said over her shoulder.

The nurse led her to a semiprivate room on the second floor; last week, when her father had escorted her to the obligatory visit with a counselor, the woman (also gray-haired, but more pleasant) had explained that since Jody was so young, and in her second trimester, the doctor wanted her to stay overnight. Did she understand, did she have any questions, had she considered her options carefully? the woman said quickly, shuffling through some papers on her desk. At the word "options" Jody glanced at her father, who'd said nothing during this interview but whose big-jawed, sullen face caused Jody's own face and tongue to harden, so that she could barely speak; she'd willed that hardness to spread down toward her sore heart, her queasy stomach. She'd swallowed with difficulty and said, "No ma'am, no questions," and minutes later they'd been back in the truck. Her father stopped at the cemetery, as he did almost every day, but Jody had stayed in the truck cab, staring dully through the windshield as if her father had stopped for gas or a loaf of bread.

"Go ahead and undress," the nurse told her, "and I'll be back in a few minutes."

Today Jody wanted to resume the pose of indifference, or acquiescence, in order to cope with what was going to happen, so she nodded slowly, unbuttoning her blouse. She stared with mild curiosity at the partition dividing the room, wondering if a girl like herself slept on the other side?—or perhaps someone like her mother, who might be dead by nightfall? Lying in bed, Jody stared at the ceiling and remembered her girlish fantasies, that night after she'd lost all arguments with her father. Sneaking out of the hospital, like someone in a movie, heading out to the main road and hitchhiking down to Atlanta, surprising Lennie at his parents' house, or at the veterinary clinic where he worked part-time . . . or maybe she and Lennie had planned her escape together, and he'd be waiting at the hospital curb when she rushed out, one arm cradling her stomach, and together they'd drive down from these hills and southward, never to return. . . . How gradually these feverish ideas had lost their richness, their possibility, a sullen hard certitude replacing her wild flights of hope, her father's cold pragmatism cancelling out the romantic dreaminess she must have inherited from her mother. How gradually but inevitably, over the agonizing lifetime of a few short days.

The nurse returned, breaking Jody's reverie. For a half-moment Jody wished the blond, frightened-looking nurse might come back, but no, she preferred this scowling gray-haired woman with her chilly dry hands. Within seconds the nurse had inserted a thermometer into Jody's mouth, prepared a tray holding medication and syringe, made notations on Jody's chart. She removed the thermometer, gave it a hard look, then transferred this same look to Jody.

"It's almost time," she said. "The doctor would normally stop by, but he's doing another procedure, so he'll see you in the O.R." She lifted something from the tray. "I'm going to start an I.V. and inject you with some Valium, and then we'll wheel you downstairs. You're getting a general, you know."

"A general?" Jody said. She winced at the needle-stick.

"General anesthetic—that means you'll be asleep," the nurse said, like a teacher scolding a stupid child. "It's because you've waited so long."

A sudden bright anger scalded her heart. "I waited because—"

"I'll inject the Valium now," the nurse said, and all at once Jody's anger dissolved.

"You're lucky, you know," the nurse said in a voice that sounded blurry and almost kind to Jody's ears. "When I was young, we didn't have this option. Couldn't just ask the doctor to fix our mistakes. A few years from now, most likely, it'll be outlawed again, and best it should be. So maybe you're learning something, eh?"

Jody felt as though she were floating and remembered with difficulty why she was here. "Where's my daddy?" she said.

"He'll be along," the nurse said vaguely, but then she began talking to a man who had entered the room—was this the doctor?—and Jody felt them urging her onto a metal-framed gurney. The nurse was talking about the doctor's schedule, how it was always hurry up and wait, but Jody felt that the woman wasn't speaking to her. The young man—or were there two young men?—laughed softly, their murmured responses inaudible as they began maneuvering Jody out of the room.

She closed her eyes. This diminished the floating sensation but heightened the sickish motion of the gurney. But then she forgot about that, too, as her mind yearned back to that intensely pleasurable first night with Lennie, last summer, when they'd gone for a hamburger and then had driven out into the country, Lennie's car swaying gently as they turned this way, that way, going nowhere in particular. When he'd pulled the car alongside an old cornfield—it was dusk by then, the dark coming on fast—Jody had known what would happen but had decided that she didn't mind, after all she was sixteen now and it was surely time. If she could believe the talk of girls she overheard at school (few of them talked directly to her, old horsey-face), the time was long past; they reminisced about "doing it" at thirteen, fourteen, bright fluttery talk that wound through their discussions of parties and ball games and Friday night dates, a world entirely foreign to Jody. Since her mother's death Jody had known how her father would react to boys around the house, and Jody had understood in any case that few of the boys from school would dream of bringing their loud sputtering cars down the McCreas' dead-end street at the edge of town, where most of the other peeling frame houses were occupied by elderly couples or lone silent men her father's age.

Which had made that evening with Lennie seem all the more miraculous, to use one of the words her mother had favored. Jody tried not to look eager or too happy when he stopped kissing her forehead, her cheeks, her neck, and asked if they wouldn't be more comfortable in the back seat—Lennie had borrowed his uncle's car, a four-door Chrysler—but as they moved into the rear of the car, Lennie easing himself on top of her, she hadn't felt weighted down but, in a pleasant way, turned inside out, as if this evening marked the death of old horsey-face, as if tomorrow she might look in the mirror and see another girl entirely.

And Lennie was gentle. Lennie was sweet. "Is this okay?" he said in a hoarse murmur. "This doesn't hurt, does it?"

She couldn't answer because she'd been seized by the image of her mother's face, during those last days in the hospital. "It's over for me," her mother had whispered, barely able to open her eyes, "but for you it's just starting . . ." Jody hadn't known how to interpret these words—were they a promise? a curse?—but that night, holding Lennie, she thought she knew. She understood how foolishly she'd behaved just after her mother's death, when she'd put away the clothes her mother made for her—frilly blouses, wool sweaters in soft pastel shades—in favor of jeans and flannel, and had thrown away the lipstick and mirror her mother had bought for her fourteenth birthday, and had let her hair go unwashed for weeks at a time. At school they ridiculed her—"when you gonna shampoo that mane of yours, horsey-face?"—but she ignored them. For more than a year she'd been the school oddity. Last April, when a boy approached her in the cafeteria, where she sat eating lunch by herself, she'd thought it was some kind of practical joke: all the time he spoke to her, she kept expecting to hear the catcalls of other kids breaking out around her, and to see the boy himself start laughing, acknowledging that the prank was over.

But Lennie hadn't been joking. No one paid them any attention, and the more he talked the more she understood that he was just lonesome, a new kid at school who hadn't made many friends. He'd enrolled in January, he told her, and was staying with his aunt and uncle for a while; they ran a medium-sized farm near town, and he wanted to be a veterinarian, and so here he was. In a lower voice he told Jody that his parents had divorced last year, and though he lived with his mother, she had some emotional problems, and she was seeing a man Lennie didn't like, and so . . . when his uncle made the offer, he'd jumped at it. He was glad to be here, never mind that he didn't know very many people. He loved the farm, he was glad to get away from Atlanta, all the noise, the traffic. . . . He'd talked on and on, anxious but friendly, cracking his knuckles, every once in a while pushing his glasses back up his nose. Jody sat there amazed, watching him. His face was ruddy, scarred from acne, and Jody understood that he'd probably approached a number of other, prettier girls—he wasn't shy—and had been turned away. Yet he had a boyish smile, and his eyes were a clear strong blue, and despite herself Jody liked him. When he began, "So, I was wondering if . . . ," she'd said yes before he finished the question, giving him a quick nervous smile, and there was a long pause and then they'd laughed at the same moment.

Jody had never dated before, and when Lennie began showing up on Friday or Saturday evenings—sometimes in his uncle's Chrysler, more often in his own beat-up Camaro—Phil McCrea had been too shocked to respond with anything but hostile silence, stomping back into the TV room and slamming the door whenever Lennie rang the front bell. Although Jody had excavated the boxes of clothes her mother had made her, she found that she'd outgrown them; but her mother's own blouses and skirts fit her perfectly, and she wore them without asking her father's permission. He'd glared at her, the first time or two, but said nothing. She still wore no makeup, but she'd bought some musk-smelling perfume at the drug store, and a cheap hairclasp of imitation pearls, and she wore her mother's delicate gold chain and cross.

Though her dates with Lennie became the focus of her life, they were infrequent. He worked hard on the farm and on his school assignments, so he called only once every two or three weeks. Sometimes they went to a movie, but more often they took long drives in the country, and after that evening when they parked beside the cornfield Lennie drove out there automatically, not asking Jody what she wanted to do. Jody told herself that she didn't mind. Would she have preferred to go anywhere else, after all? And she loved the drives they took, before and after lovemaking, and the way Lennie would flex his strong hands on the wheel as he talked about the future. He was much more serious and ambitious than the other boys at school; he already knew that he wanted to attend veterinary school at the University of Georgia and that he must do well now, as a junior, in order to get a scholarship. He loved animals and told her endless anecdotes about his experiences with the cows and goats and sheep on his uncle's farm, and how badly he wanted his own farm someday. . . . Early in their relationship Jody learned that Lennie's father, who still lived in Atlanta, was an accountant, but Lennie seldom referred to either of his parents. He wasn't yet seventeen but already he struck Jody as an adult, a man who had definite plans and a firm sense of the future. It was only a matter of time, she reasoned, before she would tell Lennie that she'd fallen in love.

This was what her mother had meant, Jody often thought. *For you, it's just starting. . . .*

The last night she saw Lennie, in August, he'd broken the news that his mother had called; that she'd been calling all week to demand that he come back to Atlanta for his senior year. The guy she'd been seeing had abandoned her—Lennie was glad of that, at least—and she needed him, she'd never lived alone before. . . . So they'd struck a bargain: just one more year at home and then she'd help him financially, as much as she could, when he started veterinary school. He had to go, Lennie told Jody, holding both her hands but gazing just past her eyes. Probably, he reasoned, he'd gotten what he needed from staying at his uncle's farm, and maybe it *would* be best if he focused on school next year. But of course he'd come to visit, he said quickly. Of course he'd invite Jody to Atlanta, once he explained the situation to his mother. They had a nice guest bedroom and he was sure there would be no problem. . . . Somehow that phrase, "no problem," had brought an icy convulsion to her heart, but she said nothing. She nodded, agreeing with his logic. She'd waited until she was in her room, alone, before allowing herself a few quick tears, a hardened clench of her long bony jaw.

Old horsey-face.

In the following weeks, she tried telling herself that she hadn't been trusting enough. That she was sour and suspicious, like her father, and she had to get over that. For Lennie began phoning her, using the pronoun "we" whenever he talked about the future, and an intimate confiding manner that he took on—somehow she knew this—with no one else. Jody could tell he was lonely; he spoke in that same rushed, anxious voice he'd used when they first met in the cafeteria. He talked about his mother and her problems, about his work and activities at school, about his new part-time job at an animal clinic, which he loved, and which would look great on his application form for veterinary school. He couldn't come north right now, he told her all during September and most of October, but he'd try to get away at Thanksgiving break, or Christmas at the latest. In fact, Jody was relieved. The longer he waited, the longer she could put off telling him about the baby, reasoning that she couldn't give him such news over the phone. But by late October she was beginning to show, and her daily ritual of assessing her naked abdomen in the bathroom mirror had become an occasion of dread rather than pleasure. She felt that time had begun to slow down, as if to force her secret gradually but mercilessly out into the open. She hadn't been surprised when her P.E. instructor, Miss Kimball, had handed her a note from the principal: "Please see me." It had been the first of many confrontations, but she hadn't seen or spoken to Lennie again. Somehow Lennie had been spared.

Now she confronted a balding green-clad man with silver tufted eyebrows who stared down at her, displaying his teeth in what must have been a smile.

"Miss McCrea?" he said. "Did you hear me?"

Her eyes had been open but unseeing. She'd heard nothing but a drone of distant voices, detached from her. Still she felt as if she were floating, her mind turned soft and gauzy. She listened with difficulty but managed to nod her head, *yes*. Then she shook her head, *no*. She understood that her eyes had filled.

"It's the shot," a woman's voice said. "Made her a little woozy."

Jody saw that her knees had been hoisted into the air, spread wide.

"Well, that's probably best," the doctor said idly, sorting through some instruments on a tray. He nodded to someone behind Jody's head.

"Now just close your eyes," came the man's voice, behind her, "and start counting backwards from a hundred. Can you do that, Miss McCrea?"

Jody said, "I don't want—"

Her throat had constricted, choking off her voice. She shouldn't cry now, she told herself, she had to tell these men about Lennie, to explain that she didn't want—

Tears leaked from the sides of her eyes but no one noticed. They were down beyond her opened legs, murmuring, and behind her the man said, "All right, here we go, then. One hundred, ninety-nine . . . "

She blinked several times, confused. She felt groggy, her throat felt very sore. Only a few moments passed before she understood what had happened. She felt no pain down there, only numbness, as if the lower half of her body had been removed. She kept blinking her eyes, trying to think what she must do. But someone was entering the room.

The gray-haired nurse. "Feeling better?" she asked, bending down.

"I don't . . . don't feel nothing," Jody mumbled.

The nurse drew back, as if repulsed by this answer.

"Your daddy's on his way," she said primly. "He's coming to see you."

Jody blinked her eyes. She said, "I told them I changed my mind—*he* made me sign them papers. I wanted the baby and I didn't want—"

"Hush now," the nurse said, touching her forearm. "Your daddy will be here soon."

The baby was what bound her to Lennie and was all that she had.

"But I wanted—"

She heard her own childish echo and fell silent. The nurse had left the room.

Jody raised her head. Already she felt stronger, and there was no pain. She did not want to see her father, she thought, nor did she want to hear what she might say to him. Instead she wanted Lennie. Probably there were good reasons why he hadn't called. Yes, probably she'd sold him short because she couldn't trust people, just as her father couldn't—my God, she was through with that! She would call Lennie and ask him to come for her. She'd go to that little motel down the road, get a room, call him from there, and wait patiently. It was only an hour's drive up from Atlanta. She had waited months to see Lennie again and could easily wait another hour.

Sitting up, she moved her legs gingerly over the side of the bed. Nothing. No pain. She felt perfectly fine. A little dizzy, maybe, but that would pass.

She saw her clothes hanging in the closet across the room: blouse, jeans, boots, and the oversized blue-jean jacket she'd worn for weeks in the attempt to hide her pregnancy. Her wallet was stuffed inside the jacket, but did she have enough money for a room? She had twenty, twenty-five dollars. If it wasn't enough, she would tell the proprietor that Lennie would pay the rest when he arrived.

She walked carefully toward the closet, more excited with each step. She felt happy. She felt that she was controlling her own life, at last. Imagine how her father and the nurse would react, coming in here and discovering that the bed was empty! But they would never understand, of course. Only Lennie would understand.

She let the hospital gown fall to the floor, careful not to look at the bandage below her waist. She felt nothing down there and would not even look. Getting into the clothes was easy, except for the jeans, which were tight. Then she did feel pain, but only a twinge. Just enough, she thought, to let her know she must be careful.

Yes, she was like someone in a movie. At the door she peered into the hall, seeing several nurses but not the gray-haired one. She took a breath, bowed her head, and hurried toward the elevators. Fortunately there were several other visitors in the hall and she blended right in. There were two women waiting for the elevator, and it opened miraculously the instant Jody walked up. The women were talking in low murmurs, and neither of them glanced at her.

Downstairs Jody walked slowly but steadily until she found the rear exit and got away from the building. Out the sides of her eyes, she looked for her father's truck in the parking lot, and then she gazed out to the oiled road; but she saw nothing. He was taking his time, as usual. Jody smiled to herself, but now she paused. She hadn't thought beyond this point. The motel was less than a mile away, but she shouldn't walk that far. She could call a taxi, but that would mean going back inside the hospital. She paused, uncertain. That was when she saw her father's pickup in the distance, rounding the last turn of the oiled road that would bring him up toward the hospital.

She veered away from the parking lot and headed in the only safe direction—toward the thick woods that bordered the hospital at the rear. About ten yards into the woods she stopped and looked back. Here among the pines and thick-leaved elms it was dim, shaded, cool, and she stared out into the lot, where sun glinted off the white gravel and the windshields, and knew she could not be seen. She might have been glimpsing another world. Her father had parked at the edge of the lot and, outside the truck, squinted upward for a moment at the hospital building, as though trying to pick out Jody's room. He didn't even glance toward the woods. His face looked stern and unsmiling, as always. He walked with slow but determined strides toward the rear entrance. Jody kept her eyes trained on him until he was gone.

She might have been someone else, she thought—a distant observer, someone her father would not recognize. For a long time she'd felt that he didn't know her, and that explained why they lived as virtual strangers in their house. Yet it hadn't always been so. Phil McCrea had been a man of few words, but not unkind and not without humor. Her mother's death had unhinged him, Jody knew. She could recall the two of them joking together in the kitchen, her father's arms slipping around his wife's waist as she stood frying eggs or washing dishes. He would whisper and she would laugh, poking him with her elbow, or dabbing soap suds onto his chin. Once they had seen Jody watching from the doorway, and her father had run over, scooped her into the air—she must have been nine or ten—and brought her back to the sink, where her mother had dabbed suds on Jody's chin, too, and both her cheeks, and her father said she looked like a little Chinaman, and the three of them had laughed and laughed. . . . Helplessly Jody had remembered such scenes when her father confronted her, last week, the moment she walked in the kitchen door from school. Their argument had been violent but brief, for he'd decided what she must do; he'd already made a doctor's appointment and had told the school principal that Jody wouldn't be back until January. When Jody responded first with anger, then with tears, saying wildly that she and Lennie were in love and he'd promised to marry her, Phil McCrea had laughed harshly. "That boy's long gone," he'd said, "and why wouldn't he be?" Jody hadn't been sure what he meant and hadn't asked. She'd stalked back to her bedroom and slammed the door, and again that terrible silence had filled the house.

For several minutes Jody had kept walking into the woods, but now she came to a clearing. Her eye took in the sloping hill of stubbled yellow grass, which was dotted with grave markers where the trees should have been. This was a cemetery without marble headstones or statuary, or much ornament of any kind. Just the brass markers, with a small stone vase beside each one. Some of these held bright plastic daisies or zinnias, others held dead flowers or were empty. Jody walked out into the green sunlit grass, blinking. She no longer felt groggy, but in her abdomen she felt a stabbing pain with every step, forcing her to limp and bringing to mind the pain her mother had undergone during her last days. Female trouble, her father had mumbled, embarrassed. . . . She looked around her but couldn't remember where her mother had been buried. After the funeral she'd refused to accompany her father when he visited the cemetery, and after a while he stopped asking her. It had been too painful, she thought. She had just met Lennie and so she'd pushed all that horror and pain away. She had not wanted to acknowledge what had happened or to be like her father, morose and silent, clinging to death.

Surveying the dozens of grave markers Jody thought that today she'd endured another, smaller death; now that her head had cleared and the pain had begun, she could understand quite easily. The thought of calling a taxi or trudging out to that motel, the thought of phoning a boy who had surely gone a long way toward forgetting her—these notions now seemed cartoonish and absurd, like some leftover daydream from her childhood years.

It took only a few minutes, after all, for her to find her mother's grave. She had remembered from the funeral that it was near the narrow graveled road that cut through the cemetery and that it had seemed set apart, by a discreet few yards, from a cluster of other markers all belonging to one family. Jody stood over her mother for a long while, her hair blowing in the mild November wind, her hands shoved inside her jacket pockets. In one of the pockets she felt the gold chain and cross, which she now grasped in her fingers like a charm. She'd felt the aching slippage of blood inside her loins, as though pulled by gravity, yearning downward to enrich the very earth in which her mother lay. But Jody ignored the pain, the seeping blood. She could not even summon any tears as she stood above the small grass-covered mound that enclosed her mother.

After a while she said, in a husky murmur, "His name was Lennie, Mama," and for the moment, at least, those words eased the pain. Then she waited until she heard the chortling engine, the crunch of gravel, and headed out to meet the one man who knew where to find her.

Sanctity

IN our small parochial school, in the regimented fifties, every child bore some kind of label. There were two or three smart, diligent girls whom the nuns held up as paragons of academic excellence. The other girls were grouped generally into the very pretty ones, the unfortunate homely ones, and the perpetual gigglers, whose bland, plump faces kept them in a middle zone of popularity, a kind of limbo devoid of either pain or hope of reward. Among the boys, there were the mighty athletic ones, ranging from the adored heroes (handsome, smooth-limbed, good-natured) to a hulking bully nicknamed Brutus; there were one or two sissies; and there was a small redheaded boy known as the "class clown" for his impudent remarks to the nuns and for certain bold stunts on the playground or in the cafeteria, which he often entered limping and slack-jawed, in perfect mimicry of the school's one handicapped nun, Sister Maureen. In our class, another boy occupied a category usually reserved for girls: the religious one. His name was Thomas Molloy.

As early as second or third grade, Thomas had quietly declared his intention to enter the priesthood, and by the age of twelve had disavowed boyish pranks of all kinds—roughhousing, obscenity, disrespect to teachers, even ordinary athletic activity. Quiet and remote, he came to life only during theology class, when he would question Sister Julian in a clear, dry voice, his hands clasped before him on the desk, his face pale as ashes. During recess he would wander from the playground, visiting a small grotto to one side of the schoolyard that contained a rock garden, a red-bricked patio, and a statue of the Blessed Virgin. Often he knelt and prayed there, by himself, while the shouts and laughter of his schoolmates echoed over the tiled roof of the school building. But nothing distracted Thomas. Facing the Virgin, he knelt arrow-straight on the patio or, during Lent, might move to the side and kneel in the rock garden, his knees pressing against the sharp edges of the rocks. Thomas was a tall, unusually thin boy whose folded hands were long and pale, almost skeletal.

Before that year when we were all twelve, and approaching the magically significant age of thirteen, no one paid much attention to Thomas. Among younger schoolchildren in that time and place, religiosity wasn't so unusual; in any given year there were a number of declared vocations, scapulars worn boldly on the outside of shirts or blouses (less pious children wore them, too, but beneath their clothing), arguments over which child's sacrifices during Lent (chocolate, favorite TV programs, and so on) were greater than the others'. Although Thomas did not participate in these more competitive and peer-conscious forms of sanctity, he was considered a typical Molloy—unassuming, soft-spoken, sharing the family tendency toward freckles and boniness—and thus earned no particular notice from the others at school. There were seven Molloy children, one in almost every grade. Like many families in the parish, they had little money—Mr. Molloy was a mailman—and were unable to afford the school tuition, partly waived in such cases at Father Bascomb's discretion. It was generally known in school which children could pay fully and which could not, but poverty in itself was no particular stigma, and the Molloy children were always neatly dressed, well scrubbed, and punctual. They blended invisibly into the social fabric of the school.

The emergence of Thomas Molloy as a special object of persecution coincided with the mysterious illness of Sister Julian during that humid spring of 1959. Though apparently they had little in common, later it became clear that Thomas and Sister Julian shared an insatiable appetite for suffering. At the end of that school year, both my parents counseled me not to brood about them or about anything that had happened. "There will always be outcasts," my mother said, with her unfailing pragmatism. "You must be kind to such people but don't let them worry you." My mother's idea was that the people she labeled "outcasts" needed desperately to call attention to themselves. "Don't be taken in," she warned me. "None of this had anything to do with religion."

My earliest reaction foreshadowed my mother's warning, in fact, as I had quickly become irritated by Thomas Molloy's behavior. A plain-faced, anonymous student in earlier years, he had begun to court disaster (it seemed to me) by dissociating himself from the daily playground activities, conversation in the cafeteria or the halls, and the routine classroom pranks that relieved, for the rest of us, the regimented monotony of school life. If the class clown, Rudy, made an obscene gesture or stood briefly and twitched his hips while Sister Julian wrote on the blackboard, Thomas refused to laugh or exchange an amused glance with his classmates. He sat stonily at his desk, hands folded, ignoring the movement and snickering all around him. During study hall, if one of the bigger boys decided to aim a spitball at the side of Thomas's head, he would turn and glare at the perpetrator, his bony fists clenched, but then would take hold of himself and return to his studies with an air of renewed serenity. Eventually he grew adept at not reacting at all: the corners of his mouth would tighten, involuntarily, or he would blink his eyes in momentary irritation, but he wouldn't even glance around, much less retaliate. Invariably this behavior inspired a further barrage of spitballs, now from all corners of the room, and I could not understand why Thomas withstood such needless indignities. He was neither sissified nor physically ugly—the usual reasons for persecution. To avoid the wrath of his classmates he had only to laugh with them or participate in some harmless bit of foolery or join them in tormenting some less fortunate soul. I remembered the Thomas of previous years as a quiet, vaguely smiling boy who had been ineffective on the playing field but nonetheless plucky, determined, and kind-natured. Thus I could not understand this sudden, aberrant pursuit of his own doom.

One day—it was the next-to-last time I spoke to Thomas—I approached him during the morning recess and asked about the book he was reading. He sat in his usual bit of shade, next to the school building, while everyone else had scattered into the sunlit playground for twenty minutes of hectic activity. Thomas sat with his knees drawn toward his chin, as though to hide or protect the book whose pages he turned quickly with his bony white fingers. Wordlessly he lifted the book in the air, so that I could read the title—*Lives of the Saints*. "Oh, that's the book Sister Julian recommended," I said awkwardly, already wishing I hadn't approached him.

"Yes, but I've had it for years," he said, in his abstracted way. "Have you read it?"

When Thomas looked at you, his gaze seemed curiously unfocused, as though he were looking somehow past your eyes, or into another dimension altogether. I found this disconcerting and vaguely insulting. As so often in those days, I wanted to grab his thin shoulders and shake him.

"No," I said, half-smiling. "I've got better things to do." I'd intended this as friendly kidding, but it sounded hostile; and Thomas's reaction tipped the balance, flooding my chest with fury.

"Like what," he said, getting to his feet. "Play those stupid games and use filthy language all the while? Is that what you mean?"

"It's what everyone does," I said, fists clenching at my sides. I was a relatively short, stocky boy, and Thomas seemed to tower over me, gaunt and spectral. His tenacious fingers clutched the book to his chest, which moved visibly as his breath grew faster. On his high cheekbones two reddish patches had appeared, like blossoms.

"Then what everyone does," he said in a brittle, quavering voice, "is offensive to God."

It was then I realized that Thomas was afraid. My anger had vanished, but out of frustration I now uttered an obscenity that had lately become popular in our class and one I knew Thomas would find particularly vile. It was a sacrilegious remark about the Virgin Mary, meaningless enough to my young ears, and I wasn't prepared for the intensity of Thomas's reaction. His pale blue eyes suddenly focused, then filled with a look of pure grief. He extended his long arm and slapped my cheek, seeming to act on pure instinct; then he stepped backward, shaking. Though this slap would become a classroom joke for the rest of that term (as the one whom Thomas had slapped, I achieved a sort of mild celebrity), at the time I felt nothing but shocked outrage. For a moment we simply stared at each other. Then Thomas turned and in his odd, loping gait shambled off toward the rock garden and the Virgin's grotto. I went back to the playground with a smeared, uneasy grin on my face, my cheek stinging.

In the weeks following this incident, persecution of Thomas began in earnest. I no longer felt pity for him, and like the others I would cheer on the bullies who rammed Thomas into the lockers whenever he passed down the hall or grabbed his lunch bag out of his hand as he entered the cafeteria and then kicked it around like a football for the next half hour. No one took up for Thomas any longer, not even the most conscientious and intelligent girls, not even the popular class president and baseball star with his quick, dazzling smile and utter lack of malice. These few would simply look away while we others luxuriated in our viciousness and cruelty.

At the time, of course, it all seemed very normal and everyday. (I seldom thought about Thomas after school hours, and I suspect that my classmates did not, either. Only occasionally, late at night when I might have an "evil" thought or wake from a troubling dream, would I see Thomas's pale accusing features there before me, disembodied in the darkness above my bed.) Nor were there any further protests or feeble retaliations from Thomas. Rather he seemed to move about in a magical enclosure, studying or eating at appointed times but in all ways removed from the actual life of the school. Often he would sit with his eyes half-shut, his colorless lips moving in silence. Even when he was not praying his eyes held that unfocused, smoothed-over gaze—like the sightless marble eyes, I thought, of the Virgin's statue out in the grotto.

One day, just before Sister Julian had entered our homeroom for theology class, a classmate tapped my shoulder and handed me a stiff, folded-over piece of construction paper. Inside was a crude, obscene drawing of a nun and a tall boy, the figures labeled "Sister Julian" and "Thomas Molloy." The sexual organs, of course, were greatly exaggerated in size and painstakingly detailed. The artist had also troubled to include the scapular around Thomas's neck, with an obscene word inscribed on it, in Gothic lettering. The classmate and several others were now urging me to pass the drawing up to Thomas, who sat across the aisle from me and on the very front row. As usual he sat imperturbably, waiting for Sister Julian with his fingers interlaced on his desktop. I hesitated, not out of kindness but because I resented showing him any attention at all—I did not want to touch or speak to him—but at last I stretched forward and slapped the folded drawing down on his desk. I will never forget that his eyes moved downward, but his head did not. With slow, precise movements Thomas's long fingers unfolded the drawing, and during the shocked few seconds (to me, they seemed half an hour) when he stared at the obscene figures, a wave of snickering and knee-slapping rippled through the classroom. Again I'd become a momentary hero, but I wasn't laughing. I watched the side of Thomas's gaunt, still-motionless face. For a moment his cheek flushed, but just as quickly it whitened to the color of parchment. I thought I detected a film of moisture, like that accompanying a sick fever, glisten briefly along his smooth forehead. Folding back the drawing, his fingers worked crisply as though independent of him. I felt that Thomas was going to become sick or perhaps fall sideways in a dead faint. In my own uneasiness, my heart-knotting paralysis of cruelty, guilt, and fear, I sensed what a relief this would be. Cold sweat dribbled down my sides. But Thomas did not become sick or fall sideways, and a moment later the general sniggering ceased abruptly. Sister Julian had entered the room.

Thomas sat facing forward, the refolded drawing on the desk beside his laced fingers, just where I had placed it. Briefly I considered snatching up the paper, then darting from the room and into the boys' lavatory; the consequences would be severe, but at least Sister Julian would not have discovered the drawing. Yet there wasn't time for this. Instantly Sister Julian sensed the tension in the room, and I watched sickly as behind her rimless spectacles her pale eyes—exactly the washed-blue color of Thomas's—followed the other children's gaze toward the drawing. Standing only a few feet from Thomas's desk, she said in her steely, staccato voice: "There on your desk, Thomas. What's that?"

My heart froze. Interminable seconds ticked by.

"Thomas? Did you hear me?"

"Yes, Sister," Thomas said. "I heard you." His voice was dry, raspy.

"Well?"

Her patience was wearing thin, I could see. In a moment she would snatch up the drawing without waiting for Thomas.

But finally Thomas said, "It's nothing, Sister. It's nothing at all."

He did not move to put the drawing inside a book or crumple it up—as I mentally begged him to do; yet I knew the moment of danger was past. A highly principled woman, Sister Julian frequently inculcated the idea of "personal honor" by accepting a student's word even if he was plainly lying—a rhetorical naivete on her part, intended to shame us all toward truthfulness. Thus it wasn't so surprising that she said quickly, "Oh, very well," and began the lesson without further ado. For the next agonized hour the drawing stayed in plain sight on Thomas's desk, a mote irritating the corner of my eye. The moment class ended, I snatched it back and hurried out the door, toward the boys' lavatory.

Nothing. It's nothing at all. As I flushed the pieces down, I stood thinking that really Thomas had not lied. I recalled hearing the renewed serenity and even a subtle pleasure in his voice.

Like the children, the nuns at school inhabited certain categories. There was the fat, "jolly" one, Sister Theodore, who frequently joined in our playground games despite her girth and her unwieldy size-20 habit (one of the girls had glimpsed the size on a small tag, high inside one of Sister Theodore's capacious sleeves); there was the quiet, intellectual one, Sister Eileen, who taught math and science; there was the self-important and rather obtuse Sister Alberta, the school principal; and there was the "pathetic" Sister Maureen, the music teacher who had suffered polio as a child, and whom all the girls adored and all the boys secretly longed to protect. Finally there was Sister Julian, who occupied a category by herself. A tall, vigorous woman with a bad complexion and abrupt manners, she had been an Olympic-quality athlete in her youth—a basketball player, a track and field star—and after college had pursued a doctorate in philosophy at a non-Catholic university in Chicago (a very unusual venture for a young Catholic girl in the early 1950's). Before finishing her degree, however, she had abruptly decided to enter a teaching order, where her leadership ability and mental acuteness had been recognized in due course. At our school, her first assignment after taking her vows, she was the only nun to whom Father Bascomb, our overworked parish priest, had ever entrusted a theology class—a move that reportedly scandalized and alienated some of the other nuns and many of the parents as well. ("Imagine that, a woman passing along the Church's teachings," my mother said in a clucking, amused way. "Pretty soon Father Bascomb will have her saying Mass," she added in a disapproving voice; but I could tell that she was secretly pleased.) By now, I was accustomed to Sister Julian: she had taught theology for three years straight, and her intense, spirited, often incomprehensible discussions of religious and moral issues now seemed the norm. We had all forgotten about Father Bascomb's mild question-and-answer sessions in which we learned that stealing a candy bar was only a venial sin, provided you gave it back and apologized; or discussed a film he might have shown about Lourdes or Fatima; or signed up to adopt pagan babies from far-off lands. Sister Julian tried to raise us to a new level of awareness—and perhaps of sanctity, to use one of her favorite words—though naturally, being twelve-year-olds, we failed her, and perhaps contributed unwittingly to her downfall during that final spring.

In retrospect, I've often wondered whether Sister Julian contributed (herself unwittingly) to Thomas Molloy's growing religious fervor during those years, much as an effective English or piano teacher can help shape a future poet or concert musician. One of the chief ironies of theology class, in any case, remained the fact that Sister Julian did not really like Thomas. Openly scornful of hypocrisy, she despised "professional saints," of whom she had encountered quite a few in her girlhood and even, she whispered, in the convent: people who were so busy attending Mass, saying the rosary, and making novenas that they never took the time to lead an active Christian life. I'd also noticed that Sister Julian, vigorous and athletic herself, found distasteful any suggestion that serving God and the Church somehow meant transcending the physical; the saints had not been ethereal, bloodless creatures, she insisted, but hearty men and women who had channeled their strength and passion into the love of God. She reminded us that St. Francis had sweated in the fields; that St. Teresa of Avila had reformed the Carmelite order almost singlehandedly, establishing convents throughout sixteenth-century Spain; that Father Jean de Breboeuf and other missionaries in seventeenth-century Quebec had endured arduous journeys and backbreaking work before they earned their martyrdom at the hands of the Iroquois. So it may have been that Sister Julian distrusted Thomas Molloy's fragile looks and pious demeanor. It was certainly true that the clear, bell-like voice he used during theology class irritated rather than pleased her. When she opened class discussion on any topic, she would ignore Thomas's raised hand at first, her eyes scanning the rest of the class; she called on him only as a last resort, scarcely concealing her impatience as he phrased one of his lucid but convoluted questions, to which she gave the briefest of replies. For Thomas's part, he did not seem to perceive his fall into disfavor, or else he did not mind. Sister Julian's quick, hectoring manner seemed to stimulate him, bringing color to his gaunt cheek, a bright film of moisture to his eyes. The rest of the class, myself included, looked on both of them with increased suspicion and mistrust. We kept our distance from Sister Julian outside of class (in any case, she seldom socialized in the halls or the cafeteria, even with the other nuns) and continued our merciless persecutions of Thomas, despite his attitude of stoical indifference. In fact, this excited our cruelty all the more.

Only a few weeks before Sister Julian's abrupt departure from the school, I came to understand fully the hopelessness of Thomas's plight. Aside from Sister Julian herself, only I perceived exactly what happened—almost, I felt, as though I'd been singled out. It was a cold morning in late March, near the end of our morning recess, and a group of boys had cornered Thomas against the school wall, in the spot where he normally sat apart from the other children, doing his reading or else staring vacuously into space and moving his lips in a soundless murmur. We all assumed he was praying, just as he often did while kneeling before the Virgin's statue in the grotto, and we tended not to bother him at these times. But that particular morning was windy and bitterly cold, despite the sunlight glaring feebly onto the schoolyard, so that our usual games were out of the question. On such mornings we would stand around in shivering clusters, hands plunged into our pockets, making raucous jokes and simply marking time until the bell rang and we could herd back inside the warm building. Thomas had ignored the cold and chosen his usual spot of shade—where the air was frigid, the wind merciless—to sit turning the pages of his book with gloveless hands.

One of the larger boys, walking by him, lifted one leg and neatly kicked the book out of Thomas's grasp, sending it a few yards off where it lay on its spine, pages flapping. "Oh, Thomas, excuse *me!*" the boy cried out and, still without taking his hands from his pockets, went over and kicked the book back toward Thomas again.

Before Thomas could get to the book another boy rushed forward—hands in his pockets, too—and kicked it back to the first boy. Squinting, I could see that the book was *Lives of the Saints,* Thomas's favorite. "C'mon, guys, that's a communion gift, he's had it for years," called one of the prettier girls, from across the playground; but there was little conviction in her voice. Soon enough there were eight or nine boys around Thomas, kicking the book among them as Thomas made ludicrous efforts to retrieve it, careening this way and that, his gangly arms and legs ineffectual against the strong, graceful kicks of the others. For their part, the boys whooped with laughter as they would during any sport, occasionally stomping on the book before kicking it again, and yelling out stray taunts and obscenities. Once or twice, when Thomas bent down to grasp at the book, someone would kick him from behind and send him sprawling. From where I stood, halfway across the playground, Thomas seemed a knot of tangled and flailing limbs inside the whirring kicks of the other boys, and I remember allowing the keen exultation I felt to block out everything else. I had already started toward the group when I saw something at a distance: it was Sister Julian, who had appeared at the far corner of the school building.

My first emotion was relief that I hadn't joined the fracas, for I knew the others were done for. The combination of hazing, destroying someone else's property, and defacing a religious book was certain to bring severe punishment to the perpetrators. I had stopped abruptly, looking back in the direction I had come in the desire to dissociate myself from Thomas's persecutors, who continued their sport unawares. Yet a moment later I looked again at Sister Julian, surprised that she had not yet called out or begun moving forward. Instead she stood motionless in the strong wind, huddled in her black winter cloak. Her rimless spectacles glinted in the cold sunlight. Just at that moment, one of the boys administered a particularly vicious kick to Thomas's stomach, which would cause him to be sent home for the rest of the day. I heard Thomas's involuntary, muffled cry of pain. Yet I did not look at him, continuing instead to watch Sister Julian who not only failed to stop what was happening but even stood (or so I imagined, from my considerable distance) in an attitude of sober, cool satisfaction, as though she were not shocked in the least. She neither spoke nor gestured, and a moment later, when the boys had finally abandoned Thomas and continued simply to kick the book around, clearly tiring of the game, she turned abruptly and disappeared around the corner of the building.

The sole witness to her appearance, I did not tell my group of bullying friends what had happened, and certainly I did not tell Thomas. In the following weeks I noticed, in a vague way, that he had stopped appearing on the playground altogether, instead spending his recess time and lunch periods in the Virgin's grotto. Occasionally a group of boys, chasing a ball or one another around that side of the building, might glimpse Thomas, sitting quietly on a wrought-iron bench near the Virgin's statue. We might call out some cheerful insult or make sniggering jokes among ourselves, but we didn't bother him there, preferring instead to continue our game and simply ignore the troubling oddity of Thomas Molloy. Yet I couldn't help noticing the subtle change overtaking him. Except in theology, he seemed to lose interest in his school work; in math or English class he would sit gazing into the distance, dreamy and abstracted, there but not really there. I knew he sat thinking about the Virgin in the grotto.

One glowering April morning Sister Julian came to our classroom in a state of unusual excitement. This was a Wednesday, our last day of school before Easter vacation. Outside it had been raining, the clouds gathered in menacing clumps beyond our classroom windows. Though the sky remained nearly black, we were relieved that just before theology class the rain had stopped; that meant we would be permitted outdoors for morning recess, which followed immediately after. Contrasted with the darkness outside, the classroom itself seemed overbright, the fluorescent lights casting an artificial glare over everything. Sister Julian went briskly to the head of the room and began to talk about the meaning of Good Friday. Her face looked shiny and bloodless in the white-lit room, and I remember thinking that her gestures were more hectic and disjointed than usual, her voice pitched in a slightly higher key. But I paid little attention to her lecture. I sat thinking about the long, luxurious vacation, about an Easter egg hunt my father and I planned to stage in the backyard for my four-year-old sister, about the new straw-colored suit my mother had bought me to wear on Easter Sunday, and which I imagined her hemming at this very moment, pins sticking out of her mouth. I preferred these thoughts to wondering about Thomas Molloy, as I had often done—what his family must be like, what unimaginable home life could produce such a mysterious, wayward child. I didn't want to consider that his family was probably not much different from my own. Whenever I remembered that our lives at home, school, and church had been virtually identical, I experienced an intense spasm of resentment and denial. Though at age twelve, of course, this felt like simple, self-satisfied hatred of Thomas Molloy.

That morning, I first became aware that something was wrong when I heard the distress and anxiety in Thomas's voice. This snapped me awake, and I saw that Sister Julian stood directly over him, her face knotted into an ugly smile. Her lips were trembling, her hands clutched at her sides.

"I don't know what you mean, Sister," Thomas was saying. "I've defined the word as best I can—"

"No, you've said that sanctity means being close to God—or *one* with God, I believe those were your words." Sister Julian spoke with cold sarcasm, the horrid smile trembling on the verge of a snarl. For the first time in months, I felt sympathy for Thomas.

"Yes, Sister, that was my answer," he said, in a wounded tone.

The room had grown quiet. Surely the entire class saw, as I did, that a film of perspiration had appeared on the foreheads of both Thomas and Sister Julian.

"Being one with God," Sister Julian repeated, derisively. She glanced around the room as though inviting us to share her scorn. "But Christ himself *left* the presence of God, didn't he?" she asked. "In order to become human, and to suffer?"

"That was different," Thomas said, in a quavering voice. "Christ needed to suffer, so that—"

"Ah! *Christ* needed to suffer!"

Sister Julian made a brief, flapping gesture with her arms; meant to convey total exasperation, this gesture usually elicited laughter from the class. But today no one laughed. We all sat watching Sister Julian's face—her clenched jaw, her steely blue eyes. I remembered her rigid demeanor that day on the playground, the sunlight glinting coldly off her spectacles.

Now I heard a small sound from Thomas's throat, "Unf," conveying impatience and frustration. "Christ came to die for our sins," he said stubbornly. "The sanctity of Christ—"

"Don't quote your catechism to me!" Sister Julian burst out. Now, at last, all pretense of teacherly rhetoric and courtesy had vanished. Her upper lip raised in contempt, Sister Julian whirled away from Thomas and began pacing up and down the room. For twenty or thirty minutes she harangued the class, speaking in a loud, savage voice about the suffering of Christ as a model for human life. This was true sanctity, she said; this was the meaning of Christ's passion. Thus Good Friday was the most important day of the liturgical year, she told us, the day when we must contemplate the terrible physical ordeal of those hours on the cross. Could we imagine, Sister Julian asked, the agony of spikes driven into a man's wrists and feet, and then the full weight of his body pulling against the spikes? Did we truly understand the physical reality of the cross, how it was designed to provide exquisite torture to every part of the body? And did we understand this as a paradigm of human life, a *sanctified* human life? Oneness with God, indeed!—here she threw a scornful glance at Thomas. No, sanctity lay in the piercing of flesh, the flowing of blood; it lay in the torturous stretching of muscle and tendon, the riot of pain in every cell of the body. . . . Dare we lose sight of this? she demanded. Did we dare to live pallid, conventional lives, ignoring the example of Christ?

By now, few of the children were listening to Sister Julian's words. Rather our anxious attention focused on her ceaseless pacing, her contorted facial expressions, the wildness of her hands jabbing the air. Several of us exchanged puzzled glances. Near the back of the room, one of the girls had begun to weep softly. As for Thomas, his head had gradually bowed under the ferocity of Sister Julian's invective, his chin nearly touching his chest. His eyes were closed, and I remember thinking that his neck might have been broken. His lips moved soundlessly, as though in prayer.

Sister Julian's tirade did not end with her discussion of Good Friday. Quickly she had lost all control (for such would be my parents' obscure explanation to me, in the days that followed: she had simply *lost control*), and somehow moved from Christ's passion into a rambling indictment of the modern world, in all its suffering and evil. She talked about Nazi Germany, about fascism and communism, about the unjust pain and suffering—the poverty, hunger, and degradation of innocent people—right here in America. I remember thinking in a confused way that she was contradicting herself, that she exalted suffering as a pathway to Christ and yet bitterly lamented the fact of suffering people, but I could not link her crazy quilt of words and thoughts into any logical pattern. Like the other children, I simply sat waiting it out. We endured a graphic description of the German concentration camps—where obscene medical experiments had been performed without anesthetic, Sister Julian insisted, on children not much different from ourselves—and of horrendous atrocities committed during fascist or communist takeovers in various parts of the world. The slaughter of innocent villagers; the torture of local leaders through burning or electrocution; chopsticks rammed inside the ears of small children, leaving them to roam screaming through the countryside. "And I'm leaving things out!" Sister Julian cried. "Things that would turn your hair white!" I remember that I sat staring at my hands—folded neatly on my desk, like Thomas's—and feeling how cold they had become. Now there were several girls weeping in the classroom, even one or two boys. Thomas still sat with his head slumped forward like a wounded bird's. Outside the sky darkened and grumbled but no rain fell. Inside, I felt that our rectangle of sickly light had begun to throb and glow, as if the classroom were only a feverish, overbright reflection of Sister Julian's troubled mind.

A few days of controversy followed, during which the school authorities offered no official explanation for Sister Julian's disappearance. (When she finally noticed how seriously she had upset the class, Sister Julian had rushed out of the room, white-faced and furious; we never saw her again.) The principal, Sister Alberta, had told one of the high school girls that Sister Julian needed a rest but would return "one of these days," and there were various rumors filtering down from the upper grades, suggesting that Sister Julian had suffered periods of grave instability in the past. In our class, the incident remained a mystery, something indeed that we seemed eager to forget. It was characteristic of 1950's parochial students that none of us raised a hand to ask about Sister Julian. To question the actions of anyone in authority, much less a religious, would have verged upon sacrilege; the mysterious turbulence surrounding Sister Julian seemed a denial of the dogmatic clarity by which we had learned "the truth" for so many years. So when my mother said briefly that Sister Julian had "lost control," I did not press her for an explanation, and I suspect that most of my classmates remained equally ignorant about what had happened. One week after the incident, Father Bascomb returned as our theology instructor and the quiescent routine of school life resumed.

The only student who seemed permanently affected by the incident was Thomas Molloy. When Father Bascomb returned as our teacher, it was clear that Thomas had lost interest in theology as well. So alert and eager when Sister Julian had taught the class, he now sat slumped inside his chair, staring vacantly at the floor or doodling on a piece of paper. During recess he remained absent from the playground, spending all his time inside the Virgin's grotto. As for the rest of us, despite the beautiful spring weather we did not immediately return to our usual playground sports but spent a few days standing together in clusters, discussing what might have happened to Sister Julian. One of the boys said there must have been something wrong with her—a brain tumor, he said confidently. (This boy would later move to Atlanta in order to study medicine, then return to our town and set up a successful practice; he still speaks confidently.) Rudy, the class clown, performed daily impressions of a raving lunatic, his tongue lolling out one side of his mouth, his eyes rolling wildly. (Rudy went on to become a car salesman; he gets a lot of kidding about the appropriateness of his position, for a former class clown.) Although we laughed at Rudy's antics, we laughed more out of habit than conviction, for despite persistent rumors that Sister Julian had gone to the state asylum at Milledgeville, had been stripped of her habit, and had quickly lost every shred of her sanity and dignity, most of us had trouble believing these lurid tales. (But for years I would be haunted by disturbing dreams of Sister Julian, locked in an institution. Her hair spiky around her head, her face pale and creased, she wore a straightjacket or soiled nightgown; in her eyes lay the random twinkling of the hopelessly mad.) Even harder to believe was the story that she had gotten hold of herself within a day or two, and had accepted a standing offer to teach at a major Catholic university in the Midwest. To us, it seemed that Sister Julian could not exist in another form: she would always remain the stern, compelling figure at the head of our classroom, haranguing us all about suffering, sanctity, and the meaning of our lives.

Soon enough, of course, our talk of Sister Julian faded, along with the tension and uneasiness that accompanied the mention of her name. Within a week or two, we stopped mentioning her at all. Easter had come and gone, it was early May, we were beginning to talk about the end of school and the glories of summer vacation. Yet we still hadn't returned to our everyday, rough-and-tumble lives on the playground, as if some unfinished business remained. During the last week of school, as a group of seven or eight boys idled near the outdoor basketball court, one of us—I don't recall which one—casually brought up the name of Thomas Molloy. Lately he'd been very quiet, very *strange*—didn't we agree? Had anyone spoken to him? Had anyone *seen* him, really, outside the ordinary round of classes? . . . Gradually the mood of our group became jocular, faintly mocking. Thomas no longer ate in the school cafeteria, someone said; he no longer ate lunch at all, but now spent all his free time in the Virgin's grotto. Thomas sat through all his classes like a corpse, said another boy. He never spoke, never raised his hand, never even glanced at his teachers or the blackboard. Rather he sat drawing aimless doodles on a piece of paper, knuckles whitened around his pencil. As the weeks passed he'd looked even thinner, sicklier. Uglier. Hey, said one of the boys, laughing, maybe he's going crazy—just like Sister Julian. That got a big laugh, especially when accompanied by Rudy's impromptu bit of mockery. Rudy hunched his shoulders together, drew his arms toward his body, lowered his eyes and sucked in his cheeks: Hey look, guys, here I am! Thomas Molloy! Then he folded his hands, lifted them quivering in the air. Oh look at me, I'm praying! I'm praying to Sister Julian, look how holy I am!

All the boys laughed, kicking aimlessly at pieces of gravel. We stood around watching Rudy, hands in our pockets.

Now Rudy stuck his tongue out the side of his mouth, rolled his eyes upwards so that only the whites showed. Look, I'm the religious boy, the crazy boy! Oh look at me!

Then someone said, coolly, Where is the little creep, anyway.

Where do you think? said another boy.

That hypocrite, said another. Skinny-assed little *fart.*

Our wills were one, it seemed, as we moved slowly off the basketball court, around one corner of the school building, and to the edge of the rock garden surrounding the red-bricked patio, the grotto, the Virgin's statue. Only last week the Virgin had been crowned "Queen of the May" by one of the senior girls, in a ceremony that annually formed the last major assembly and religious event of the school year. The weather had remained bright and cloudless, and the Virgin's coronet of tiny red and pink roses still looked fresh at her forehead, though slightly lopsided in the spring breeze. As always, the Virgin's marble stare was aimed serenely, implacably into the far distance. Our group had stopped for a moment, perhaps abashed by the Virgin wearing her crown and by our memories of the hushed, respectful ceremony a few days before. But gradually we focused on Thomas, who knelt at the very edge of the patio, just a few feet from the pedestal supporting the statue. In the brilliant wash of May sunlight he looked frail, spectral—for the first time I thought consciously that he didn't seem human. So what did it matter, really, I asked myself, what happened to Thomas?—

he was such a hypocrite, he was so *strange*. Even Sister Julian had noticed, after all. Even Sister Julian had disliked Thomas Molloy.

Now we stood at the edge of the rock garden, simply watching him. One of us said, Hey, jerk-off. Whatcha doin', jerk-off. The rest of us snickered. We shifted our weight from foot to foot, uneasy. Thomas ignored us, of course. He kept his hands folded, his gaze trained on the Virgin's statue. At some point, I noticed that one of the biggest kids—the class bully we called Brutus—had bent over and picked up one of the white stones. Hey guys, he said, we oughtta stone the little fart to death. It's what he wants, isn't it? He wants to be a martyr, isn't that right? A few of us snickered, but this time with less conviction. Thomas's perfect stillness, his imperturbability, was unsettling. All at once, we began to feel chagrined, even foolish. Of course, I thought resentfully, that's exactly what Thomas would love: we'd stone him, get expelled from school, and Thomas's lily-white soul would ascend straight to heaven. That would play right into his hands.

Ah, the hell with him, one of us said. He's not worth the trouble.

Relieved, the others grumbled in agreement. Somebody suggested touch football, so we turned and headed off toward the field on the other side of the school building.

But something made me stop. I stood watching as the others went out of sight, aware that I was taking deep, angry breaths and that my fists were clenched at my sides. I turned around and waited there alone, staring at Thomas. How I hated his smugness, his piety! How good it would have felt if Brutus had done what the rest of us lacked the nerve to do—put all his weight behind the stone, sent it white and sparkling through the air! I could imagine Thomas falling sideways, one arm jerking upward in alarm. I could hear our laughter and imagine how good it felt, how full and joyous.

Eagerly we bent down to the rock garden, again and again, cradling the jagged stones in our palms for a moment, lovingly, like misers dipping into piles of gold coins, before hurtling them toward Thomas. There were jeers, laughter. We shouted obscenities as we threw the stones. This seemed what we'd been born to do, and we cheered when one of us scored a particularly vicious hit above Thomas's eye that sent blood streaming down his face; and cheered again as he lifted his pathetically frail arms, a futile defensive gesture, only to topple sideways and expose his body to the torrent of stones now firing from seven or eight sturdy arms and joyous hearts. Greedily we watched as Thomas crumpled, his long limbs curling into a wretched pile at the foot of the Virgin's statue.

I stood there, panting. I no longer felt angry but simply desperate. Again I walked to the edge of the rock garden and spoke Thomas's name.

This time, he acknowledged me. He lowered his hands, rose gracefully from his kneeling position, and turned to face me. But instead of the calm, placid gaze I had expected, he looked at me with quiet but intense disgust, his eyes like hot coals.

"Well?" he said. "Did you want something?"

His scornful voice reminded me of Sister Julian's. I felt my face reddening as I reached an arm out, aimlessly, as though wanting to placate him.

I said, stammering, "I—I'm sorry about that drawing, I shouldn't have—And about what—what happened."

Thomas had folded his arms; I detected, or thought I did, a faint sneer at his thin, colorless lips.

"What are you talking about?" he said.

"I mean—about Sister Julian. It's tough, what happened to her. . . . "

Motionless, he watched me. I was blushing, I might even have been trembling. Why hadn't I simply gone back with the others, why wasn't I playing football on the other side of the building?

As though taking pity on me, Thomas shook his head. "Don't worry about it," he said. "She probably deserved it."

"What?" I said, shocked.

"We all deserve it," Thomas said flatly. "Whatever we get."

He opened his locked arms and briefly turned his palms upward, a gesture of futility, or dismissal. He had no interest in discussing Sister Julian—or in talking at all, for that matter—with the likes of me. As though he were alone, he bent down matter-of-factly and brushed at his knees. Then he turned quietly and walked off.

I never spoke to Thomas again. He stayed in our school, he sat only a few feet away from me in a couple of classes, but I tried to pretend that Thomas Molloy simply did not exist. The next year, when our class transferred into the junior high school across town, we learned that Thomas would not be joining us: he had won a scholarship to a Catholic boarding school in San Antonio, Texas. Father Bascomb had been trying for years to get a boy into this school, and at last he had succeeded. He told us how proud he was of

Thomas, whose high grades and religious commitment should be an inspiration to all of us. We stared at Father Bascomb, noncommittal; we said nothing.

Even among ourselves, we never referred to Thomas, but surely we all felt a guilty pleasure in our victory. For we had managed, at long last, to expel Thomas Molloy from our midst. He was gone and we were still here, unscathed. Whatever we had set out to do, we had done.

I still think often of Thomas, though not as often as in the weeks after our last encounter, when his dry, remorseless voice had echoed repeatedly in my head, a tormenting refrain. *We all deserve it, don't we? Whatever we get.* More than two decades have passed, and even now I wonder what Thomas meant by those words—if he really knew, at the age of twelve, what he was saying. I fall into brief, wondering daydreams, unhappy reveries. I have nightmares in which Thomas is viciously stoned to death by dozens, even hundreds of boys, and all the boys have the same face: mine. At certain times I've had the perverse notion that I feel closer to Thomas, wherever he is, than I feel to my family and friends among whom I've lived for all these years.

My wife, who insists that I "think too much," often senses this. She has grown impatient with my nightmares. "Stop worrying, will you?" she might say querulously, at four in the morning. "Stop brooding about everything, try to relax." She possesses a conventional pragmatism not unlike my mother's, and I prefer not to argue, so I seldom answer her. I can hardly discuss my nocturnal glimpses of Sister Julian, raving in her locked cell; or the recurrent image of Thomas's bloodstained hands, lifted in prayer toward the empty blue skies of a spring morning. Dreams, after all, have a sanctity all their own, and thus I keep these things to myself, continuing to reflect, to sort out the endless possibilities.

And often I wonder: when Thomas reflects on the past, wherever he is, does he suffer, does he hate, does he forgive? Does he simply pray?

Sometimes I think: All of these, surely.

And at other times: Or none.

Leavetaking

EVERYONE was surprised that Matt would leave home, especially at such a time of life. His wife, Cyndi, had recently given birth to a healthy boy; it was their first child and they'd gone through Lamaze, no anesthetic, Matt holding her shoulders and shouting encouragement. Only four hours of labor and afterward Cyndi had lain there with a quiet smile. Matt had begun weeping.

During the last month of his wife's pregnancy Matt had taken a leave of absence and his boss, also Matt's best friend, had heartily approved. This was a progressive company, a manufacturer of paper products, and Matt had been a valued employee since the year he graduated from college. Two years later he became a manager and began working fitfully toward an MBA. He took classes at night. In one of these classes he met a woman three years older than him named Veronica with whom he'd had a brief, blistering affair.

She was dark and sensuous, very fickle—exactly the opposite of Cyndi, whose silken blond hair, perfect skin, and air of serene expectancy had won his boy's heart overnight. They'd met in high school but, as they often said, might have shared the same cradle. Her pregnancy had ended Matt's single indiscretion. After scrupulous thought he'd uncovered no reason to tell her.

Soon enough the coming baby took all their attention, but only weeks after the birth he told her about the trip and promised to be gone only a few days.

"What about the office?" she asked. "Your leave is up next week, isn't it?"

"Yes, but—" He felt panic, but not guilt, at her discovering that he'd discussed the trip with Rick before telling her. "It'll be okay," he said. "You know how Rick and Janice feel about us."

Matt and Cyndi had known the Jamesons ever since moving south from Pennsylvania. This was a small city, not far from Atlanta but rural in mood, texture, rhythm; people took their time, they looked you over. It hadn't been easy to break in, and even Cyndi might have lost patience if it hadn't been for Rick and Janice, who had "adopted" the young Culver couple—eventually, this became a joke among the four of them—right from the start. One element of Cyndi's present dismay, he knew, was the implied disloyalty to Rick, whom she once accused Matt of respecting more than he respected her. This had been their first and only serious argument, several months ago; his inability to respond to the charge had silenced her, and she'd never raised the issue again.

"Look, I know this is hard to understand," he told her, "but it has nothing to do with you. I just want some time, that's all. I need my mind cleared."

"I know it's nothing to do with me," she said. She sounded resentful. "It's the baby, right?"

"It's not Cameron," said Matt, who liked using his son's name.

"Are you sure?" Cyndi said. "Janice said that when Lyle and Chuckie were born—"

"Cameron isn't Lyle or Chuckie," Matt said. "And we're not the Jamesons."

Cyndi stood next to the kitchen range, where she'd been clearing up after dinner; she'd just fed Cameron and put him to bed, and Matt detected the odor of sweet milk about her. He wanted to reach out, cuddle her as he'd just seen her cuddling with Cameron. Yet this went against the rhetoric of the situation—tomorrow morning, he was walking out the door—so he did nothing.

"I don't mind your doing this," Cyndi said, finally, "but there's something strange about it. It's too abrupt. We haven't processed it together as a couple."

She loved jargon; she was always reading self-help books about personal growth, marital problems, parenting. Matt often teased her for being gullible, for believing everything she read.

"How can we process it?" he asked, genuinely puzzled. "It hasn't even happened yet."

Needing to talk with someone, Cyndi took up with the Jamesons the issue of town gossip about her and Matt. He'd been gone three days; at the college library, where she worked as a cataloger, she felt that people averted their heads when she approached, that even the students seemed suspiciously polite. "It sounds like paranoia, I know," she told them. "I'm projecting onto the landscape. But still, what do you think? Have you heard anything?"

Cyndi knew that Janice would laugh, and reach out her thin, beringed hands to clasp Cyndi's elbows; she did exactly that, but this time she didn't end by calling her a "little idiot." Instead she murmured, "You've got a right to be worried, of course. Rick and I were discussing it just this morning."

It was now past nine o'clock and the baby was sleeping. The Jamesons had stopped by after dinner—just popping their heads in, as Rick always said, but Cyndi knew they were genuinely concerned. Matt had called each morning, willing to talk for only three or four minutes. Cyndi strained to catch the background noise—Matt's sister had three rowdy youngsters—but heard only the deadened, melancholy buzzing of empty space. It was all she could do to keep from crying out, much less ask when he was coming home, much less call him back on some pretext to find out, once and for all, if he'd been lying; but so far she'd managed to do none of these things. Matt asked about her, then about the baby, then about Rick and Janice. As if he were reading from a list, she told herself, but she'd hidden the resentment even from her best friends. It alarmed her, now, that she couldn't express her feelings to Rick and Janice, but instead had brought up such an irrelevant topic as what the neighbors thought, as though she gave a damn.

"As far as the office is concerned," Rick Jameson said, "he's taking a few days off for a family visit. It's hardly anything scandalous," he added, smiling. A tall, solidly built man with hair that looked, in certain lights, blue-black, he had an amiable, reassuring manner; Matt liked to kid that he could have been a game show host. ("I'll be glad to, if the price is right," Rick had said one night, winking.) Cyndi agreed with her husband that Rick was the kind of level-headed, selfless man that kept the planet turning: he always came through.

"I really appreciate this—your checking on me," Cyndi said, looking from Rick back to Janice. "Being our adopted parents is a full-time job, isn't it?"

Janice laughed again, her mouth and eyes stretching in that wide, many-wrinkled smile Matt had once described as "spectacular." There was no question of Cyndi feeling jealous; not only were the Jamesons a dozen years older, but they seemed immeasurably wiser, more experienced. In fact, both she and Matt idolized them. Until recently, before the baby took all her attention, Cyndi often woke from daydreams to discover, a bit chagrined, that she'd been thinking about Janice and Rick.

"Don't worry," Janice said, "now that the boys are in their teens they live their own lives—by their choice, not ours—so we have to meddle in *some*-body's affairs. Right, pardner?"

Janice, seated beside her husband on the Culvers' living room sofa, poked him in the side. She often called him "pardner."

Rick nodded in that sleepy, amiable way of his, closing his eyes.

"Please don't use that word—*affair*," Cyndi said, with an exaggerated groan left over from her high school years.

Janice's smile brightened and Rick's vanished in the same moment.

"Paranoia's one thing," Janice said, adding a dismissive laugh, "but please, no full-fledged insanity. Like we've been telling you, the smartest thing is to take him at his word."

"That's what the books all say," Cyndi agreed, not caring if they teased her.

"It's really not so outlandish," Rick said, rather somberly, "considering the changes he's been through. From a male perspective, it's quite normal."

"That's what I keep telling myself," Cyndi said.

She offered them coffee, but as if this were a cue they rose at the same moment, saying they had to get going. They each took her hand and squeezed it, in turn; Janice pecked her cheek and whispered, "Don't worry." After she closed the door behind them, though, Cyndi had a sense of her own perversity, for in fact she felt much worse than before they'd arrived. It wasn't just loneliness: it was the sense of unshakable unity the Jamesons always gave her, which had seemed inspirational in the past but only depressed her now. Also, she reasoned, Rick and Janice had no sense of the pain, the immediacy, of what was happening; it was as unsharable as, for instance, her emotions when she nursed the baby. Grief or joy, she thought, reduced alike to a privacy that was hard-edged, absolute. Had such a wedge come between her and Matt, driving him away? She moped back toward the bedroom, flicking off lights as she went, reflecting that the Jamesons—and perhaps even Matt—would laugh if they could read her mind at this moment. It was her lifelong complaint that people did not take her seriously, and of course they did not take the complaint seriously, either. Left alone, she thought obsessively of her husband, yet sensing that for him she had all but ceased to exist.

Matt hadn't been lying about going to visit his sister. He'd pointed the car toward Pittsburgh and had driven intently, like a man wearing blinders, but as he reached the city's outskirts twelve hours later, his resolve collapsed. It was also, he thought, as though his mind had come awake, burst free of some long stupor. He pulled at random into a parking lot, then sat facing a squat stucco building with grimy windows and a red neon sign: BEER. He spent two hours inside the tavern, drinking steadily. In his rush to leave home that morning, he hadn't bothered to shave, and by now he could feel a thick stubble at his jaw. He wore jeans and a windbreaker, and understood that he fit in perfectly with this crowd of steel and factory workers, many of them as young as himself. No one looked twice at him. His eyes stung from the long hours of driving, and about ten o'clock he paid his tab and found a cheap motel not far from the tavern. The next morning, after downing a cup of coffee and taking a few deep breaths, he made his first brief call to Cyndi. It was then that the lying began.

He showered and put on fresh clothes, but still he didn't shave. By eight he was back on the road, driving south in exactly the direction he had come. Yet he wasn't going home, he knew; he was just driving. This time, though, he went slowly; he took side trips into the countryside, drove idly through small towns, spent time in a string of diners and bars that, after a while, blended together in his mind. While driving he played the radio, he ate junk food, he tried not to think. He'd left Cyndi the new Toyota they'd bought last summer, and for this trip had taken the old Chevy Nova he'd driven to death long before his marriage. Anytime he heard an odd squeak or rumble he feared the car would break down, stranding him. He felt a vague, pleasurable anxiety in being vulnerable to the car, and he drove it hard, as though testing its loyalty. He felt that the car was an ally, somehow; that it sided with him against whatever had so suddenly propelled him outside his own life.

When he reached Atlanta, after three days of this, he exited the interstate and began driving around midtown, aimlessly. It was nearly eight o'clock but this was early summer and a pale dusk lingered, as though suspended out of time; Matt crooked his arm outside the window, tapping the car's roof to the beat of the radio, glancing around at the people strolling the sidewalks, clustered near cars parked on side streets or on the porches of restored older homes set discreetly back from the street. There were elderly women sipping iced tea on the porches, there were young men in T-shirts and carefully ripped jeans idling at streetcorners, there was a woman with shimmering blond hair who was several months pregnant and carried another baby on her back, Indian-style. Matt drove slowly, his perception hungry as he took in these many people whose lives had nothing to do with him. He felt a peculiar mingling of loneliness and exultation. Several times he and Cyndi had discussed moving to the city, finding new jobs, perhaps renting a house in this very section of town, since it offered such a variety of people, such a free style of life; many of the city's artists lived in midtown, alongside older residents who'd lived here for generations. The blend worked, somehow; a quirky harmony had been established. Both Matt and Cyndi disliked the newly built subdivision in which they lived and had bought their tidy three-bedroom brick—one identical to the eighty-odd other houses in the subdivision—with a sense of cheerful capitulation. It wasn't only that they'd begun "succeeding" in life, Matt thought now, and that certain behavior was expected of them; it had been what they expected of themselves.

Turning onto Peachtree Street, he saw an ancient buff-colored hotel he'd admired each time they visited the city. Badly in need of restoration, yet still grand with its baroque ornamentation, its balconies and cupolas and abundant wrought iron, the building had a seedy but undeniable glamor. Matt was pleased, too, by the general mustiness inside, and by the carpeting in the lobby, once plush and expensive, now trampled to a dim coral-brown. An elaborate floral pattern was faintly visible beneath Matt's boots as he stood at the reservations desk, waiting for the unctuous clerk to hand him a key. The lobby was dim and hushed. No one seemed to be around. He went upstairs in an old gilded cage of an elevator, feeling absurdly happy despite the roach scuttling across his path as he stepped into the hall and toward his room. He sat on the bed and picked up the phone to call Cyndi, feeling his mind going hard, opaque; but he'd just called that morning, he reasoned, and he put the receiver down. He poured himself an inch of bourbon from the bottle he'd bought that morning, somewhere near Greensboro, North Carolina. Then he lifted the phone again and called Veronica.

She had a sly, teasing style with Matt that had always excited him. Tonight, as during those raw, bewildering nights of their first passion, she could sit back, flick her long hair behind her bare shoulders, and gently laugh at him. Her laughter was like murmuring, he thought; it seemed to come from underwater. Clearly she liked him, and she would never deny that somehow he brought forth her extravagant passions; but also, he felt, she treated him like a child. Once he'd pointed this out, in a wounded voice, and she'd laughed at him again.

Tonight she listened to him, patiently, but finally she sat back, her dark eyes flickering with amusement. "So here you are," she said, smiling, "having your midlife crisis at age twenty-six."

She was subtle, he thought. Malicious. Despite himself he felt his face reddening. "I'm twenty-four," he said. "You know that."

She reached out, chucked him briefly under his chin. "Hey. I think you should lighten up."

She handed him a hotel matchbook and waited with the cigarette in her mouth until he struck the match, bending toward her.

"Such a gentleman," Veronica said, exhaling.

Matt grinned. He shook his head. "What the hell am I doing," he said, but it wasn't a question.

"I've wondered that, myself," she said, her first reference to their parting eight months before. There had been no parting, in fact; she'd been preparing for her move to Atlanta, and it was the week Cyndi had come home from the gynecologist, bright-eyed with her news, and Matt had simply stopped calling Veronica. Tonight he'd gotten her number from Information, like a stranger.

"I'm sorry," he said.

She laughed again. Then she held him again, and he felt her body trembling.

The next morning, after she left, he poured himself another inch of bourbon and sat thinking. Fifty miles to the west of this town, this bed, were his wife and son, his home and job, his future. He swallowed the bourbon in a single gulp and wondered if he'd lost his mind. What bothered him most was his lack of guilt, even as he sat deliberately recalling his Catholic boyhood—Christ, he'd been an altar boy!—and his good grades, his election to the Student Council, his father's sternly loving pronouncements on hard work, responsibility, commitment. He tried to flagellate himself with these memories, but he couldn't summon any pain. He was perfectly content, he thought, to be sitting here on an ordinary weekday, a working day, getting blitzed in a hotel room at ten in the morning. Even when he watched his own reflection in the bureau mirror, the unshaven and rather haggard young face did not alarm him. It seemed his true face, which had found him at last.

Veronica had written her office number inside the matchbook, and now he lifted the phone and dialed.

"Is something wrong?" she asked.

"I wanted to hear your voice," he lied. "That's all."

She paused; he knew he'd caught her at a busy moment.

"But you're all right?" she asked.

"I'm sorry. I shouldn't be bothering you."

"You're not bothering me. It's just your voice—it's sort of deadened or something. Why don't you take a nap?"

"Maybe I will. You're coming at seven, right?"

Another pause. "I said I'd come at seven, didn't I? I don't break dates."

"I'm sorry," he said. He felt nothing.

"Take a nice warm bath. Then a nap."

She worked for an accountant, and Matt could hear a vague clacking noise in the background. Adding machines?

"I don't know why you put up with me," he said. "Either of you."

She laughed; when she laughed her voice became musical, slightly wicked. "Maybe we should go into therapy, old Cyndi and I. Joint sessions."

"Not you," he said quietly. "Me."

He pictured her throwing her eyes upward, flicking the long dark hair behind her shoulders, now covered, he recalled, with red silk. She'd stood at his mirror applying lipstick that matched the blouse, exactly.

"We were going to lighten up, remember?" she said. "It's a little early in the day for Sturm und Drang."

"You're good for me," he said, sincerely. And he felt something at last: self-pity.

"Don't I know it. Matt, I've got to go. See you at seven."

"See you at seven."

He went to the window. People of all kinds strolled up and down Peachtree Street. If he went downstairs and drifted onto the sidewalk, he would blend in easily. No one would notice him. Why did it please him, thinking this? He wanted, he thought, to drift out of his own life. Quietly. Painlessly. Last week, talking with Rick about this trip, trying to describe his eerie restlessness, he'd wanted to ask: How do you do it, you and Janice? How do you stay so damned happy? And he'd wanted to ask, wildly, whether Rick had ever felt—even for a moment—that he'd stopped loving Janice. Yet the shame of this idea silenced him. Now he thought of Cyndi in her pastel clothes, her silken blond hair reflecting the light. He pictured her at home, at this moment, awaiting his call. Each time they spoke the conversation became more strained, as though he'd lost the knack of conversing with his own wife. Matt the loving young husband, like Matt the altar boy, had departed him like a ghost, so that talking to Cyndi he felt like an impersonator, trying to catch the right inflection, the right tone. Talking with Veronica was easy—her quick passion, her irony, even her cruelty helped pull him together, define him. She gave him that face he'd glimpsed in the mirror: a cheater, a liar. A fraud. Someone who could drift down into that crowded world and not be missed.

Now, on the sidewalk below him, there was sudden commotion. He heard what sounded like a woman screaming, and he had to open the window and crane his neck outward before he saw what had happened. A blond-haired girl of nineteen or twenty lay sprawled on the sidewalk, screaming and moaning, her hand clawing the air. The gesture seemed aimed directly at Matt, but he saw that she was simply trying to get up. She wore a hot-pink dress, very short and very tight, and iridescent-silver stockings. Blood streaked down the side of her head and throat. A short, wiry black man in a cream-colored suit stood above her, a baseball bat raised in his hands, as though to strike her again. Around the pair a few pedestrians milled uncertainly. Matt heard the black man shouting at the girl, repeating a litany of obscene names, while the girl kept screaming up at him, clawing the air. She seemed terrified but also furious, as though refusing to capitulate. Out of nowhere Matt thought: *Put your head down, don't say another word. Play dead.* When she dropped her arm he felt relieved, for she had seemed to be gesturing up at him, accusing him. In the distance Matt heard sirens. He saw the black man dart away down the sidewalk. Matt stepped back from the window, feeling suddenly overcome with nausea.

Minutes later he'd thrown everything inside his bag and sat at the small desk beside the bed; in the top drawer he found stationery and a pen. For a few moments he sat earnestly bent over the blank paper, like a student. Then he looked at the phone. He glanced away. Worse than a cheater or liar, he thought: a coward. He deliberately left the blank stationery and the pen out on the desk, as though that meant something.

Each morning, Janice stopped by for coffee, something she'd seldom done in the past.

"You don't really have to do this," Cyndi said guiltily, on the fourth day of Matt's absence. Janice worked full-time (though "unofficially") in her husband's office, and joked that she was the lowest-paid co-president in the history of American business; if she was lucky, Rick took her out for an occasional lunch. But Cyndi knew that Janice loved working, that she and Rick were a "team" in the way that Cyndi and Matt had never been, and that Janice didn't have time for coffee klatches.

They sat in the Culvers' sunny breakfast room, picking at the blueberry turnovers Cyndi had made at six that morning, knowing that if she didn't do something—some kind of busy work—she might run screaming out of the house like a madwoman.

"Listen, I remember what it's like, being cooped up with a baby," Janice said. She was not really eating the pastry, and Cyndi recalled suddenly that Janice disliked sweets; why hadn't she served something more wholesome, like bran muffins or fresh fruit? Cyndi didn't want her pastry, either. Since the baby's arrival she'd been watching her calories. It was Matt, she thought bitterly, who loved blueberry turnovers.

"You're good for me," Cyndi said, reaching out and touching her friend's forearm. "You're my way of testing reality."

Without warning, she began to cry. Janice pulled her chair closer, drawing her arm around Cyndi.

"Still no progress?" she asked gently.

Cyndi shook her head; she used a napkin to wipe her nose. "This is the first morning he hasn't called. Here it is, ten-thirty, and he still hasn't called." She crumpled the napkin and dropped it onto the plate. She cleared her throat. "Not that it matters, really. Even when he does call, he won't talk to me. He always sounds so—so distant."

"That's what he needs at the moment, isn't it? Distance?"

"What about what *I* need?" Cyndi said. The casual pragmatism she'd always admired in Janice now struck her as cruel. "I mean, I believe in open marriage and everything, but—"

"Just try to keep this in perspective," Janice said, almost sternly. "For one thing, he's very young. You can't appreciate that, of course, but I do. In the last couple of years, a lot of weight has settled on his shoulders. He doesn't have much experience, he doesn't know how good his life is. Just give him time. Try to relax, and give him time."

Cyndi sighed. "Maybe I'm expecting too much."

"You're idealistic," Janice said, "like most people your age. In time you'll see that you can't communicate openly with your husband—not all the time. And even less, maybe, as time passes."

Cyndi stared at her friend, dismayed. She pictured Rick standing behind Janice, laughing amiably, closing his eyes.

Janice lifted her eyebrows, inquiringly. "What?" she said.

"Nothing. I was just thinking." But in fact a raw, burning anger had welled in her abdomen, seeming to flood that empty space abandoned by the baby. She couldn't share the anger with Janice—she felt that somehow Janice had sided with Matt—and once again a great loneliness overwhelmed her, such as she'd never experienced before her husband and baby had entered her life.

"It's not quite fair, is it?" she said, but not really to Janice. "I mean, the whole situation."

Janice gave her wide, crinkling smile. As always she appeared the picture of reason, of sane good health. "No, you little idiot," she said. "And it never was."

Matt pulled the Nova into the driveway just before lunchtime. The car was filthy: its fenders streaked with mud, the windshield spattered with insects. Getting out, Matt didn't look much better. Cyndi parted the living room curtains an inch or so, feeling immensely relieved and yet offended—even shocked—by her husband's stubbled jaw, his wrinkled clothes. He'd gone into the world with a boy's shining face and pressed underwear, she thought, feeling angrier each moment. She didn't want damaged goods.

On the breakfast room table, the plate of blueberry turnovers sat like an invitation. Matt's eyes lighted when he saw them.

"I made them for Janice," Cyndi said quickly, wrinkling her nose. It was clear that her husband hadn't bathed this morning. He had a musky, unfamiliar scent about him.

"They look great," he said. "I'm starved."

He sat down at the table and began eating, like a boy home from school.

"Don't you want to see the baby?" she asked.

He looked at her, blinking. "Of course, but isn't he sleeping?"

"That didn't used to stop you."

He chewed thoughtfully for a moment. "Cyndi, I just walked in the door. Give me some time."

She didn't want to give him time, nor space either. When he finished the turnover and went into the kitchen for milk, she followed him. In here the musky scent seemed stronger. He wore jeans, and a yellow T-shirt he hadn't worn since last summer. After pouring the milk, he took off his watch and put it beside the sink, then emptied both his pockets onto the counter, as he did each evening after work. Cyndi thought, *He's home.* She noticed among the coins and wadded-up dollar bills a small matchbook bearing the name of an Atlanta hotel. Matt's eyes caught the matchbook at the same moment, and he seemed to freeze.

"Never mind," she said. "I knew you weren't in Pittsburgh."

Her anger had drained away. She felt tired.

"What?" he said. He looked panicked for a moment, then disgusted. He picked up the matchbook and fingered it, then put it back inside his pocket.

"I'm not sure where I was," he told her.

They hadn't gone to Cameron's room, but back to their own bedroom. For the next couple of hours, amazingly, Cameron stayed quiet, as though conspiring in his parents' swift reunion. Matt half-sat, half-reclined in bed, thinking about his son. When he did go into Cameron's room, it would be like seeing him for the first time.

Cyndi lay quietly beside him, giving him a look he couldn't read. Her manner had changed when he came out of the shower, pink-skinned, his face as smooth as the baby's. He'd shaved so quickly, in fact, that he cut himself; Cyndi had torn off a small piece of Kleenex and dabbed it in place. Now she craned upward, squinting at the spot on his jaw.

"I think the bleeding stopped," she said. "Does it sting?"

"No, it'll heal fast," Matt said. "I always do."

She'd asked several times—even during their lovemaking—why Matt had left them. Each time he became more irritated. He hadn't left anybody, he said; he just took a trip.

Now Cyndi said, thoughtfully, "I guess you were just acting out, right? Some kind of hostility?"

"Cyndi, I don't know. I told you."

"Don't you want to know?" she said. Her tone wasn't bitter, only curious, as if his attitude amazed her. It occurred to Matt that they would never understand each other.

"No," Matt said.

Satisfied, she snuggled against him.

"But you won't need to leave again, will you," she said. Her voice dipped on the last word; she was too afraid, he thought, to make this a real question.

"No, not ever," he said gently, feeling that he was lying, knowing he wasn't.

Last Night

"YOU said you would, last night. You *promised.*"

"Lauren, we've been through this so many—"

"Then why did you promise? Why?"

Her voice rising, almost a shriek, though they'd been talking for less than five minutes. He almost hadn't answered the phone.

"No, I didn't promise," he said awkwardly. "Not exactly."

To get away from you, that's why. So I could go home, get some sleep, get away . . .

To his surprise, she laughed. "That muttering of yours, I love it. That guilty mutter." She laughed again.

He had to give her that: she could still surprise him.

"Lauren, one more night, one less night—what difference does it make? I know you're having a rough time, but why prolong it? Everybody says the same thing, I told you that—Tim and Edie, Debbie Coyne—"

"*Your* friends," she rasped out, whether in grief or fury he couldn't be sure. Didn't suppose it mattered.

And how am I guilty?

But now he knew: grief. Because she was crying. That near-inaudible wheeze of hers, breathing slowed, punctuated by the girlish sniffling that made his chest throb painfully. He changed the receiver to his other ear, the cordless phone trapped between chin and shoulder as he paced his bedroom. Wiped both clammy palms against his jeans. Reached for the dumbbell he'd been using before she called, began curling it with his left arm. He'd had nothing to drink last night, which had helped him to leave Lauren's and to sleep here safe at last and to start working out again after his two-month hiatus. Women weakened him, always. While he listened to Lauren's ragged near-silent weeping he kept curling the dumbbell, feeling the heat and moisture at his forehead, under his arms, but this was a good sweat, a clean sweat, which he welcomed like a boyhood friend unseen for years.

Not my fault . . .

"Lauren?" he said finally. "Are you still there? Listen, I think we'd better hang up. I think that's definitely best."

She waited. Then: "I'll kill myself," she said. "If you can't keep a promise, then no one can. So it's pointless. Continuing to live is pointless."

He pictured her on the edge of her bed: her head canted forward, mane of heavy black hair unwashed for days, soiled yellow bathrobe with those darkish red stains down the front. Nail polish, he hoped; or ketchup. He imagined her there with her hair hanging down across the receiver, obscuring her face, the room itself obscure and shadowy because she hadn't opened the blinds. The bed unmade, musty, giving off the same stale smell as her hair. Saturday morning.

He breathed deeply and said, "I can't do it, Lauren, you'll just have to work through this. One more night won't make any difference."

"And you're fucking Debbie Coyne, aren't you!" she shrieked. "So naturally she tells you to dump me—God, you're both such assholes!"

Weeping. Raving.

He hung up.

Downstairs, he took the two half-gallons of Scotch he'd bought yesterday out of the pantry, uncapped them, held them upside down over the sink, one in each hand. As the pale-caramel liquid sloshed down the drain he held his breath, shunning the smell. He felt a tart sweetness at the back of his throat. An ache. The phone began ringing. As a joke, and to distract himself, he lifted the bottles up and down as he poured, as though they were dumbbells, counting each repetition to drown out the phone until the ringing stopped and all the Scotch was gone and the bottles weighed next to nothing. He laid them in the sink and grabbed the edge of the counter, expelling his breath. He should go to the gym, probably. Get out of the house. The liquor store was on the way to the gym, but he could take another route. The phone started ringing.

He went to the park. A crisp bright day, early March, and everyone was out. Families having picnics in the grass. Couples walking their dogs. People jogging. He started jogging himself, along the eight-block perimeter of the park. An ordinary guy, people must think, mid-thirties, nicely built, especially strong in his broad back and shoulders. Curly dark-blond hair, white headband above blue eyes, ordinary T-shirt and nylon running shorts, legs well-muscled too and covered with a reddish-blond fuzz. Clean-cut. All-American. Jogging, it was easy to hold in the sagging gut, and he figured that four weeks of running plus an hour's daily training in the gym would get him back in shape. A lone female jogger coming from the opposite direction smiled at him, as though confirming his optimism. A pretty dancer's body, flying auburn hair, ears wired to the tiny Walkman clipped to her waist. He grinned back and thought for a second she might slow down, but no. Nonetheless he felt better. Lighter, freer. He held in his gut so tightly that his stomach muscles felt like hot coils.

And he ran. Kept running.

True, last night he'd made a promise. They'd gone for a pizza, and of course Lauren ordered a half-liter of red wine and wanted him to have some—she hated to drink alone—and he told her casually that he was staying away from liquor for a while. (She didn't know about the Scotch, of course; didn't know that *he* drank alone.) So she'd finished the wine by herself and he'd had to help her out of the restaurant. In the car, she began crying. At her apartment door, she insisted he come in; wasn't the whole purpose of this dinner for them to talk? They hadn't *talked* at the restaurant. That had been chit-chat. That had been nothing. How dare he pretend that he didn't understand! So he'd mumbled all right, a few minutes—but then he had to get going.

Inside, curled next to him on the sofa—he lacked the energy to get up and move to a chair—she picked another fight. She accused him of cowardice. She said he was afraid of intimacy. "My father was like that, too, and God, did my poor mother suffer!" she cried. She stared at him with her slightly enlarged green eyes, the pupils dilated like a cat's. "Am I responsible for what your father did?" he asked. "It's what he *didn't* do," she said. "He wasn't there for her." "Then she should have divorced him." "They're Catholic, for God's sake. They were married in nineteen-fucking-forty-six!" He looked over, startled. He'd never heard her use that word before. She narrowed her eyes slyly as if she'd been saving the obscenity all this time, to surprise him.

Heartened by her energy, her anger, he decided to speak his mind. To appeal to her intelligence, the fast-tongued wit and toughness he'd first admired in her. Where had that woman gone? he wondered. She'd amazed him, that first night two months ago, at Tim and Edie's party. Somehow he'd pegged her as a stewardess, or maybe an interior designer. Something feminine, sexy. Her close-fitting black silk sheath that had eased her ample breasts upward, an offering. Her heavy black hair, so black it might be dyed but so what, thick and lustrous and swept back from her face, giving an effect of wildness, daring. The dramatic eye makeup, unfashionable but somehow right on her, eyes heavily lined in black, lashes thick and waxy. And her perfume, heavy and floral, or was it fruity. He imagined bowls of raspberries, glistening. "I'm an electrical engineer," she'd said matter-of-factly, and at first he'd thought she might be joking. But he knew better than to laugh where women and their occupations were concerned, so he had not; he questioned her seriously, earnestly, though something in her dark bright eyes made him think she was amusing herself. He didn't care. He told her about his own job, in computer sales; downplayed his accomplishments; flashed his boyish grin at strategic moments. In the coming weeks he would learn that she was more successful than he, which somehow pleased and excited him. They made love wildly for five or six weeks, and when she crouched over him with that heavy black hair brushing his eyes, his opened mouth, he'd thought that yes there were degrees of pleasure that edged close to insanity, surely, and for those weeks he was near-insatiable and so, it seemed, was she. They seldom went out. Her place; her bed, which it was pointless to make because they used it so often. But then, changing as abruptly as the weather, she'd become someone else.

She turned possessive. Whiny. Complained if he showed up immediately after work, before she had a chance to relax, but complained even more if he went home and failed to call. One night she called him on one of these occasions and started screaming. Asshole, bastard, just taking advantage, taking her for granted!—the usual. He'd had a relationship like this once in college and had sworn if it happened again he'd break things off early. Which he did, or tried to do. At first, to his surprise—there were always surprises!—she'd accepted the idea that they should part. She'd nodded her head. Intelligent. Thoughtful. The next day she sent him flowers at work, then phoned in the evening and asked if she could stop by. They were standing in his kitchen, having a glass of champagne and talking, he thought, companionably, when suddenly she came toward him and with a single gesture, quick, snaky, she had jerked down his zipper, taken out his penis, fallen to her knees. He'd had to struggle to detach her, he'd thought helplessly *My God it's like having a tick* and then he saw the drop of blood suspended from her lip and glanced down in horror. But he was all right. She had not bitten him. Instead she was biting herself, her own lip, so hard that the blood had formed a sudden swelling bead at the side of her mouth. He stared in disgust, *vampire bitch goddamn you why did you* but of course he kept silent. For a while she'd screamed the words at him, the names, the accusations, and then somehow he'd gotten her out of there. Had called Tim and Edie, who commiserated, who apologized, saying they'd known her only a short time themselves; she was a friend of one of Edie's friends who had been coming to the party, and so— But they were sorry. Really sorry. And yes, of course, there was nothing else he could do. It was the only sensible thing. A clean break. Right away. "And don't let her put a guilt trip on you," Edie had said. "Thanks," he responded. "I won't."

The next day, Lauren had called and apologized. It was Saturday and he'd been feeling perplexed and depressed and had made himself a Scotch and soda after lunch. And another, and another—the usual. He did not believe he was an alcoholic because both his parents were teetotalers. He was just depressed; it was just a bad time in his life, and he told this to his friends, who must have considered him a normal social drinker. He told them yes, he was going through a tough time, and Edie responded at once, calling it a "yuppie crisis," success and money and youth but no meaning, no love, no nourishment of the spirit, and in fact their talk had prompted her decision to throw a party. Invite a few women he might like. He'd made fun of her for the word "yuppie," no one used that anymore, for Christ sake's Edie get with it, and she'd laughed and claimed to be an old married lady, okay, but still she knew some people, and did he want a date or not? So he'd thanked her, and later, when Edie apologized, he said it wasn't her fault. He didn't say that he'd always expected to have a marriage like his parents', which had been unruffled, without any expression of anger or discontent from his earliest memories to now, but of course his standards were too high. No one measured up to their parents, these days, much less exceeded them. All that was over. At least he recognized now that he brought out the worst in women—they tended to idealize him, think him sensitive—*If you can't keep a promise, then no one can*—and so they drained him of his energy, of what youth and possibility he might have left.

He'd been thinking this, last night, sitting tensely on the edge of Lauren's sofa. How to get out of this mess. How to feel that he hadn't taken advantage, hadn't lied. For she'd loved the sex, too, hadn't she, and wasn't it she who had changed? No, he'd done nothing wrong, except maybe what the nuns in grade school had called lies by omission, since she didn't know about the yuppie crisis, the insomniac nights, the solitary Scotches at 5 P.M., at midnight, at any time during one of his derailed weekends at home. But surely she had her secrets, too? Shit. He couldn't let her weaken him, bring him down.

"Lauren, you've got to understand—"

Reading his mind, it seemed, she'd come closer, grabbed his forearm. Her hair and skin smelled stale; she wore the perfume but now it seemed a mere pitiful stink, the raspberries gone rotten. He held his breath for long seconds to shun the smell, glancing up every few seconds from his heavy-lidded guilty gaze in the hope that her eyes might become just a degree or two less desperate and sorrowful, releasing him.

But no. She fixed him with that aggrieved wild stare and he felt his body going hard, stonelike, everywhere but his crotch, which now felt gelatinous, shrunken, unprotected; he felt that he was becoming paralyzed, turning to stone, his very jaw a chunk of immovable rock so that he could not speak. But she could.

"All right then," she said, easing the pressure on his forearm, drawing her fingertips lightly along his wrist, his hand. The calm in her voice surprised him: the resignation. "All right, but promise me something, okay? Please come tomorrow and stay the night—just one last night. We won't have sex, I don't want that, I just want you to be here. To hold me. If I'm going to lose you, at least I want that night to remember, with no arguing or passion or worry. Just peace. Just being close. Together. One last time."

Then she'd gone silent, as if letting the words take effect. He'd never felt more uncomfortable in his life. Her little speech had sounded both dignified and pathetic, somehow beyond reproach, so he'd said yes, all right, I'll be here at seven. She'd smiled, expelled her breath in relief. Reached across and kissed him on the cheek. Said, "Well then, tonight I'll let you go on your merry way. But thank you, in advance. Thank you for tomorrow night."

He fled, making resolutions all the way home as if it were a new year, a new century. Back on the workout regime, starting tomorrow. Cut liquor out of his life. Cultivate his friendships with sensible people like Tim and Edie, give his parents a call, his old college roommate out in California, maybe give Debbie Coyne a call, too, why the hell not? Get his life back on track. Nonetheless he knew by the next afternoon that he shouldn't have hung up on Lauren. That wasn't fair. That was getting off on the wrong foot, jump-starting your life at somebody else's expense, and so he sat at the pass-through bar to the kitchen with his hand on the phone, debating. He felt exhausted: after his run in the park he'd gone to the gym, spent not an hour but almost two, had come home and showered and made most of the phone calls he'd promised himself. His parents had sounded befuddled but pleased, and he'd felt a pang to think how long it had been since he'd called them. Idle chit-chat about his job, about the weather here in Atlanta, there in Tulsa, about the doings of various family members—great-aunts, cousins—whose faces he could scarcely recall. Once he'd taken a girlfriend home from college for Thanksgiving break—she was a stylish, strong-willed girl, his type, and had grown up in New York. During the drive back to campus she'd said, "Your parents are so—so *innocuous,* somehow," but that hadn't sounded right and she'd added quickly, "Or I guess I mean innocent, really. Innocent. So sweet and nice. They haven't spent much time outside of Tulsa, have they?"

He hadn't dated this girl again, but now he sat pondering the word, *innocuous,* and of course it was the perfect word. His parents did not argue, did not complain, did not get angry. Had no bad habits. Nowadays, in retirement, they piddled in the garden and visited with relatives (they had few friends) and occasionally attended a church social, a dinner theater. Innocuous. He did not understand his flexing fist, his urge to pound the countertop, the sudden uprush of feeling that might have been grief or rage but in any case seemed inappropriate. *Inappropriate behavior.* He'd read this once, in an article about alcoholism and drug addiction in the family. *Be on the look-out for inappropriate behavior, such as unreasonable outbursts, secretiveness, spending too much time alone, unexplained absences. . . .* But no one was on the look-out, of course. He had no family.

Except for his faraway parents, and when they hung up he'd had the sudden thought that there was something deathly about them; their lives were so static, unchanging. In the past, he'd found this thought reassuring, but now it filled him with terror.

Innocuous. Deathly. *Inappropriate thoughts.* Why should a healthy man of thirty-four sit alone on a Sunday afternoon, worrying about such things?

Out of old habit, he got up from the stool—it was 5:30—and went into the kitchen, bent down to the cabinet, and then remembered that he'd poured out the Scotch that morning. His stomach felt sore. He'd worked out too long, too hard. You couldn't escape your life, he thought clearly, relieved that there wasn't any Scotch. He went to the phone and punched Lauren's number.

When he got there, exactly at seven, she'd worked a transformation that amazed him. The rugs were vacuumed, the tabletops shone, the rich scent of warm tomatoes filled the kitchen. "I knew you'd come, even after you hung up on me," she'd said shyly at the front door, not quite meeting his eyes. She wore a simple navy dress with a white collar, ordinary white pumps—an outfit, he couldn't help thinking, that his mother might wear. Her hair had been smoothed back neatly from her forehead, clipped in back with a barette. Following her into the kitchen, he caught a whiff of unfamiliar perfume—a whitish lemony scent—before the tomatoes drowned it out.

"It's lasagna," she said shyly. "I haven't made it in a while, but I hope . . ."

"You shouldn't have gone to the trouble," he said. "Really."

Odd, they sounded like people on a first date. He wanted to inject some note of caution into the proceedings, a reminder that he was merely fulfilling her request, his promise. Nothing more. But he needn't have worried. After checking the oven she turned and said, again with that demure, averted look, "I wanted to. Like I said yesterday, I appreciate your coming this one last time. It's a nice thing for you to do."

She went to the refrigerator. Even the way she moved seemed girlishly simple, and he wondered that he'd once made love so fiercely to this woman. He stood at the kitchen doorway, feeling disoriented, then noticed that she'd brought out a bottle of wine.

"None for me, Lauren, I'm really cutting back. I spent most of the day at the gym, and I—"

"It's a special Beaujolais," she said, disappointed. "The man at the liquor store said . . . " She broke off, shrugging. "Well, I'll put it on the table. Maybe you'll change your mind."

During dinner, he changed his mind. He could not control the strange jumpiness in his body, his awkward anticipation of holding this woman all night: he'd assumed that she'd be the angry, grief-stricken Lauren, the woman he'd known lately, and not this meek, grateful creature. So he thought, *Well, it might as well be the last night for this, too,* and nodded when she offered to pour him a glass, and then a second. The wine did relax him. They talked of ordinary, everyday things—their jobs, some renovations she had in mind for the house—and their talk was, he couldn't help thinking, as innocuous as the conversation with his parents had been.

By the time they went to bed, he felt that all was well. She'd opened a second bottle of wine, even though she wanted none for herself. "I'll have a headache tomorrow," she said, smiling, "but you go ahead." He went ahead. The tension and depression he'd felt earlier that day had vanished. In the bedroom, she behaved coyly as a bride, telling him that she had "something to do" in the bathroom and to make himself comfortable. This was his only moment of panic: he remembered the diaphragm she sometimes wore. She'd once claimed that the pill disagreed with her, made her sick, and he'd suspected briefly that she was trying to get pregnant, for she didn't always use the diaphragm.

But she hadn't gotten pregnant, at least.

He got into bed, keeping his shorts and T-shirt on—he hadn't worn a

T-shirt to bed since he was a kid—and clasped his hands beneath his head, waiting. When she came out of the bathroom, wearing not the negligee he had feared but the old stained housecoat, her makeup rubbed off so that her face looked shiny, stark, and yes, ugly, he felt relieved but also slightly offended. She'd overdone it, a little. Yet she was trying to please him. He lifted the covers on her side and said, "Be my guest."

Quickly she removed the housecoat—she wore an ordinary white bra and panties underneath—and snapped off the bedside lamp. They slid close together and he felt her eyelashes brushing against his shoulder. "I've been looking forward to this," she murmured. They snuggled together like children. She had turned off the heat, as she always did at night, and the room was already chilly. Yet her legs and back felt warm, pliant. Despite himself, he felt a hardening at his groin, so he used an old trick and forced his mind into the past, into ancient and harmless recollections.

Himself as an altar boy, lighting the candles before Mass.

He and his friend Charlie, sneaking small giggly sips from the wine cruets when the priest left them alone in the anteroom that adjoined the altar.

The blessing that the priest—a scowling, red-haired Irishman—had given them after Mass, his hand slicing the air in the quick approximation of a cross. The blessing was perfunctory, impatient. The Mass was over, the priest was already thinking of other things.

When he came back to the present, he understood that his erection was gone, but when he thought about the woman he held in his arms, the woman he'd inadvertently harmed, he felt again that harsh stirring at his crotch. Lauren had fallen asleep. He resolved again to think about the distant past. The innocuous past. It seemed to him that these were the last hours of one part of his life, perhaps of his youth itself. But tomorrow he would begin anew. He would give Lauren a peck on the cheek and then leave by the front door, free. If he felt tempted to drink any more he would join AA or see a shrink, or both. All this would begin tomorrow, tomorrow, and he let the word echo in his head until it lost its meaning.

He woke several hours later, his head throbbing, a sour taste at the back of his throat. The room was very cold. Still motionless in his arms, Lauren felt strange. Too quiet, her skin clammy beneath his hands. He rose from the bed, like a man still half-dreaming. But his stomach had knotted fiercely, throbbing, and soon enough the pain, the hot sickish knowledge, had surged into his aching throat and widened eyes. Standing, he flipped on the light and stared at her, then stomped barefoot into the bathroom and saw the long, empty pill container, lying sideways beside a letter with his name written across the front in a large, slanted, girlish hand.

He ran out, his stomach writhing. In the dining room, he reached for the phone but halted, remembering the chill silence of her flesh. How she surprised him, always!—he was wild with amazement, with feeling. Too much feeling, inappropriate feeling, he didn't want—

He went to the refrigerator and took out the wine bottle and, his hand shaking, filled a glass halfway. He kept looking at the phone, perched on a side table in Lauren's dining room. He had turned on the chandelier in there but not the kitchen light, so he felt himself in shadow, protected. He glared out from the darkened kitchen like an animal in hiding. He watched the phone as though it were an enemy that might surprise him, too. He drank. His mouth felt large and wet, greedy as a lover's. He was young and innocent and he would take his fill, he reasoned, before starting his journey out of this comfortable darkness.

I Am Dangerous

OR WAS. This happened in a movie theater, 1973. I know the year because I'd just broken up with the love of my life, had my heart broken, etc., you give the cliché and I suffered it, blood and bone, skinless heart, and you don't forget such things.

I'd gone to the movie to do just that. Forget. This was the Silver Screen, an Atlanta theater that showed old movies, "classics" from the '30s, '40s, and early '50s. Two in the afternoon, a weekday, I'd cut one of my classes since grad school now seemed meaningless, even laughable when I pondered the notion of "Dr. Knowlton" leading his own graduate seminars one day. (I'd been wild for the Civil War since I was a kid and wanted to talk about it, talk about it forever, but otherwise I really had little interest in history, a fact that would become clear a year later when I flunked my prelims and moved back home to Augusta: but at least my heart was mended by then.) The fantasy had included Sheila, of course, the dazzling faculty wife, the prize on my arm, Sheila who had informed me the week before that she was moving to Asheville, North Carolina, she wanted to develop her talent, not our relationship, she was rethinking her life, she was rethinking *me,* I was too intense I didn't give her space I just gave lip service to feminist ideas, etc., but the upshot was I'd been dumped, just like that, so the idea of "Dr. Knowlton" seemed ridiculous enough when I felt like walking scum, I almost said like an amoeba but that's an insult to amoebae, walking scum will do, so as usual when everything turned shitty I went off to the movies.

I hadn't even checked what was playing, but it turned out to be *The Heiress* with Montgomery Clift and Olivia de Havilland, which was perfect because there the woman gets it for a change. Olivia's the plain-Jane daughter of a rich doctor who disapproves of her new boyfriend, the too-handsome Monty, but Olivia believes he's *not* a gold-digger and even the audience isn't sure unless you've already read the Henry James story it's based on, anyway he proposes and she accepts but makes a fatal error, telling him she's giving up her inheritance, who cares if Daddy approves, all we need is each other, etc., so naturally on the night of their elopement he never shows up. It's a painful scene when poor dumb Olivia finally gets the picture, but I knew it would make me feel better, I guess I'd lucked out that it wasn't *Of Human Bondage* or something like that, so I bought the ticket and a large popcorn and headed inside.

The opening credits were rolling, white letters on a black background, and the theater was very dark. I couldn't see a thing and literally had to feel my way down the aisle. When I got to my preferred area, right-hand side about ten rows from the back, I waved my hand sideways toward the aisle seat and it seemed to be empty. So I sat, started munching popcorn, and was already feeling better. As the credits wound up and the opening scene began, my eyes started adjusting to the darkness, and to my left I saw that the theater was deserted—just rows and rows of vacant seats. I'd been here before when there were only ten or fifteen people, but had never seen the place completely empty. After a minute, though, I became aware that I wasn't alone, that in fact I had sat down next to someone—an auburn-haired girl, it was, who sat frozen (or so I imagined) in the seat to my right. Tasting panic, I swung my head around, quickly scanning the theater, and realized that, yes indeed, we were the only two people there.

I felt embarrassed. No, I felt mortified. She probably thought I was making a move or something, otherwise why would I choose the one seat next to her, when I had my pick of five hundred others? I thought I would explain, telling her I hadn't been able to see, I didn't mean to violate her space, and probably it would be best if I made some little joke, like "You keep the right half of the theater, I'll take the left," and then got up and changed my seat. But something stopped me. She did seem frightened, sitting there motionless, scrunched about as far away from me as she could get, and of course her arm nowhere near our common armrest. Did she think I was dangerous? Some sex-starved wacko wandered in from the street? What kind of man goes to the movies at two o'clock on a weekday? And *The Heiress* wasn't exactly a male sort of picture—I must have ulterior motives. All this ran through my head but by now, of course, it was too late to say anything. I'd made a show of stretching out, and digging into my popcorn, and giving every possible sign of being sanely involved in watching the movie.

Which meant, of course, that the movie was ruined for both of us. We were both pretending to watch but were distracted out of our minds by our sitting there together, two strangers, alone in this big theater, neither of us willing or able to change our seats without making, I guess, some sort of unwholesome admission about ourselves. She was probably imagining, "He'll think I'm some weak scared female if I get up and move, or leave, and he's probably just an ordinary guy, maybe he didn't even *mean* to sit by me." And I was thinking, "If I move now, she'll think she ran me off, that I really *was* coming on to her but got discouraged because of the way she's sitting there with the coat wrapped around her, her arms folded tight over her chest, like she has gold bricks under there." Every few seconds I glanced over from the corner of my eye and she did look attractive, small-framed with reddish curly hair and glasses, not dorky glasses but little round rimless ones, she might even be pretty but this frozen posture of hers was so annoying, so unnecessary. I didn't think she'd even blinked or breathed since I sat down.

By the time Olivia had gotten infatuated with Monty, though, I'd given up all hope of following the movie. In fact, something odd happened: I'd started enjoying this bizarre situation, sitting next to this paralyzed girl, more than I'd have enjoyed the movie itself. I couldn't deny it: her fear had caused me to swell with a sense of power. Now I was glad I hadn't changed my seat during that first minute or two, when I had the chance. I sat there with a little smirk on my face—the expression a dangerous man would wear, I guess—and had fantasies of turning casually to her and saying, "We've got to stop meeting like this." Or, "I always take this seat—always. *But I guess you knew that.*" Or, more suggestively, "I almost wore my raincoat, too. If I'd known you would be here . . . "

But of course I didn't speak, just sat there snickering to myself, feeling crafty and superior. During those minutes Sheila left my thoughts for the first time since our loud, lacerating argument the previous weekend.

The fight had started after Sheila gave me the shock of my life. People break up every day, so why was I shocked?—it was the very weekend, such is my luck, when I'd planned to suggest that we move in together. This was April and since Christmas everything had been perfect, we'd spent nearly every hour together when we weren't in class or working our grad student jobs (mine in the library, hers at a woman's clothing "boutique" half a mile from campus) and almost every night together, too, alternating her place and mine. I preferred my own surroundings, my own bed, but Sheila liked everything to appear *equal*. Fifty-fifty. A two-way street. Exactly half the time, she said, I should adapt to *her* reality. She wasn't going to become my appendage. She wasn't a stick of furniture. Nor was she a dishwasher: we shared all such chores. If we were running late and I had to leave for class before the dishes were done, she'd stop washing, too—she wouldn't finish without me. Two days later when I came back they'd still be there, in six inches of scummy gray water, and we'd pick up where we left off, Sheila acting like it was the most natural thing in the world instead of this stingy, obsessive game.

"Hey, let's don't keep score," I said once, when she complained that lately I'd been having three orgasms to her one, but that remark got me frozen out for nearly a week.

Sheila was a petite, dark-haired girl with big glowing eyes that could shine with tears one moment and turn to black ice the next. Her tiny white shoulder, with its lovely curve inward to her fragile collarbone and perfect small breasts, could suggest the heft of an iceberg when it shifted away from me in bed, the smooth expanse of her back an untouchable white negative to my warm, aching fingers. Okay, I'd say snidely, but not out loud, we'll buy a ledger book and have running tallies of money spent, dishes washed, and orgasms owed, just please don't leave me here drifting on my side of the bed.

Except for such incidents, though, our life both in bed and out had made Sheila, for the past few months, seem the one safe haven in a world I sensed increasingly as fraught with peril. Already I knew, though I hadn't admitted it to myself, that grad school wasn't going to work out, and my parents' acrimonious divorce when I was a teenager hadn't held out a great deal of hope for the consolations of domestic life. Yet with Sheila, who had seemed when I met her so glamorous and turbulent—she was, after all, an actress—it seemed that I had calmed and won over some element of life that had always seemed threatening and untameable, and far more powerful than I could ever be. This was the reason, I guess, for the stranglehold of emotion I experienced whenever I saw her on stage. Never did I love her more passionately, more recklessly, than when she was playing someone else. These were drama department productions, edged with the self-consciousness of apprentices straining for greatness, but Sheila (the department's acknowledged "star") always outshone her surroundings. The role itself didn't matter. The angry befuddlement of Hedda Gabler, the serene altruism of Cordelia, the dazed self-immolation of O'Neill's mother as she journeyed into night—no matter whom she played, Sheila's hot glistening eyes and wavering flutelike voice brought all her characters to the same fever of incandescent passion, whether of rage or love or soul-destroying hatred, the words or situation mattering so much less than Sheila's tiny flamelike radiance on the stage, pulsing with energy, irresistible. Like everyone else in the audience, I watched her every move. At times it seemed Sheila fed on the inconsequent energies of the nameless crowd huddled invisible beyond the footlights, our power willingly sacrificed to hers, so that she might express the bold words we dared not imagine, the frightening passions we dared not feel.

It was after one of her performances (as Nora in *A Doll's House,* the slam of that infernal door still ringing in my ears) that I decided the time had come: I wanted her to move in with me, I wanted to buy her a ring if she didn't think it was too bourgeois, I wanted us to start thinking about getting married. I knew what she would say—that I was trying to "trap" her—but I would point out this wasn't a final commitment, we weren't saying "I do" but only "maybe I will," and if she wasn't happy she could always move out. But before I could even pose the question, she turned her small pert head and gazed off into the distance (we were in a crowded Italian place, red tablecloths and glowing candles, one of our favorites because it was both cheap and atmospheric) and paused a beat, two beats, before saying in a soft, rueful voice, "Chet, I've decided to move—I'm moving to Asheville."

It didn't help that I knew she was acting, even now—that her timing had been flawless, both the pause and the tone of her delivery precisely calibrated, the script improvised but self-conscious, the taut face she now turned toward me (still flushed from that night's performance) ready for its close-up as I sat there chumpy and nameless, expected to make the best of a thankless bit part. I could feel the blood draining out of my head, and I think my mouth was open.

"But—but what—" I stammered. "Why would . . . "

Sheila's phantom director had decided she ought now to take pity, let her eyes fill with the generous, fond remembrance of our shared but insufficient love, maybe reach across the table and squeeze my hand. Sensing this, I withdrew my hands to my lap where they curled abruptly into fists.

"Come on, don't look so grumpy," Sheila said. "You know what this means, don't you?—it's a chance that won't come again. It's only for a year, Chet, and it doesn't have to change anything. It's not even that far from here—you can come up on weekends. We'll have a great time! The managing director called last night—he's the *nicest* guy—"

And she went on to tell me about this experimental theater company that offered a fellowship each year to a promising young actor. She'd get to do a broad range of work, cutting-edge people came down from New York every season to check out the company's new productions, it was all so exciting so fantastic and I was happy for her, wasn't I? I didn't want to hold her back, did I?

These weren't answerable questions so I just said, dully, "You didn't even tell me you'd applied. Did you."

"Chet, I apply for all kinds of things—all of us do. The competition is so fierce that you don't really expect—" She stopped herself. She moved back slightly in her chair—just an inch or two. "You don't take me seriously, do you?" she said. The corners of her eyes slanted upwards when she was angry, as though pulled by strings. Or when she was pretending to be angry. Her cheekbones seemed to sharpen. "Did you think acting was just a hobby, just a college 'major,' and that once I graduated I'd take some ordinary job and get married to some—" She broke off. "Didn't you think I was *serious* about my work? Chet?"

I stared at her. Despite the ache in my chest, I offered my line with an understated drollery. "I guess I was too ordinary. To understand such things."

She rolled her eyes; she grinned, as though I were being a difficult child.

"Come on," she said again, "don't act this way. This has nothing to do with *us*—it doesn't have to change anything."

"Right," I said mildly. "You mentioned that."

I went home that night in the kind of raving, wild-eyed despair you can feel only in your twenties. Back in my cramped apartment, dustballs in the corners and the usual pile of dishes in the sink, I felt like a student out of Dostoevsky, ready to murder the next old lady I came across. Instead I cleaned the apartment, slowly and methodically, and for the rest of the weekend stared at a half-written paper on the tricky relationship between the last Russian Czar, Nicholas II, and his cousin George VI, who refused the Czar and his family sanctuary in England. They were massacred a short while later, of course, and so much for family feeling. In my own misery I felt strangely attracted to the topic, but the words wouldn't come.

Monday rolled around, and though I had an appointment with my graduate adviser I spent the day in bed. I tried calling Sheila until past midnight, growing more jealous and desperate with each call, but no answer. Fortunately, these were the days before answering machines, for no telling what message I might have left. The next day I tried calling my older brother in Tampa, but his wife said he'd just left for a business trip and would be back Thursday night. (I didn't know his wife very well, so I couldn't dump on her.) My two best friends in Atlanta, roommates who lived in my building, were also out of town, on a camping trip with their girlfriends. Since I had no taste for solitary drinking, the only escape I could imagine by Tuesday afternoon was a trip to the Silver Screen, where I found myself sitting beside that poor woman, both of us alone and in the dark, both frozen into roles we hadn't chosen and didn't quite know how to play.

The surge of adrenaline I'd experienced, that primitive sense of power you feel when someone else is afraid of you, was short-lived. As the movie plodded forward, the painful throbbing of my heart had reasserted itself, my mind's eye assaulted by lurid images of Sheila with someone else ("the managing director called last night—he's the *nicest* guy"), though I was trying hard to follow the movie. Even when I succeeded, Olivia's trials brought no relief. It didn't matter, of course, that she was a woman: we were going through the same thing, we were both romantic fools, we both deserved our fate. But as the movie wound up, I knew that Olivia had quickly outpaced me in hardening herself, as she finally succeeded in doing, to the likes of dimpled Monty. By now, Olivia's rich father had died, and though the two never reconciled he didn't disinherit her, after all. She was now a rich woman, possessed of a mansion on Washington Square and a mountain of cash, but alone. After Monty, no other man had come along. In the final scenes, Monty comes back to town, claiming he'd gone away to seek his fortune, wanting to be worthy of her, though by now we have to assume he's just the same opportunist as before, returning only because Olivia now has the money and no hawk-eyed father to mess things up. That's when it dawns on you: why shouldn't she marry him? Wouldn't that be better than living alone in that hulking mausoleum of a house? Isn't a late-arriving, imperfect love better than none at all? And it seems Olivia decides that's the case, for she agrees to see Monty and then accepts his ardent proposal, telling him to come back for her later that night. They're going to elope! That wild, passionate honeymoon of Olivia's long-ago dreams is going to happen after all! But the movie ends with Monty knocking frantically on the bolted door, and Olivia ascending the staircase alone, a candle in one hand, her eyes glazed with a look of suicidal determination. Now that her heart had died, Olivia had closed up shop. She didn't want Monty and she didn't want anybody else, either. She couldn't trust or love anyone again, so her life was over. The movie was over, too.

Slowly the lights came up, and I shook myself out of the foggy mixed emotions that had descended during those last scenes of *The Heiress*. Despite myself, I'd finally gotten involved in the movie and had forgotten about the poor scared girl sitting next to me. I sat forward in my seat, ready to bolt out of there, but something held me back. Though we were strangers, it seemed rude to just get up and walk out, especially since the girl still sat there, staring at the screen, arms crossed, making no gesture toward leaving. Whether I liked it or not, our being there alone in the theater, just the two of us watching the movie, had created a bond between us. I had to say something.

So I decided to explain, finally, about sitting next to her—just to be sure she understood.

"When I first came in," I said, turning stiffly in her direction, "I couldn't see—" But I stopped. The girl still hadn't moved, but there was something I hadn't realized: she was crying. Not sobbing, not shaking, just staring motionless at the now-blank screen with tears streaking down her face. She didn't look at me or acknowledge me in any way.

If I'd had any sense, I guess, I'd have just mumbled "Sorry," and quietly gotten up and walked out. But again something held me back. Though I wasn't thinking this at the time, not in so many words, I could plainly see—any idiot could have—that she'd been badly hurt, that here was another human being, suffering. Maybe her situation even resembled mine, maybe she'd gotten her heart smashed to bits. Now that the lights were up, I could see that she *was* fairly attractive, her reddish hair done in a sort of Orphan Annie cut, her skin milky-pale with freckles, her body underneath the raincoat graceful-seeming, slender. Not beautiful, but cute. Maybe a cheerleader in high school, perky and popular, with a name like Cindy, or Susie. But now her damp blue eyes looked almost deadened by pain. The tears kept coming, but she didn't wipe at them and still hadn't acknowledged me.

"Um, I guess the movie really got to you—yes?"

No answer.

"I hope I didn't—I mean, I didn't mean to violate your space, or to bother you—"

I broke off, understanding that I was bothering her now. But I couldn't stop.

"See, I guess it sort of got to me, too, because I've been going with this girl, her name is Sheila . . . " And I kept talking, though the girl gave no indication that she was listening at all. She just kept staring at the blank screen, quietly weeping. But for some reason the situation no longer felt awkward. I sat there and in a calm, reasonable voice told the girl everything that had happened between me and Sheila.

It didn't take long—maybe three minutes, five minutes. It must have been a relief, it must have felt wonderful, otherwise why would I have done it?—though I can't quite remember what I felt. It must have been the kind of emotion peculiar to one moment, urgent and essential and deeply strange, never to be experienced or even remembered again. The romantics among you, at this point, listening to this in the same way I was watching *The Heiress,* might be supposing, or hoping, that I invited that girl in the theater out for coffee, and we hit it off and eventually got together, happily ever after, etc. But I'm afraid not. Once I got to the part where Sheila told me about moving to Asheville a big lump rose in my throat, surprising the hell out of me, and I realized I was about to cry, too. So I got up and ran out of the theater. I went home and called Sheila, tried to talk her out of moving, failed, asked if there was another man involved in all this, was told there wasn't, and decided I would try to make the best of a long-distance relationship. She moved a few weeks later, and the situation gradually unraveled: I drove up every weekend, of course, but then she insisted on every other weekend—she needed space, I was smothering her—and by the middle of the summer the visits were worse than the time I spent alone in Atlanta. Each time we made love, it became for me a desperate effort to reclaim her, while for Sheila it just seemed a chore. On that Sunday afternoon in August when she finally said, "Chet, we've really got to talk," I was almost relieved.

Romantics are said to be incurable, so I did go back to that theater, sometimes several times a week, but I never saw the girl again. She'd never spoken a word or acknowledged me, but still I knew that I'd failed her. Or maybe I'd spared her? Who knows but that we might have fallen in love, that I craved the treasures of kindness, sympathy, understanding she kept so well-protected under her raincoat, and that once I'd taken my fill I might have skipped out, no less treacherous than Monty Clift, just one more of the random dangers you find in the world's every corner, even in an empty movie theater on a weekday afternoon? Instead I got married, had kids, became reasonably happy teaching history to bored middle-schoolers, though I know by now that the history books are nothing but lies and I can't teach the kids anything worth knowing. I'll never know their private histories and they'll never know mine, and what other kind of history is there?

Even my wife, a self-confident woman famous for her loud, bracing laugh, has no idea that late at night, on the rare occasion when she cries in my arms, I'm sometimes holding an actress I once loved, at other times consoling a nameless red-haired orphan I found stranded that day at the movies and with whom I shared an intimate couple of hours unequaled in my life before or since. We're playing our own parts, that girl and I, struggling through our own lines as well as anybody, but neither of us, I hope, can quite give up that moment in 1973, when our hearts stop as we watch Olivia de Havilland mounting that darkened staircase, alone. Her face has become ours: eerily bright in the candle's flame, fronting the darkness as she ascends implacably, ignoring that faint but dangerous knocking from the terrible world downstairs.

And we ignore it, too. We stay with Olivia. We watch her every step of the way.

Primordia

May 10

SOMEONE bends toward him out of the dimness, saying Andrew's name. A man, a large man, intruding gently into Andrew's dream from the depths of a chair, a wingback chair as large and rumpled and comfortable as the man himself. The man says, "Andrew, _______." And then: Andrew, _______."

Weakly, Andrew smiles. He wants to acknowledge the man, his kindness, his willingness to spend time with Andrew here in a darkened room on such a brilliant morning. When Andrew came in, the man was going from window to window, drawing all the curtains.

And yet, though he hears his name, the man saying his name, everything that follows seems garbled. Deep, wavering sounds, like words spoken underwater.

Weakly, Andrew smiles. He feels like crying. Perhaps he is already crying.

The man's white shirt, a size 17 or 18 or maybe larger, lifts out of the room's dusk and floats toward Andrew like a billowing sail. Andrew blinks. The room has begun rocking, a ship in a terrible storm, and Andrew lurches forward to feel the man gripping him under one arm, to hear him saying, "Andrew, ____________________." They are both standing up. Now the water seems calm beneath their feet.

"Andrew, you're feeling better . . . ?"

They stand precariously balanced, linked by the man's firm grip: Andrew a few inches taller, wearing an impeccable bone-colored suit, his face bloodless and smooth, rather owlish in thick spectacles with heavy brown frames, staring down at the ample, kindly Dr. Goode, a man in his shirt sleeves (the shirt's back and underarms wet with perspiration), a bit heavy with middle age, his hair colorless, thinning, receding. The older man supports the younger with his large capable hand and with an expression turned suddenly grim. Andrew stares back, mesmerized. Now Dr. Goode's words come clearly to Andrew, as if spoken within Andrew's own mind.

"Andrew, you're feeling better now? Are you? I think you've done extremely well today."

Andrew accepts this morsel, like an animal who has lived up to his trainer's expectations. "Yes, thank you," he says. "But I'm sorry about—"

"Don't apologize," Dr. Goode says, almost sternly. His grip tightens beneath Andrew's arm. "You've done *very* well. Far better than I had hoped."

"And now—?"

"And now, since I have a better idea of what you are suffering, I can help you more easily. And in a shorter period of time."

They are both standing. Andrew understands, startled, that it's time for him to leave.

"You want me to leave . . . ?" he says shyly.

Dr. Goode would never say *Yes, I want you to leave,* even though the hour is over. He is too polite, too considerate. Instead he smiles reprovingly, like a wife to her overworked husband: "You've made good progress today. You don't want to become exhausted. . . . "

Involuntarily Dr. Goode steps back, unprepared for Andrew's desperate lunge toward him. Andrew takes hold of his shirt-sleeve; his eyes have filled again with tears. "You won't make me leave?" he begs. "I can have another hour, right now? Another hour . . . ?"

February 12

A faculty meeting.

No, not a faculty meeting: a committee meeting. Eight of Andrew's colleagues, gathered around a seminar table, discussing the relative merits of E. M. Forster and Virginia Woolf. Only one can be included in a course they have approved for the next academic year. The arguments drone on, endlessly, punctuated by words like *tradition,* and *modernism,* and *accessibility.* Andrew keeps track of these words as they float about the table, when necessary seizing one to place inside a sentence of his own, but since he is facing the window, and since the weather today is dark, frigid, glowering, his gaze keeps straying to that vision of a windswept, deserted campus, with an occasional leaf scuttling across the lightly accumulated snow, naked forks of trees in the far distance, the turbulent lead-colored sky. This is Andrew's favorite kind of weather. It annoys him that he must keep following the brittle thread of conversation, and that the meeting shows no signs of ending, and that one of his colleagues across the table, Monica Frye, keeps trying to get his attention by smiling at him, uncomprehendingly, and giving him quizzical looks. She is a small, dark, quick-tempered young woman, hired this year along with Andrew, and she pretends they share a cynical camaraderie that Andrew doesn't feel. *Last hired, first fired,* she'd said one day, jokingly, giving Andrew an unpleasant pinch beneath his forearm. *Our common fate,* she'd laughed. Weakly, Andrew had smiled. Now he is trying to ignore her, picturing himself as a young man trapped in a committee meeting that will never end, staring dreamily out the window as if his consciousness has gone out of him entirely—out toward the pale windswept hills, the lowering vault of sky, the heartless weather.

It is four-eleven in the afternoon, somewhere in Georgia.

Later he will say to Dr. Goode: *This moment is important, since today it happens for the first time.* He will think back to the event as something shapely and discrete, rising into consciousness—like any perception—in due and gradual proportion, not impinging upon his eye but gradually coaxing it outward, almost with a kind of logic, an aesthetic propriety. As a professor of modern and contemporary poetry, as a gifted poet himself, he naturally looks back on any surprising event as no surprise at all, but rather as something canny and sleek and eminently sensible, partaking mysteriously—like some teasing non sequitur out of Eliot or Robert Lowell—of a larger, more finely constructed whole. In such a light will he consider his experience, later; at least during that first and rather successful visit. *A deft turn of consciousness,* he will tell Dr. Goode, *unpredictable but right.* He speaks with a sober, wondering joy. His first visit, yes: early in April. Or perhaps, he will wonder, it was something about the weather? *It seldom snows here in Georgia, especially this far south, and the weather had put me in a kind of trance, the voices of the other committee members began to fade, and even the face of that woman, Monica Frye, no longer seemed quite real. . . . It was all receding, fading away, and my vision was drawn outward, into some wavering new dimension that was not the landscape outside but something like the landscape, corresponding to it, darkening and glowering and filled with stray, indistinguishable shapes. . . .*

But in the seminar room, something else is happening.

Something hideous, like an insect but really too large for an insect—more like a large rat, a rodent of some kind—has appeared in Andrew's eyesight, creeping up the wall. It is only a few feet away from the window, and Andrew's eyes have jerked away from the nacreous landscape and onto that formless blotch crawling up the wall. . . . Despite his later recollection, his insistence that his attitude had been calm and unsurprised, Andrew has let out a gasp, sitting back abruptly in his chair, and has visibly paled. He has disrupted the committee meeting, of course. Monica Frye was watching at the moment his eyes jerked aside, and she glanced over her shoulder, following Andrew's gaze; but seeing only a blank expanse of wall, she looked back at Andrew, alarmed. The other committee members are looking at Andrew, and at each other; they are murmuring in low voices, behind their hands. Finally Monica, the only woman in the room—aside from Violet Laughton, who is not *really* a woman—stage-whispers across the table, "Andrew, what's wrong? Are you ill? Andrew . . . ?"

The rodent is making slow and deliberate progress across the wall. It continues upward, at an angle, as if aiming for the upper left corner of the window. But Andrew has decided that the creature is not a rodent: it is an insect, after all. It has a pair of long feelers, like extended whiskers, and it has the shiny brown surface of a roach. It has innumerable spindly legs, their concerted effort moving the creature up the wall, implacably. It does not seem to bear any malice toward Andrew, or toward anyone, but only to be intent on its own immediate designs. Andrew sits and watches, horrified. He finally responds to someone's hand under his arm, and to a voice hovering nearby, just beyond the range of his awareness.

". . . Andrew? Please try, please *try* to get up. Can you hear me? Can you . . . ?"

Her voice enters him, slowly. The committee meeting has ended, she will inform him later, and they are all standing around Andrew, alarmed and upset and not knowing what to do. They are leaving the initiative to Monica, who always pretends that she knows Andrew better than she really does—better than anyone does, here at Fairview College—and so she tries to coax him out of the chair, to make him speak, make him acknowledge her. After a few minutes she succeeds. He does begin to come around, slowly.

"Andrew? How are you feeling? Andrew . . . ?"

Groggily he turns his head in her direction—later he will remember the way his neck ached, as if he'd been struggling from a terrible stranglehold, some antediluvian paralysis—and he looks up at her, blinking. He blinks several times. Allows her to lift him slowly out of the chair, as though he is an invalid, murmuring something about overwork, about a doctor, about the need for sleep. . . .

He allows Monica to lead him from the room, murmuring words of comfort. He shuffles like an old man but cannot resist—they are at the doorway now—taking a last glance over his shoulder, toward the opposite wall and window. The wall stares back at him, innocently blank. Outside the window, the afternoon glowers and darkens.

After only a day, or two days, Andrew's life returns to normal.

April 6

"Everything was receding, fading away, and . . . and there was nothing I could do. . . . Somehow the first incident didn't really frighten me, I even felt rather good about it—rather privileged, you know, as if I'd been chosen for an experience denied to other people—and I also felt, I suppose, that I really was in control of the dream—the hallucination—that I could snap myself awake at any moment. . . . But then came the second time, and the third, and it seemed to be getting out of hand, it was no longer pleasant, and yet I was completely powerless. You understand, don't you? Powerless?"

During the first session Andrew sits forward in the chair, as if he might leap up at any moment, his elbows on his knees and his head bent, watching his own hands as they knead together, nervously. It is a familiar posture. In his own chair, ample and relaxed, Dr. Goode pays more attention to the young man's posture, and to the workings of his hands, and to his irritated rasping voice—implying that he doesn't really belong here, it's simply *unfair* that a young man of his caliber should be sitting here—than to the rambling monologue itself. From the first moment, when Andrew made his awkward, self-conscious entrance, Dr. Goode has known that he is desperately ill, that here is a young man who would come to Dr. Goode, surrendering himself to the care of another man, only as a last resort. He takes note of the lean, angular body, the furrowed brows above thick-framed glasses, the olive-dark skin that nonetheless appears bloodlessly pale. And the way he sits on the edge of his chair, talking in a voice by turns anguished and a little smug, both expressing and refusing to acknowledge his pain, his helplessness, his need of Dr. Goode.

"Perhaps, Andrew, if you could describe exactly what happens during one of these episodes? Not what you see, but what *happens* inside you, what kind of transformation takes place . . . ?"

The young man glances up, apprehensive. There is a flash of resentment in his eyes—something Dr. Goode also sees often, as if the patient would resist such a probing, intimate question, if only he could afford to. Dr. Goode waits patiently—with his inquiring, slightly widened eyes and the scarce hint of a smile—for the moment of resentment to pass. He is happy to wait, as always. There is no limit to his capacity for waiting.

Again the young man has lowered his eyes, and now he begins shaking his head, slowly. "That's part of the problem," he says in a flat murmuring voice, "the weirdness of it, the ineffability. . . . But it seems that everything fades away, everything real, and in its place there's only a blur, a kind of gray area, that's only a prelude to the hallucination, the vision. . . . I don't know." He keeps shaking his head, mournfully. "Maybe it's like watching a film, and then having the focus tampered with, and the images on the screen become a senseless, vaguely moving blur, nothing you can understand, but when you think the focus is returning, and everything will come clear, then something terrible and unexpected happens, like that insect I told you about, or the snakes. . . . It's like entering some other dimension, and I'm powerless to see or hear what's really happening around me, or to shake myself awake. . . . I'm completely powerless."

"And how do the hallucinations end, then?"

He shrugs his shoulders. "They just end. They don't have any shape, any dramatic climax . . . They merely come to an end, after five or ten or twenty minutes. Usually I wake to someone shaking me, asking if I'm all right. . . . It's humiliating."

And he lifts his anguished eyes to Dr. Goode, in the manner of all new patients. *There's my problem, now what's to be done? When will I be cured?*

Dr. Goode smiles, noncommittal. His clothes are rumpled, his face is rounded and benign, the wisps of hair combed across his scalp give him a rather comical, grandfatherly look: and yet, seated in the wingback as though he might have sat there for centuries, he has a solid, vatic, almost godlike air. He is pleased, at the moment, that the young man does not seem to notice.

Dr. Goode asks: "And why is it so terrible to feel powerless? Why does it frighten you?"

Andrew stares blankly, as if this is the first question anyone has ever asked that he could not answer promptly.

"Why . . . ?"

Dr. Goode nods, as if this were the answer he wanted. He scribbles something onto the legal pad held in his lap.

"It's possible, you know, to overestimate the value of power," Dr. Goode says softly.

March 30

Late that night, he wakes suddenly. Fumbles for the switch of the reading lamp over his bed, feels for his glasses on the bedside table, strains to hear a sound already fading from his awareness, a low and desperate sound, as if someone were softly moaning, whimpering. . . . He does recognize the sound, of course. A man's voice, whimpering with fear. His own voice.

He sits up in bed, absorbing the silence of the bedroom, the darkened apartment, the universe outside. He breathes shallowly, his heart pounding. All the universe seems peaceful, still. Only he sits awake, wide awake, perspiring and twitching with fear.

He cannot remember the dream, nor can he connect with his dream-self of a few moments before, writhing in that darkness, that featureless terror. . . . Never before has he wanted to remember his dreams, nor has he considered them important. Twenty-nine years old, educated at excellent preparatory schools and then at Harvard, Andrew has filled his life with work and books and constant, meticulous thought: *conscious* thought. He and his mother are the only living descendants of a very old, very genteel New England family, and great things had always been expected of Andrew. He had expected great things of himself. His assets are a sharp, aggressive intellect, an impatience with slowness or irrelevance, and a discipline that keeps him working around the clock, even on weekends or during the few holidays he spends with his mother, in the hulking Victorian mansion that has housed generations of the dwindling Thatchers and that Andrew intends someday to occupy himself. Later in his career, after his reputation has been made. After his monumental study of current poetics—tentatively entitled *The Visible Muse: Contemporary Excursions into the Self*—has been completed, and he can teach anywhere he chooses. He will return to New England, of course. He has come this far south with the idea of serving his apprenticeship, and with an air of philosophical resignation—the Thatchers have always been known, in public life and private, for a certain pragmatic wistfulness—for after all, he thought, one must begin somewhere, and he was not proud. He had planned to move here and to work very hard; to isolate himself from all distractions; and to look back on this experience, someday, as among the most serene and productive of his life.

That night in March, recalling his grandiose plans and his own complacency, feeling his heart pumping desperately in the residual fear of some dream, some ghastly and unremembered dream, he startles himself by laughing aloud. He gets up and crosses to his desk, an enormous roll-top that has been in the family for more than a century, pushes aside the manuscript pages of his book—he hasn't written a word in six or eight weeks—and rifles through assorted stray notes for poems and essays and reviews, and for a possible second book (an idea that now seems laughable), until he finds what he is seeking: a brief list of phone numbers. He grips the telephone and quickly, nervously dials. He cannot remember the last time he actually picked up the phone to call someone, but knows he must not be alone, not at the moment. Not tonight. It is three o'clock in the morning and he is prey to the most whimsical, most primordial terrors, and he must not be alone. . . .

He says quietly into the receiver, "Hello, Monica? This is Andrew Thatcher—Andrew. Yes. Listen, I was just wondering. . . . "

May 10

So Dr. Goode has given him another hour. It might have been his lunch hour, or an hour for reading his mail, or resting, or meditating—but he has given it to Andrew, after only a moment's hesitation. And Andrew, for his part, has calmed down considerably. Each settled in his chair, they sit talking like old cronies. Or so Andrew thinks, as if unaware that *he* is doing all the talking—rambling on in that easy, glib style his students find so entertaining, so "brilliant"—while Dr. Goode merely sits listening, his plump hands raised before his face with fingertips lightly touching, his brow knotted with concentration, giving Andrew an occasional nod or smile to keep him talking.

Andrew has returned to normal, but now the second hour is nearly past. This realization (he has glanced over, carelessly, to the small gold clock on Dr. Goode's cluttered desktop) sends a queer jolt of panic through Andrew, stops his voice in mid-sentence.

They wait—one minutes, two minutes.

"I forgot what we were talking about," Andrew says at last.

Dr. Goode shrugs. "That doesn't matter. What are you feeling now?"

Andrew gulps. He gives a little laugh. "I don't want to leave," he says hoarsely. "I feel so much better, as if I'm returning to myself—but out there—out there—" He gestures vaguely toward the door.

"Out there?" Dr. Goode echoes, his eyebrows raised. "But what could happen, Andrew? What could happen 'out there'?"

"Anything," Andrew whispers.

April 2

Mid-afternoon, a Saturday. Sunlight. This spring day is warm, overwarm, and soon after exiting from his apartment Andrew removes his jacket, takes a squinting look upward at the sun, feels himself firm and fixed and even comfortable in his resolve. Even rather pleased with himself—a familiar emotion from the past. He has made a decision, an intelligent decision, and yes, he is quite pleased with himself. As a boy he'd been "withdrawn" (so people said), and as an adolescent, quite "obstinate" (so his mother insisted, with her indulgent smile). In graduate school he was "arrogant," or "egocentric," or "probably a genius." So people had said, his acquaintances and colleagues and students. Only last night, Monica had brought that back to him, all of that. His past, his memories. *You're a genius, I know you are, and what's been happening isn't part of an "illness." It's only a manifestation of your genius. . . .* They sat on Andrew's little, hard, Victorian couch, her hand resting lightly on his tensed knee, her small supplicant face turned upward to his. But his own face was slightly averted, for at that moment he had been thinking: *knowing this woman is a grave mistake.* One moment of weakness, and this was his punishment. But how to get rid of her, now? How to put things back as they were?

He took her advice as a sign, and determined to do the opposite of what she told him. This is part of the pleasure he feels, today, strolling down the sidewalk from his apartment on this overwarm afternoon—for how drastically the weather has changed since that frigid, glowering day in February, the day when all his troubles began. Now the hot sticky air has made his skin redden alarmingly, especially on his cheeks where two rosy splotches have appeared, as if he has a fever or a rash. He is headed for a telephone booth on the corner (making a kind of ritual of this phone call—for he might have phoned Dr. Goode, after all, from his own apartment). He ponders the marvelous illogic of his decision, the aesthetic *rightness* of his decision. . . . Monica Frye had said he was not sick, only a genius, needing only her own understanding and attention and respect. And love? And worship? Andrew had not wanted to laugh aloud, and indeed he had not. Commendable. So he *was* sick, then—that was the direction he had taken. But Andrew doesn't mind: he has made a decision, he is following it through, he is in complete control of his life. Dr. Goode, recommended to him by the Fairview College health center, has the best reputation of any psychiatrist in the city. Andrew has high respect for reputations. He has already spent much of his adult life, after all, carefully laying the groundwork for his own.

He doesn't know exactly when, or how, the nightmare sneaks up on him. When he thinks back, everything will seem hopelessly jumbled. There are boys, yes, three or four boys, lean and bare-chested and calling to one another in loud, high voices, playing in an empty lot across the street—throwing a bright green frisbee back and forth between them—and he is already in the telephone booth because he has to squint past the grime-stained glass to make them out, focusing on one tallish, blond-haired boy in particular, his hands raised, teeth flashing in a heartless youthful grin, transforming Andrew's squint into a wide-eyed helpless stare when he feels, out of nowhere, the sudden sharp stab of lust. Is he already holding the telephone? Perhaps he has already spoken with Dr. Goode's secretary and perhaps *they* are already hanging down on all sides of the telephone booth, writhing, tapping their little mallet-like heads against the glass in the effort to get at Andrew? Perhaps his glimpse of the boy, of those young supple muscular white arms raised to catch the frisbee, the teeth flashing in the merciless sunlight, had not been the source of his discomfiture, but only a puzzling further twist of his fate, an ugly signature to an event he would never, never be able to remember clearly?

Snakes. Thick-bodied, coiling, in constant motion. Coming from somewhere above, lowering their soft, dark, undulating bodies down all four sides of the phone booth as Andrew stands gaping, turning from one side to the next, the boys' shouts from the lot across the street like beckoning voices only half-heard by a bewildered dreamer. The phone fallen useless to his side, dangling by its steel cord. Snakes, yes. *Them. They.* Tapping their hard little heads against the glass.

"I think—I think I must be an evil person," Andrew will whisper to Dr. Goode.

And Dr. Goode will reply, in an odd half-petulant voice, "But there is no such thing as evil. There is only health and its opposite. Well-being, and the absence of well-being . . . "

May 15

Everything jumbled together, confused, images and dreams and stray disconnected thoughts, all so chaotic that fear itself is losing the power—has already lost the power?—to harm him, so of course he goes to the end-of-year faculty party: not that he has much choice in the matter, thanks to this damnable entanglement with a woman named Frye, a busy little wisp of a woman named Monica Frye who has him, who feels sure that she has him, and who *will not* leave him alone.

"You're feeling better this week, aren't you," she says offhandedly, adjusting his tie, not really wanting an answer. There is something wifely about her, something proprietary—as if they'd been together for years. Already they are half an hour late; in recent weeks Andrew has been uncharacteristically late for nearly everything—classes, meetings, his countless dates with Monica that he never remembers having made—because he is wading, struggling, trudging through his newly dazed and darkened consciousness, fearful of every dim corner and every looming, indistinguishable shape in the far distance, fearful especially of himself. Mirrors give back to him an undersea monster, trying horribly to smile. So he avoids mirrors, he avoids vision itself except for his attempt to squint past those distances of murky waters, to glimpse what might be lying in wait or advancing cunningly toward him. Yet nearer, always at the fringes of his immeasurable self, chattering at him and adjusting his tie and peering curiously into his fixed, deadened retinas, hovers the inexplicable Monica, ubiquitous and unceasing, a gnat he'd like to slap away and yet he can't summon the energy, or doesn't dare. At least she is dependable, he often thinks, leading him through his paces, coaxing and cajoling, unlike Dr. Goode who after all has given up. Who hadn't given him another hour but had merely stared back at him, his brow creased. Who hadn't called out or done anything at all when Andrew turned with childish violence and stumbled from the room, whimpering.

This evening, dry-eyed and expressionless, his head sloshing with dirty water, he submits to Monica's nattering and fussing and yanking; he even tries to pay attention to her odd little voice, at once steely and whining.

". . . So who cares what they think?" she says, rather crossly. Frequently she argues with herself; Andrew has wondered, idly, why she thinks she needs him at all. "I mean, what do they know? They don't understand you, they're all parochial and narrow-minded failures, they wouldn't know a real talent if it came up and slapped them in the face . . ." but her eyes don't even brush his, she is still fiddling with the tie, she doesn't need him or his attention or his bemused curiosity at all. Staring, Andrew thinks: Who is she? But his curiosity quickly wanes.

"Come on," she says, taking him by the arm, "I can't wait to see their faces when we walk in. We'll show *them,* I guess! I can't wait to see their faces!"

Andrew could easily wait to see their faces, but his habit of acquiescence allows Monica to pull him along; a moment later they're in Monica's car—he's grateful that she prefers to drive, since he has surely forgotten how—and then they're at the curb of a brick house, smallish, painted a neat glaring white, the home of Violet Marie Laughton (rumor has it that the name is a fanciful invention of Violet's, a rumor given weight by the fact that no one knows anything of Dr. Laughton's past, and since she is chair of the English Department, no one has ever dared to ask), a woman in her late sixties who has developed, over the last nine months, a livid, barely concealed hatred for both Andrew and Monica.

At the curb Monica hurries around to Andrew's door and carefully opens it, then even more carefully pulls him out and stands him on the sidewalk as if handling some particularly unwieldy mechanical contraption. Standing there, Andrew blinks at the dusk settling gently upon the world. It is the gradual, mellow, deep-blue dusk of late spring, so why should Andrew feel terrified? When they reach Violet's black wrought-iron gate, behind which a small vicious-looking terrier is barking fiercely, he turns to Monica, his cheeks blanched and his eyes deadened with fear, to whisper hoarsely, "Monica, I—I've changed my mind. I'm not feeling well, and I really don't think—"

And Monica does an amazing thing: she slaps him. A quick, sharp, housewifely slap across his sagging jaw.

"There's no reason for you to be afraid," she hisses. Her eyes blaze at him, one small hand curling under his forearm as if to yank him through the gate. "*They're* the ones who should be afraid—it's *them,* Andrew! But they don't know anything, they're too dull and narrow and stupid to be afraid—don't you understand that? Don't you *see* that?"

June 2

Later Andrew would think upon the events of that spring, all those puzzling, fearsome events, and would decide that a phase of his life had come to an end. A phase he would think back upon—oddly enough—as relatively unimportant, performing no significant function in his life, embodying no instructive fable or cautionary tale. A waste of time, simply. A worthless experience. It seemed that nothing had happened back there, down there: nothing at all worth remembering. Of course he would finish his book, working steadily and brilliantly through that mellow New England summer, and of course it would be accepted by a prestigious university press. Of course he would obtain a teaching position for the next academic year, and at a much better university (despite the absence in his dossier of any recommendation from his colleagues at Fairview), and soon it would seem obvious—had it not always seemed obvious?—that his future was assured. *A brilliant young man. A brilliant career.* Yet he did not need his new measure of success to know that his nine months in the deep South—in that awful hole of a college, where one's sanity might sink down into darkness as into quicksand, as into the stagnant waters of a bayou—had been worthless. He had known this only a few days after that doomed faculty party, where he had fainted once again in meaningless terror, prey once again to his meaningless visions; had known it, in fact, the moment he understood, sitting behind the wheel of a northward-pointed car and feeling the miles hurtle away beneath him, that he need never return to that place again, that he need never again be infected by its close, stifling, evil-smelling atmosphere—like some malevolent force of gravity it had been: sucking at his feet, his mind, his sanity itself!—and that, free of it, he could easily resume his former life. His normal life. A life in which there was very little to distress him, where time lost meaning and power because he immersed himself in work, in which a young man's mind—working crisply and efficiently—need never be bogged down in dark or terrifying details of personality and, in fact, need never be really conscious of "his" personality at all. The meditative faculty was dangerous, after all, when not attached to some external object; free time was dangerous. The time he had wasted, for instance, sitting in the office of that quack, Dr. Goode! Dredging up all sorts of muck, making himself thoroughly miserable! All his life Andrew would feel amazement that he could ever have been—even temporarily—so stupid.

May 10

"What were you like as a child?" Dr. Goode had asked, looking up sharply as Andrew fumbled for an answer.

This was during the first hour, before Andrew had become angry and before Dr. Goode had become impatient; before they both had become deeply, inexpressibly weary.

"A child . . . ?" Andrew says, wondering. The word feels strange upon his tongue.

"Yes. What were you like?"

It is a reasonable question, and Andrew—brilliant Andrew—has been confidently replying to questions since early childhood, always correctly. But now he stammers, halts, blushes. For the first time in his life, he doesn't have the answer.

May 15

No, he thinks vaguely, in response to Monica's question, he *doesn't* see; doesn't really understand. Smiling the bland smile of an invalid, squinting as if facing the terrible brightness of a searchlight, Andrew allows Monica to lead him slowly around the room; and he hears the amiable, vacuous chatter all about him; and can even pick out certain phrases, certain voices. *Really? You didn't know? Yes, Andrew is almost finished with his book, I typed a draft of the final chapter only last night. . . .* Supercilious, sardonic, arch: Monica's voice, so Andrew believes, will never cease; even after her death, will play and replay through the minds of people she has known; will eventually travel through outer space, perhaps, plaguing other worlds. *No, I certainly didn't know,* says Violet in her low, throaty murmur. *I wasn't aware that he'd been doing any work at all.* Some part of Andrew wants to say: *Touché!* He enjoys Monica's baffled pause; he finds himself, in this sparring between her and Violet, serenely impartial. But no sooner does their conflict get interesting than Homer Choate, a fiftyish Shakespeare man with an odor of failure about him—or is it the odor of cheap cigars?—seizes Andrew's free arm and begins to talk about . . . what? Allusions to Shakespeare in contemporary poetry? An alleged instance of plagiarism, on the part of a leading English poet, from one of the earlier works? *The Two Gentlemen of Verona,* had it been? Or *The Rape of Lucrece?* Still smiling, still squinting, Andrew shakes his head as if in amiable confusion, but the man's grip on his wrist grows tighter, his fetid breath wafts closer to Andrew's quivering nostrils, and the swordlike thrusts of talk between Violet and Monica make a harsh, grating music inside his head. The entire roomful of chattering heads, swirling somewhere about him, just beyond the range of his awareness—for it seems that everything, everyone, is *just beyond* the range of his awareness—all begin falling into a pattern, a sudden clarifying *Gestalt* that might erase his fear and confusion, might calm the warring acids in his stomach, but just at the brink of this clear perception, this revelation, something catches his eye and throws him into confusion once again: a large punch bowl, filled with a foamy green mysterious liquid. It sits there, harmlessly, in the center of a long table strewn with napkins and paper cups and paper plates. A sweetish-looking green punch, harmless. He remembers, he tries to remember . . . but no, he does not remember. He shakes his head, confused. Monica has taken his arm once again, has begun walking in a new direction: toward a knot of people standing near the fireplace. Numbly, Andrew follows. No, he thinks vaguely, he *doesn't* see; *doesn't* understand . . .

June 2

As he drives, his gunmetal-gray Peugeot crammed with his possessions—clothes, books, a handful of antiques he'd been afraid to entrust to the movers—his anger stays focused on Dr. Goode: Andrew had been so upset, so confused, that he had not even checked the man's credentials. An M.D.? A Ph.D.? Perhaps the diplomas were forged. And that mysterious attitude of his: benevolent, even saintly. Beatific. Waiting in serene, watchful silence for Andrew to speak. To utter his own wisdom, to give his own answers. The mask had been convincing, Andrew has to admit, but now he sees the truth: the silence meant that Dr. Goode had nothing whatever to say. A charlatan, a poseur. Probably not very intelligent. Andrew drives intently, his eyes narrowed against the bright New England sunlight (the summers are so brilliant, so breathtaking in this part of the world!—and here he is, less than a hundred miles from home!), his fingers whitened in their grip on the steering wheel, his thin lips quivering in an odd blend of anger and relief. But never mind, that residue of anger would drain away before long—once he sets to work, once he begins to forget. The dark, primordial apparitions; the feverish, unremembered dreams; Violet Laughton and Homer Choate and all the others, especially that despicable Monica Frye yammering constantly in his ear, like a buzzing gnat that cannot be dislodged. . . . And sitting there with Dr. Goode, humbling himself. Fainting at committee meetings, at faculty parties. Watching an ordinary grinning shirtless teenage boy, his teeth—so white they seared Andrew's vision—glinting in the sunlight, and feeling that inexplicable swelling in his groin, that urgent terrible lust. Through all these gruesome events a tiny voice within Andrew had cried out plaintively: Not me, not me! Not Andrew Thatcher! Something is wrong, some terrible mistake has been made, that isn't me and I really can't be blamed. . . . Now, half a continent away and the distance increasing with every minute, that weak intimidated voice has shaded into one of contempt, even of a certain gloating triumph: it had *not* been Andrew, after all. His own sanity had prevailed.

Every few minutes he glances into the rear-view mirror, anxiously, and there he is.

May 10

Andrew looks up at him, glumly. His embarrassment has subsided, his skin has faded from that painful dark-mottled red to an ashen paleness, his hands rest on his lap with their long pale skeletal fingers neatly interlaced. Dr. Goode stares back at him, ignoring Andrew's dour, rather menacing look, smiling that slight enigmatic beatific rather teasing smile—the corners of his mouth raised almost imperceptibly into his plump cheeks—and lifts his feathery eyebrows inquiringly.

"Well . . . ?" Dr. Goode says.

"I don't know," Andrew says at once, bitterly. "I don't *know.*"

May 15

What can a person know, anyway? he thinks as Monica leads him around the room, shoving him into the faces of colleagues he half-recognizes, faces that smile uneasily at him while he stares back blankly, almost rudely, following his own ruminative vaguely comforting train of thought. Really, what can a person *know?* Which experiences deserve one's attention, which can safely be ignored? Which images, visions, dreams? He had wanted to ignore the little rodents, the snakes, the black swiftly-moving spiders that scuttled this way and that, disappearing beneath sofas or into the cracks of doorways the moment Andrew glanced around. Were these things important? What disturbs him is that the party where he now finds himself, and the people with whom he is expected to chatter inanely, are *not* important: he can ignore them. Must ignore them. And if they are unimportant, does this mean that his own abstraction, his own trance-like stupor, *is* important . . . ? Must somehow be interpreted? He is intrigued, in his vague way, that the others do not seem to mind his behavior, or at least have become resigned to it; even Monica doesn't seem to mind. She is quite content to drag him around this room with her, endlessly. Somehow they are back with Violet again: Violet who so plainly hates them both; Violet who had excited such a reciprocal murderous hatred in Monica this past Monday morning, when Monica received her notice of non-renewal (Andrew had received his own in the same mail) in the form of a brief, coldly worded letter that lacked even the few insincere pleasantries and compliments such letters normally contained. Andrew had not been angered by his own letter, which was identical to Monica's, but Monica, invading Andrew's apartment that evening, had railed against the nerve of "that woman"—"that miserable bitch"—"that stupid illiterate whore." Andrew had listened blandly, without comment. He listens blandly now, his eyes wandering unmoored about the room—from Homer Choate, puffing a nasty cigar near the fireplace, to a couple of history professors already at the door, escaping early with their wives, to the sad remaining few still scattered about Violet's austerely furnished living room, and finally to the long table of refreshments, abandoned now, the food mostly gone but the bowl of green sick-looking punch still there, still untouched. Though the room is hazy with smoke and overwarm, a chill runs through Andrew.

The conversation between Violet and Monica seems oddly civil. It seems they are discussing headaches, Violet speaking in a low, pleased, hypnotic murmur about her trouble with migraines, the useless painkillers, the hours of lying in hellish abandon atop her daybed. No wonder Monica has warmed to this subject, with its lurid images of Violet's suffering and helplessness. Monica, darkly solicitous, asks if Violet has tried Fiorinal? Percocet? Once, when Monica had been suffering with a mysterious headache of her own—but Violet cuts her off, laughing indulgently, like an old roué whose nightly lover is pain. *Nothing works—nothing,* she says in her husky satisfied voice, and then goes on to talk rather sentimentally about the *value* of pain, the *importance* of experiencing pain. And though he is half-listening, half-interested—especially since Violet is so often a simple bore, a heartless uncomplicated angular bitch of a woman: perhaps she has been drinking this evening—and though he might have had, under other circumstances, something intellectually penetrating to say about pain himself, since he considers it valueless and degrading and can prove he is right, at this moment he in turn interrupts Violet, raising his arm and clearing his throat and causing both women to look up at him, startled, as he says in a strained voice, ". . . something to drink. I think I'll have some of that punch—over there." And tries to point, holding out an arm stiff as a mannequin's.

Yet they are relieved. They are pleased and greatly relieved, and their smiles seem to give him a little maternal nudge toward the table, the punch; then they resume their conversation. He walks stiffly, their attitude reminding him briefly of his own mother, whose nature is not "maternal" but proud, grim, and proprietary, and in a flash he recalls—yes, he recalls it now!—a birthday party she'd given him, he'd been ten or eleven, and she had served a green thick foamy punch just like the one now before him. He peers down into the punch bowl, faintly smiling. Is *this* an important memory? Is *this* worth remembering? His little friends gathered about him, none of whom liked him though they enjoyed parties like all normal children so here they were, each ladling out a cup of the punch made of—what? lime sherbet and soda?—and then standing about, sipping, like parodies of adults holding cocktails. His mother standing off to the side with a maiden aunt of Andrew's, whispering about his accomplishments at school, his prizes, his constant reading in the afternoons and evenings. *Little Andrew and his poetry books . . . He does nothing but read, you know.* Fatuous for his aunt's benefit, his mother knowing nothing about poetry except that it was important somehow, a vital thread in the history of highly placed New England families like their own. So it would be poetry. Fine. (Her husband, Andrew's father, had been a successful banker; but he was dead. Unremembered.) And little Andrew had stood there in his navy blue shorts and suspenders and spotless white shirt, gazing down into the punch as if into an oracle. His future, where would it lead him? . . . And did it matter, he thinks now, whether he had really thought such a thing or not, at the age of ten or eleven? Must he seize the memory and make sense of it, or simply let it go?

Staring into the punch bowl: something happens as if to answer his thought. In the punch—cloudy, opaque, the green of witches' teeth—there is motion. Sluggishly, just beneath the surface, something dark and shapeless: its bulk stirring, moving upward. It appears to struggle, wanting to rise—massive, many-armed, horrible to contemplate—and yet Andrew can make out nothing clearly. It stays just beneath the surface, teasing him. What will happen? he thinks in wonder. Probably nothing. Oddly, he is unafraid. Yet mesmerized. Transfixed. In a flash he recalls a particular night—was it only last week?—when he'd driven desperately into Atlanta with the idea that something must happen. Soon. Now. He went to a "singles" bar: nothing happened. He went to a "gay" bar: nothing happened. *Is nothing ever to happen?* he had thought, panicked. Andrew nursing a drink, watching other people (who were they? *what* were they?) out the corner of his eye: a ridiculous sight. A ridiculous concept. Closing the door of his apartment behind him, late that night, he breathed a long sigh of relief. He thought he might weep; he thought he might cry out; he thought he might even—in his loneliness, his desperation—fall to his knees and pray.

Nothing happened.

Now this terrible, bulky, dark, inexplicable thing moves inside the bowl of sickly-green punch, and Andrew, his eyes rimmed faintly with tears, trembling but unafraid, utterly fearless, plunges both his arms into the depths, determined to seize or placate or destroy, determined to stop the terrible thudding of his heart. Primordia. Pure featureless terror. But when he lifts them out his arms, his hands, are empty. His expensive cream-colored jacket is wet to the elbows with a greenish mucous-like liquid—mysterious. He releases a small wail of despair.

Behind him he hears voices: "Andrew, ______!" "Andrew, ______!"

He turns abruptly to shake his arms at them, a threat. *Get back! Get away!* Now the tears have welled; they streak his face. But whoever these creatures are, they won't stay back. They approach him, implacable.

"No—no," he stammers, blinded. "I don't see, I *can't* see—Please, no—who are—*what are*—"

And his eyes close, involuntarily. Something dark, stifling, permanent weighs on his eyelids, on his consciousness itself, and he abandons himself to it, gratefully, knowing there is nothing left to fear.

June 2

No, he muses, trying to ignore that image of Dr. Goode moving ponderously about the room, drawing all the curtains until nothing was left except the dimness and themselves, *no,* he thinks, a charlatan like Dr. Goode had nothing to offer him, had not been quite real. As he checks his reflection in the rear-view, aware that he is driving too fast, his mind working like a machine and already certain of its own future (*a brilliant young man,* people had said: would always say), it seems that nothing *had* happened, after all. Signs for the smallish New England city where he lives, where he belongs, have been appearing regularly for the past hour or so: *64 miles, 27 miles.* He is almost there. No, he thinks to himself, clearly: nothing had happened. He was free.

Alliances of Youth

THEY were in league against me: I felt that from the moment I arrived.

Aunt Veronica, whom I could never call "Ronnie," so ample of bosom and leg, swathed in layers of heavy, stifling black despite the September heat.

Carole Ann, Barrie's "long-time fiancée," as the local newspaper had it (this far south, a small-town paper could still employ such a euphemism), a woman who, strung along by my cousin for more than two decades, now had a sallow, absent look, as though the years of waiting had cast a glaze upon her features.

We stood in baggage claim, three entirely dissimilar women unrelated to one another except through Barrie, who had died unexpectedly of heart failure three days before, at the age of thirty-eight. Yet almost at once I did sense a relation. When I left the South, twenty years ago, Veronica had been a grim, commanding woman who felt that no one—and certainly not the slight, rather fey Carole Ann—was good enough for her darling Barrie, while Carole Ann, thinking very mistakenly that Veronica's inelastic will alone stood between herself and connubial bliss, had played the miffed and ill-used heroine to the hilt. (Barrie, mischievous as always, loved telling me of their latest contretemps—a snide remark at the dinner table, for instance, from his mother, followed by Carole Ann's swift, disdainful exit from the room. At that time, I was hardly an unwilling confidante.) Encased in her heavy mourning, Veronica now looked stolid but rather pitiable, like a fallen idol, while Carole Ann, still pretty in her way, gave the impression that Barrie's death had not really surprised her, but had only confirmed a long-acknowledged fate. It was a static quality, I suppose, that somehow united them; something in their empty, fish-eyed stares.

"You both—you both look wonderful."

They didn't respond, at first; and I stood rooted, a bit shocked that I'd spoken insincerely.

A long moment, then a wan smile from Carole Ann.

"We're glad you could come. We decided to invite you, if we invited anyone."

"It's going to be small, mostly family," Veronica added, as if issuing a pronouncement.

I wasn't really "family," of course, since Veronica already had Barrie when she married my Uncle Rex; in fact, Barrie once said that his mother had warned him of me. "Warned you? What do you mean?" I asked. Barrie glanced away, slyly. "*You* know," he said.

"Really, I think it's just us three," said Carole Ann.

I spotted my bags, slowly approaching on the conveyor belt, and used the moment to ponder their invitation once again. At best, I'd felt they acted out of some dim, vestigial notion of Southern propriety; at worst, out of a long-cherished and perhaps unconscious malevolence. Their apparent collusion edged me toward the latter. (Although the question I should have been pondering, of course, was why I had accepted, and so eagerly.)

During the long drive into the hilly, parched-looking countryside, we tried to make pleasant conversation. They asked about my teaching, of course, and I launched into a glowing description of the private girls' academy in Bucks County, Pennsylvania, where I'd spent most of the years since my rather abrupt departure—though I deliberately did not tell them that I'd become headmistress more than three years ago (perhaps because this connoted a certain prim, fussy self-sufficiency, along with a hopeless spinsterhood). They seemed impressed and interested, though I felt that Veronica saw through me. She drove in her cold, efficient style, her profile etched in steel as she listened, the large diamond Barrie had given her on his eighteenth birthday (one of his eccentricities, of which he was so vain, was the habit of buying Veronica a present for his own birthday: "a compensatory gesture," he'd said one year, bowing gallantly) glinting near the top of the steering wheel. Carole Ann sat crushed between us, slump-shouldered, fiddling with a kerchief in her lap. I kept putting fingertips to my brow, to the back of my hairline: the humidity and heat were nearly overpowering. Veronica kept the windows of her late-model Cadillac rolled up, but had not turned on the air conditioner.

"It must be strange, coming back home," said Veronica in a still, even voice. "Things must be quite different up there."

"Yes indeed," echoed Carole Ann. "I remember that winter, after Barrie went up—why, the stories he told! The terrible snowstorms, and all the traffic. And the people being so unpleasant."

"Except for Ruth, of course," said Veronica, indulgently. She smiled across at me. "Of course, he didn't mean you."

Carole Ann wrinkled her brow, as if dimly aware that her meaning had been distorted.

"No, of course not," she said. "Heaven knows, Ruth is one of us."

"Though he did express his fears, Ruth, that you'd been 'converted.'" Veronica gave her dry, croaking laugh.

"Well, I have my work," I said, with calculated brevity. Had they brought me here simply to find out, at last, what had transpired during Barrie's month-long stay in Philadelphia, nearly two decades before? I'd received letters from both Carole Ann and Veronica shortly after Barrie returned home, Carole Ann's wondering coyly and Veronica's demanding outright to know what was the matter with him, what happened to the charming Barrie they'd known and loved, had I gotten some kind of power over him? I hadn't answered the letters.

"Yes, you have that," Carole Ann said philosophically.

A thin film of sweat had covered my face; I felt that I could scarcely breathe.

"One thing we don't have up north," I said, trying to sound polite and offhand, "is this terrible heat. It's a sweltering day, isn't it?"

An interminable two hours passed before we reached the house. Carole Ann remarked that she didn't mind the heat, though she spoke absently, as if her thoughts were elsewhere. Veronica raised her eyebrows, sympathetically, but didn't reply. Nor did she offer to start the air conditioner.

The house, more than a century old, had been in the family for less than thirty years, my late Uncle Rex having been prompted by his new wife and a cynical, precocious, eleven-year-old Barrie to set them up in proper style, with all the trappings of Southern gothicism. Shading the sinuous front drive (full of potholes, and threatened on both sides by thick crabgrass and kudzu) were a number of stately, decayed-looking trees; there was an imposing front veranda, complete with white columns and a creaking swing; from the third story, turrets jutted out like gaping, disconsolate eyes. There was even, dear God, a tight-lipped housekeeper, her black hair parted severely down the middle and plastered against her skull, whose every gesture seemed distinct with menace. Before leaving school for the airport, I'd joked with one of my colleagues that I'd be staying in a "mouldering mansion" while down South, and had given a mock shudder. In truth, I'd carefully prepared myself for the dispiriting atmosphere of this house that Barrie somehow could never leave. I was not prepared, however, for the nature of what Veronica, with uncharacteristic vagueness, termed "the arrangements."

Quite simply, they had arranged that Barrie's remains should be displayed in the front parlor. To an outside observer, this might seem merely old-fashioned; or, at the worst, fantastically distasteful. I felt confirmed, however, in suspecting that the two women were somehow ranged against me, for neither of them told me that Barrie's open casket waited in the house. This might have been merely stupid of Carole Ann, but it was certainly disingenuous of Veronica. I could imagine her playing and replaying in her mind the rather embarrassed, unsavory scene that did in fact occur.

It was later that evening, some four or five hours after I arrived. I'd wandered downstairs after my nap, hoping for some sign of dinner, for I'd awakened ravenously hungry. Near the base of the stairs, the main hall had entrances on either side to a pair of great front rooms, identical in size and shape (at the time this house was built, symmetry had been the chief criterion of good taste), both high-ceilinged, stiffish, cool. Before proceeding back toward the kitchen, I peered expectantly into the dining room with its magnificent cherrywood hutch and table, its stately chairs poised upon ball and claw, its heavy draperies. Though the room looked well-maintained, I felt that no meals had been taken here for a very long time. (Even ages ago, when I was a mere girl who felt herself a shadow in the house, all except holiday meals were in the big breakfast room off the kitchen. But Barrie and I, occasionally alone in the house, would hold elaborate mock-formal dinners in here, Barrie got up in his dead stepfather's old tux, in which he looked astonishingly handsome, while I wore some jeweled and high-necked thing of Veronica's, laughable because it was several sizes too large. Though her dresses, I supposed, would fit well enough now.) Unsettled, I stepped back into the hall, but could not resist the other room, either; the ancient, sumptuously decorated "parlor" where infrequent guests of the family were entertained, where Carole Ann for long years had tortured the grand piano with her tinkling melodies, and where Barrie and I, though nearly out of our teens, had played hide-and-seek among the hulking furniture, the ornately carved screens, the window seats so capacious that their drawn curtains might conceal a dozen men. It was in this room, as imposing now as when I was a girl, that I saw flanking one wall a plain low table that supported, unmistakably, a large and dully gleaming coffin with its lid opened wide. Before I had time to think, to react with my customary caution or mistrust, I was standing above the coffin, staring balefully down. Twenty years had passed since his visit to Philadelphia; after that we had exchanged no letters, not even a card or photograph at Christmas. Yet here he was, my Barrie, unchanged but for a few silver streaks in the dark, well-cut hair, a couple of shallow creases in the broad forehead, and a slight puffiness to the cheeks and sealed eyelids. The severe, midnight-blue suit only enhanced his youthfulness. He might be a boy, temporarily well-behaved, dressed for a birthday party; he might be the same lovable, prankish Barrie, lying so utterly still only to open his sparkling cornflower-blue eyes to shout "Boo!" and release an impish laugh.

My Barrie.

Behind me came a soft footfall, but I didn't move my damp eyes even when I heard Carole Ann whisper, in a reverent tone, "He looks wonderful, doesn't he, Ruth?"

I'd been about to reach down, stroke the side of his cheek or the lovely dark hair; but now I breathed deeply. I cleared my throat.

"Of course," I said, with sudden bitterness. "But why wasn't I told?"

"Told?"

"That he was—that he—"

A tiny, sharp exclamation escaped Carole Ann: "Oh!"

I shook my head, uncaring that two or three tears had streaked across my cheekbones, deriving a morose pleasure from Carole Ann's apparent shock. Did she think me incapable of tears?

"Never mind," I said, wiping roughly at my face. "I just didn't expect it."

"Oh, Ruth, I just assumed that Ronnie had told you. I mean, when she telephoned—"

"She said the arrangements were made. She didn't specify."

I tried to keep the rancor from my voice, for I felt a grudging conviction that Carole Ann was innocent in this; that she could be charged, at the worst, with an unthinking complicity. It had always been the dragon Veronica who ran this house and the lives of its tenants.

Carole Ann had begun to whimper, almost noiselessly. A dry, desperate sound, not unlike a hiccough. Stiffly, I turned and took her small ringless hand. She was gazing woefully down at Barrie.

"He's so—so beautiful, isn't he?" she said, in a kind of disconsolate rapture. "Even now?"

"Yes," I said, uncomfortably. I wanted to release her hand, but now I felt trapped in the gesture, as though committed to some unspoken bond. I felt the need to keep talking.

"He never aged, somehow," I added. "He looks twenty-five, twenty-six at the most. He looks like a college kid."

If my tone had become sardonic, it didn't faze Carole Ann. "Oh, I know," she whispered. "Whenever people met us, they'd always ask if Barrie was a college student—and of course he'd say yes. On the spot, he'd invent some fictional college and go into all kinds of detail, saying with a straight face that he majored in astrology, or sexology, or that he'd gone out for cheerleader this past spring but had lost. And he'd look so downcast. And the poor guest would just stand there, gaping."

Despite herself, Carole Ann wore a faraway smile. She reached down, lightly touching Barrie's fingers with her own.

"That sounds like Barrie," I said. "But what *did* he do with himself, all these years?"

Carole Ann frowned, as if this were an odd question. "Do? Well, you know, Ruth, just what he always did, even when you lived here. Supervised the house and the landscaping, helped Veronica with her finances, her investments. . . . Played master of the house when anyone came to visit—friends of Ronnie's, you know, or old cronies of your uncle."

Her voice had tightened, as though she felt the need to defend Barrie.

"He stayed very busy, really," she said. "Toward the end of the week he'd usually go into Atlanta, to meet with Ronnie's broker, or her lawyers . . . sometimes he'd be gone until Sunday night."

"Big cities fascinated him, didn't they?" I said, but I confined my sarcasm to a curling lower lip, which Carole Ann couldn't see. After all, she'd been hurt enough. I added, gently, "He loved Philadelphia, too. For the brief time he was there."

It was then that Carole Ann, still gazing down at Barrie with her eyes misted over, almost casually said. "Yes, he talked about that all the time, and about *you*. He truly admired you, Ruth. Your independence, I think. And your being so smart."

I laughed, sharply. I dropped her hand.

"Oh, now don't act so surprised," she said, and I could not help but recognize that particular asperity in her voice: the familiar, brittle jealousy that Carole Ann had suffered almost from the moment she met Barrie.

"Carole Ann, I really don't think—"

"No, I know that he worshiped you," said Carole Ann, giving me a look of rueful honesty. "I always felt that I had to measure up to you, somehow. And that I'd always fail."

"Carole Ann, please don't cry," I said tightly.

"It was always 'Ruth this, Ruth that.' Always 'the time I visited Ruth, in Philadelphia.' There were days when I wanted to say, Go on back up there, then! Go live with your wonderful cousin!" She sobbed for a moment; then her voice came low and penitent. "But I was afraid he'd do it. And guilty, too, because I could never make him happy."

My gaze fell again to Barrie, in whose stilled features I no longer saw the bright, high-spirited child I'd known. I wanted to slap the waxen cheek, demand an explanation as I've done so many times with especially sullen or willful students back at school.

"But I guess—I guess Barrie was already happy," said Carole Ann, sadly.

And I replied, sharply, "Maybe not."

In any case, neither of us was really listening to the other. Carole Ann kept touching Barrie's fingers with an insipid, forlorn look of pity.

"Listen, it's nearly seven," I said, irritated. "Where is Veronica? What time do you people eat dinner?"

My appetite is the one thing I can depend on, for it carries on efficiently, not to say relentlessly, regardless of the state of my mind or health. It has proved equally impervious to depression, stressful conditions, sudden shifts of environment, or poorly cooked food. All these appetite-suppressing elements were present during my visit, and still I ate. That first night, an underdone roast beef. The following day, just before the two o'clock funeral, a luncheon of inexplicably greasy fried chicken, charred black in places, served with large helpings of tepid and watery black-eyed peas. Coffee that no amount of cream could lighten, leaving a bitter residue near the back of the tongue that lingered for hours. Since several guests had been invited for the funeral baked meats later that afternoon, I dared to suppose that the housekeeper, Mrs. Hodges, might make a special effort to see that the ham was served hot, the fruit salad and butter kept cold; but this witless assumption quickly died when she issued from the kitchen, wearing a fearsome scowl and a filthy apron, carrying a platter of ham that might have been sliced with a hacksaw. No one dared to comment, not even Veronica; we took the large, oddly shaped hunks of meat with an air of deference and gentle thanks. After the ham came an unexpectedly festive dish of sweet potatoes covered with marshmallows, though the marshmallows unfortunately had not melted and proved to be quite stale. Then the warm fruit salad. Then the black-eyed peas, again, even more watery than at lunch. Finally, more of the coffee into which one poured cream as into a bottomless well.

Yet I sampled everything, and even had seconds of the peas. Since my arrival, I'd begun to experience a peculiar lack of self-consciousness: appraising my naked, rather bloated frame in the bedroom mirror that morning, I'd thought only in passing of how radically this image of middle-aged complacency, which would soon present itself for the last time to Barrie, differed from the thin, nervous, laughing girl who'd once chased him about this house. Nor had I cared to present any but my rather abrupt, moody self to those long-suffering partners of his existence, Veronica and Carole Ann. And now, surrounded by strangers, having just seen my life's single bright object of passion dropped into black earth, I contentedly ate. It was mostly an awkward, stiff company, so there was little to do but eat. There were people like myself, who knew no one, and others who seemed to know each other all too well. So there were two kinds of silence, uneasily blended. Veronica tried to maintain a semblance of conversation, but the results were brittle and uncertain, like the notes of a child struggling through his first piece on the piano.

"He looked lovely, don't you think?" she said for the third or fourth time, though "lovely" had no place in her usual vocabulary.

"Oh yes!" breathed Carole Ann, whose fork, bearing three black-eyed peas, trembled aloft.

The local minister, a young, full-faced, rather wistful and hapless young man named Reverend Cray, vehemently nodded. "A fine-looking young man," he agreed. "So pleasant and well-mannered."

He gave a benign, avuncular smile, though he appeared at least a decade younger than Barrie had been.

"And so talented, too," said a neighbor (the nearest house was three miles away) who'd been introduced as Mrs. Nesbitt. She was a bony, perky woman in her sixties; her black cloche sported a plum-colored feather. "Bursting with talent, really."

This boundless hyperbole distracted my attention from the sweet potatoes. Innocent and ignorant, "family" flown in for the funeral, I could ask: "Really? What talents were those?"

Mrs. Nesbitt, it was clear, owned an intractable faith in her own observations; she smiled brilliantly. "Oh, all sorts of things," she said. "He could do—well, anything he wanted. We always said that."

Mr. Nesbitt was a quiet, silver-haired man who resembled a rabbit. "A right nice boy," he said, looking melancholy. "And in the flower of his youth."

Even his wife seemed startled by this unexpected poetry. "Yes," she said, her eyes bulging. "He could have done anything."

"He was always so helpful," someone else said.

"And such a good sense of humor!"

"Very selfless, too. Especially for such a young man."

"Oh yes—so sweet and thoughtful. Why, one day, for no reason at all, he came over with some flowers—a bright bunch of zinnias."

"So charming. Quick-witted, too."

"And handsome—let's not forget that! Those big blue eyes."

"Always smiling, always humming a gay tune."

"And never a cross word. Not in all the years I knew him."

"Never!"—the word came like a chorus, an emphatic *amen*.

Then Mrs. Nesbitt, who still looked a bit dazed by the bright bunch of zinnias, said rushingly to me: "And you were terribly close, weren't you? Despite your having moved so far away?"

This was not a question of course but rhetoric, another item in the litany of Barrie's praise, but as my appetite became sated so had my indulgence proved short-lived. "Close?" I said. "Hardly. We hadn't communicated in many years."

All seemed to slump a little in their chairs—all but Mrs. Nesbitt.

"But I know you were!" she cried. She wagged her finger, as though I were being naughty, and performed her favorite gesture of ducking her head, as one ducks when laughing uncontrollably. With each duck, the purple feather came closer to her untouched cup of coffee.

And now Veronica, unexpectedly, took my side. "It *has* been quite a few years," she said, "since we lost Ruth."

"Oh yes, it's been *too* many years!" echoed Carole Ann.

I looked at them, the familiar pang of suspicion—of jealousy—smarting no less keenly now that Barrie was gone. They'd never forgiven me for leaving, of course; for nearly succeeding in drawing him out of their lives forever. Against only one of them I might have succeeded, but as an alliance they were unbeatable, as through these long years of mutual dislike and mistrust they had doubtless come bleakly to know. I had crawled out on my limb, had played my long shot, and had crashed. Now, of course, they were mocking me, indulging their sweet privilege; why else had I come?

"But it's true that Barrie and I were close, long ago," I said to Mrs. Nesbitt. "That's why I'm here."

Reverend Cray bobbed his head. "Family feeling," he said, sagely. "It doesn't fade away."

Both Veronica and Carole Ann glanced in my direction.

"But you knew, Reverend Cray," I said politely, "that we weren't blood relatives?"

"Well, I suppose—I mean, I had always gathered—" Flustered, he broke off.

"See, what did I tell you?" Mrs. Nesbitt said gaily, if somewhat cryptically, to the company at large.

"But they were just like brother and sister," Carole Ann said. "They grew up together, sort of."

Reverend Cray, who had recovered himself, smiled at me. "I didn't know," he said.

Didn't know that we weren't blood relatives, or that we had grown up together, sort of? I frowned at him.

"Ever since then, she's been a schoolteacher," Carole Ann said. She had assumed the knowledgeable, slightly pompous air of a tour guide through the family's history.

"We've certainly missed her," Veronica sighed. "And so did Barrie."

"Oh yes!" added Carole Ann.

There was a scattered murmuring of agreement, but the group's attention had wandered. Reverend Cray was downing the last of his coffee, and Mrs. Nesbitt delicately patted her mouth with her napkin. The meal was over. Mrs. Hodges had entered from the kitchen, bringing along her air of intense disapproval, and had begun clearing the dishes.

My heart pounded. Various rebukes, sarcasms, and imprecations rose in my throat, but I could not choose among them. The moment passed. All at once I felt Barrie's presence—blithe spirit extraordinaire, prankish poltergeist, presiding genius over this comedy of errors. That drizzly morning in Philadelphia, outside the train station, he had indeed said to me: "I'll miss you, Ruthie. God knows I will." A tear had gleamed in his eye, and I'd wanted desperately to lash out—to say something witty and devastating, something unanswerable. But the opportunity passed, and I'd watched his fawn-colored raincoat recede, with a swarm of fellow travelers, into the cavelike recesses of the station. Shakily, I had walked away. Shakily, I now stood up, and before hurrying from the room I said, in a quavering voice, "Excuse me, I'm going to be sick."

* * *

But I was not sick; I didn't take the time. I left by the main entrance and began striding rapidly along the winding front drive. I didn't care that Veronica, Carole Ann and the others might be peering out the windows, clicking their tongues. I rushed along, at once bold and furtive. The graveyard was less than a mile down the main road.

The day was sultry, the reddish-brown earth seemed to radiate waves of moist heat, and my stomach did feel queasy. I took deep breaths as I walked; with one palm I wiped the sweat from my cheeks, my forehead. They had lowered Barrie's silver-toned casket into the cool, deep-delved earth, six or eight feet down, and now I saw him lying in that utter dark, crisply attired in the midnight-blue suit, imperturbable. Reverend Cray had mumbled a few words, reading from a damp, much worked-over sheet of legal paper crushed in his hands. Veronica's head was bowed. Carole Ann had groaned, like a wounded animal. Oh Barrie, how cleverly you have escaped us all!

Reaching the main road, I slowed my pace; I even considered turning back. A quick, murmured explanation, and everyone saying that *of course* they understood. But no. Something I preach to my girls, endlessly: Follow through. There is no awkwardness, no indignity like a half-completed gesture. Halfway along a tightrope, one doesn't hesitate or look down; one doesn't pause to reconsider—! Not even if there's a net, which there isn't.

When Barrie and I were young, we used to play a game that Barrie called "Trust." It was the simple game of standing perfectly straight with your eyes closed, the other person behind you, and letting yourself fall backward, freely, trusting him to catch you in his arms. In truth, I disliked this game. Not because Barrie delighted in teasing me—shouting happily that I was a coward on those days when, unable to entrust myself even to Barrie, an insuperable reflex made my arms spring out behind me during the free-fall; or, when I was more reckless or brave, waiting until the *very last* moment, when I had fallen within inches of the ground, before scooping me in his arms and lifting me, shaky and pale, into a standing position. I'd considered it a given, I suppose, that I was cowardly, and that my salvation depended on the unearned beneficence of my cousin—which he might justifiably withdraw, at a moment's notice. Rather it was Barrie's turn that made me uncomfortable. He would accept the vulnerable role with alacrity, often clasping his hands behind his head, or stretching them forward like a somnambulist.

Or he would stand with his arms crossed upon his breast, like Queequeg in his coffin. Miserably I watched his stiffened spine, and the dark-haired, vulnerable-looking back of his head. Sometimes, as he fell backward, he would let out a mock-scream, or would yell out, "Geronimo-o-o-o!" He never showed the slightest hesitation or fear, and afterward, his head cradled in my arms, I would see his great blue eyes, upside-down, opened wide in delighted laughter, for evidently I looked even more pale and terrified than when I'd taken the fall myself.

Invariably, when Barrie began to fall, two things would happen. First, I would feel suddenly incapable of catching him, sensing that my arms were not quick or strong enough to prevent his crashing to the ground. Second, I would feel a sudden reflexive twitching in my arm muscles, an unexplainable urge to *withdraw* my protection and deliberately allow him to fall. This never happened, of course, but on several occasions the impulse was quite strong. Hopelessly in love with him even then, I nonetheless disliked the free, unthinking way he entrusted himself to my care. Though he never allowed me to fall, either, I could never attain this certitude, this abnegation of control. When for no particular reason Barrie abandoned this game, never to mention it again, I felt an immense relief.

It was this same relief, I suppose, that I would experience years later, after that terrible winter of my nineteenth year, and for which I now had such a dire, unappeasable longing. Having reached the top of the next hill, I looked back; I could just glimpse the house, glimmering whitely through the tangled mass of trees. A few steps down the other side, and it was out of view. Over the next hill, I knew, lay the scattering of gravestones—too small, really, to be called a cemetery—adjacent to a now-defunct Baptist church, its paint peeling, the wood itself rotting away. The same church on which, in his extreme youth, Barrie had heaped such open, cheerful scorn. One evening, just at twilight, we had been riding along this road with Veronica, in her stately, slow-moving car, on our way to a restaurant in the next town. Passing the church, we saw a gathering of some thirty or forty people having a cook-out, on the small strip of ground that divided the old building and the graveyard. Barrie, who despised organized religion, had made some typically scathing remark—"Wouldn't it be nice" (I think it was) "if some sort of concentration camp could be set up, where they could truly flock together. Like sheep." And I giggled, nervously. "Remember, we have to live among these people," Veronica had said, sternly. "Why Mummy," Barrie said, with his best mock-aghast expression, "those weren't people—those were *Christians.*" And our laughter had drifted out the back windows of Veronica's car, into the bluish twilit air.

The innocent, conspiring laughter of children, ringing out into some clear, long-past, irrecoverable evening—that sound for two decades has accompanied my heart's convulsing, blended surreally with images of his wide, ingenuous, matinee-idol face, lit with tenderness, mischief, or the slightly aggrieved look of bewilderment that was Barrie's response to the vast and hostile world surrounding us; or with his fine alto voice singing "Clementine" as we tramped together through the woods on midsummer mornings, a voice that cracked sentimentally on the refrain, "You are lost and—gone—forever—oh, my darlin'—Clementine—" and brought hot stinging tears to my eyes.

My Barrie.

I heard only vaguely the singing of tires on the main road as I turned to face the graveyard. It looked smaller now, emptied of the preacher and the mourners and the inevitable small-town gawkers and hangers-on. The old church building, mostly denuded of paint, seemed to sag in the moist late-summer's heat. Atop the reddish mound of Barrie's grave were the several dozen sprays of flowers, exotic and somehow minatory, as if they might be carnivorous; and arched over them the undertaker's canopy, a bright unnatural green, with gleaming aluminum stakes and a fringe of gold tassels. It all had a look of misplaced festivity—some lost gypsy caravan, stranded amid ruin. Around it the older graves (each decorated meagerly with its own clutch of flowers, fresh or sun-weathered) had a pathetic stoicism as the red earth received their slow deliquescence. I stared, disconsolate, remembering a visit we'd once made to a farm in the next county, where one of our school friends lived, when Barrie had turned to me and said, with a grave flourish, "Behold our Ruth, amid the alien corn!" By then we were in high school, though, and I didn't laugh. For a moment Barrie's face had that bruised, sagging look that came whenever I stepped back, primly, and let him crash to the ground—as I'd begun doing, so often. Less than two years would pass before I fled the South.

Still at the roadside, blinded, I could move forward only with an awkward, jerking motion. With open flat palms I wiped my eyes. The warm air felt heavy, gelatinous. Each step took a conscious effort as I picked my way through the maze of stones and flowers.

From behind came a solid, whacking sound: a car's door, slamming.

"Ruth— Please wait—"

I half-turned; I didn't want to face Veronica.

"Are you all right? Ruth?"

"Yes," I said coldly.

We stood a few yards from Barrie's grave, two women who had been violently weeping. For when I allowed my hot glance to brush hers, I saw that her eyes, too, were red and swollen.

I distrusted this. Even though her shoulders sagged; even though one of her brown-mottled hands reached out, in a half-imploring gesture.

"Everyone—they're all quite concerned, back at the house," she said, in a queer, ingratiating tone.

"Are they?" I answered.

"Ruth, you mustn't be angry with us," she said, so pathetically that a sudden chill passed along my arms.

"I'm not angry," I said, trying to sound casual; but it was hopeless. "All right, I'm angry. But not really with you."

She took a step forward, then reached out and let her fingers lightly brush my knuckles on one hand. Her face had the awkward, near-desperate look of one who seldom resorts to touching another person.

"Thank you," she said. "That's what Barrie would have wanted."

We both looked back to the canopy, the mound of earth and flowers.

"I mean—he would have liked to see us here, together like this," I heard Veronica say.

What had been Barrie's power, I thought, whose passing could reduce his strong and coldly disposed mother, whom even he called "the dragon," into this grief-stricken, ordinary woman?

"Yes," I said.

"I—I hope we'll become closer, you and I," she whispered.

"Yes," I said, absently.

She opened her purse, extracted a couple of tissues, and handed me one. She blew her nose.

"You know, he never got over you, not really," she said. "In the last year or two, his heart condition slowed him down quite a bit; he stayed home a great deal. And he spoke of you even more frequently than in the past. Sincerely, too. Not with that odd sense of humor."

Something of the old Veronica surfaced as she spoke that word, "odd," but then she wiped her nose again and went on, her voice hoarse with emotion.

"I knew then that I'd never reach him," she said. "It was always you."

My eyes had fastened, mesmerized, on a clutch of white roses near the center of Barrie's mound—about where his heart would be. When Veronica had phoned to report his death by heart failure, I'd thought with quick, malicious zest: Of course, his heart! That little-used organ! I stared at the white roses, stricken.

"I hope you'll try to understand, try to—to forgive me," Veronica said, faltering. "I was always very attached to Barrie, you know, particularly after his father died and I married your uncle. I—I didn't love your uncle, Ruth, but he loved me, and I knew he would take good care of us, and I didn't know what else to do. But when he brought us back here, back to—to this kind of life—well, I wasn't used to it. I was accustomed to city life, you know, and so was Barrie."

She paused, swallowing hard. I wanted to stop her, say it was all right; but I couldn't resist her uncharacteristic meekness, her air of penitence. She resumed:

"Try to understand, Ruth. Everything went so well, for a year or so, but then Rex got that telephone call about his brother and sister-in-law, dying in an auto crash somewhere in Texas. I'd never even met them, or seen pictures. And one day Rex comes home with this young girl, thirteen years old—exactly Barrie's age—and announces that she'll be living here, too. Barrie's cousin, he said. Another member of the family." She paused, perhaps aware that an ancient rancor had crept into her voice. "It was quite a shock," she said, subdued. "Particularly when Barrie took to you that way, seemed to come alive in your presence. I'd stand at my bedroom window and watch the two of you, out back, sitting under a tree and reading poetry to each other, or chasing through the woods, laughing, or playing some silly game or other. Children, I kept saying. They're just children. But it did no good. My—my hatred," she said, groping, "it grew like a cancer." A bleak satisfaction had filled her voice. "Yes. A cancer."

"Veronica, you don't need to—"

"No, Ruth, it's all true. You know it is. He adored you, he preferred you even to me, and certainly to Carole Ann, but by then something had happened—I didn't know what, and I don't mean to pry—but you seemed to lose interest, to be nourishing some secret disappointment of your own, and within weeks after finishing school you were gone, just like that. *Gone.* You were eighteen, your trust fund had come due, you suddenly decided to go to college, to move far away. . . . " She spoke dazedly, as if still not quite believing this had happened. "And you were at your very prettiest then, too, as Barrie mentioned more than once. But after you left, of course, I didn't get him back, and of course Carole Ann never got him. No one did. He stayed the way he was, that willful attractive teenaged boy, and I was left to hate you, that's all I could do, and then, as the years passed, even that hatred grew abstract and lifeless, unsatisfying. I didn't even have *that*—"

Weeping, she'd lifted the tissue to her eyes. The wattled flesh shook along her throat and jaw. I reached out and patted her shoulder, awkwardly, but then withdrew my hand.

I said, in a careful, measured way: "It hasn't been easy, I'm sure, for any of us." I had an almost irresistible urge to become, like Veronica, garrulous and self-pitying; to portray that plump, authoritative, bitterly isolated woman of recent years; to summon up that scene of parting, in Philadelphia, when I had been too weak and cowardly to do anything but send Barrie away. And soon after that, the schoolmarm. A bit later, the witch. Veronica might well sense a kinship, however distasteful.

She looked up, timidly. "Did you ever—I mean, in Philadelphia, were you eventually able to—"

"No," I said.

Why wouldn't she leave? How to get rid of her? I wanted to stand here, alone, mooning over those halcyon early days; paying homage only to *that* Barrie, sweetheart and brother, confidant, my soul's guide, who answered to my complex of girl-adolescent longings with just the right blend of love, foolishness, and glamor. I would forget those other Barries—the amiable idler who could never abandon the hothouse protection of his mother's possessiveness, of the South itself; the young man who flirted so openly (and so exotically, to my sheltered awareness) with other men, and who took off sometimes, alone, for Atlanta—"where the boys are," he said once to me, winking, leaving me too stunned to feel jealous; the inert, absurdly youthful figure I'd gazed upon yesterday, his eyelids sealed, dressed in midnight blue. No, I would not think of them.

"Veronica," I said. "If you don't mind, I'd like to be alone for a little while."

This confused her. "You want—you mean, *here*—?"

"Yes." And I turned again toward the grave, starting away from her.

Then I heard, from behind: "You'll never give up, will you!" A fierce, accusing voice.

"Veronica," I said sharply, turning, "you must understand that this picture you have—this vision of things—is greatly distorted. I mean, Barrie was fond of me at one time, yes, but he didn't—I mean, he never—"

I couldn't finish.

Veronica, her face taut with fury, stood her ground. "What *do* you mean?

I breathed deeply. "We loved each other, in a strange way, but we were weaklings. *You* were the strong one. You deserved to win, and you did."

Her mouth twitched, as if she were choking on her own malice. "You're one to talk about distortion," she said, bitterly. "You've been gone for twenty years, and not so much as a letter, a phone call. What do *you* know about him? About me?"

Unconsciously she had clasped her hands together, as if she were strangling some invisible assailant.

"You didn't have to go through what I did, Ruth, right up until the end. Why, only last week I passed by his bedroom, he was lying fully clothed on top of the spread, even his shoes on, he didn't see me, he lay there staring upward at the ceiling and talking to himself, in a dreamy voice. It was a voice I'd never heard before, not ever; he'd never shown me that side. He was reciting a passage, I realized, from that Brontë novel—you're the English teacher, you should know—where the hero cries out, 'Oh, Cathy, be with me always—take any form—drive me mad! I *cannot* live without my life. I *cannot* live without my soul!'—you know how it goes, I'm sure. He lay there repeating it over and over, I'll never forget those words!"

Tears wandered down her face, a strange route of dried reptilian skin, puckered by grief. Her shoulders shook, her eyes were half shut, yet she looked imperious as ever with her clenched hands and her gritted teeth.

"Over and over," she said, "in that sad, dreamy, faraway voice. 'Oh, Cathy! Oh, Cathy!'"

Abruptly, I turned aside. I hurried to the grave. To my relief, she didn't follow; but neither did she go away. We would never escape each other, I thought, any more than that unholy alliance, love and death, might ever dissolve within the compass of idle passions, idle dreams. Not quite alone, I stood staring at a mound of dirt, in the middle of nowhere.

Other Books by Greg Johnson

Pagan Babies, a novel (1993)

Aid and Comfort, poetry (1993)

A Friendly Deceit, stories (1992)

Distant Friends, stories (1990)

Fiction Titles in the Series

Guy Davenport, *Da Vinci's Bicycle: Ten Stories*
Stephen Dixon, *Fourteen Stories*
Jack Matthews, *Dubious Persuasions*
Guy Davenport, *Tatlin!*
Joe Ashby Porter, *The Kentucky Stories*
Stephen Dixon, *Time to Go*
Jack Matthews, *Crazy Women*
Jean McGarry, *Airs of Providence*
Jack Matthews, *Ghostly Populations*
Jean McGarry, *The Very Rich Hours*
Steve Barthelme, *And He Tells the Little Horse the Whole Story*
Michael Martone, *Safety Patrol*
Jerry Klinkowitz, *"Short Season" and Other Stories*
James Boylan, *Remind Me to Murder You Later*
Frances Sherwood, *Everything You've Heard Is True*
Stephen Dixon, *All Gone: Eighteen Short Stories*
Jack Matthews, *Dirty Tricks*
Joe Ashby Porter, *Lithuania*
Robert Nichols, *In the Air*
Ellen Akins, *World Like a Knife*
Greg Johnson, *A Friendly Deceit*
Guy Davenport, *The Jules Verne Steam Balloon*
Guy Davenport, *Eclogues*
Jack Matthews, *"Storyhood As We Know It" and Other Stories*
Stephen Dixon, *Long Made Short*
Jean McGarry, *Home at Last*
Jerry Klinkowitz, *Basepaths*
Greg Johnson, *I Am Dangerous*

Library of Congress Cataloging-in-Publication Data

Johnson, Greg, 1953–
I am dangerous : stories / by Greg Johnson.
p. cm. — (Johns Hopkins, poetry and fiction)
Contents: A house of trees — Hemingway's cats — Uncle Vic — Evening at home — Scene of the crime — In the deep woods — Little death — Sanctity — Leavetaking — Last night — I am dangerous — Primordia — Alliances of youth.
ISBN 0-8018-5375-3 (alk. paper). — ISBN 0-8018-5376-1 (pbk. : alk. paper)
I. Title. II. Series.
PS3560.03775I2 1996
813′.54—dc20 95-52621